DILEMMA
By: Latifa Sanchez

Latifa Sanchez

This is a work of fiction. Any references or similarities to actual events, real people, living or dead, or to real locals are intended to give the novel a sense of reality. Any similarity to other names, characters, places, and incidents is entirely coincidental.

Concrete Rose Publishing LLC
5 Corman Road
Mattapan MA 02126

ISBN: 1-4196-9162-7
EAN13: 9781419691621
Cover Photography: Mike Lewis of Image Impressionz
Cover Design/Graphics: Natasha Adams
Models: Alicia Meyers, Chezley & Chelston Mitchell, Danielle Johnson

Copyright © 2008 Latifa Sanchez. All rights reserved. No part of this book may be reproduced in any form or by any means without prior consent of the Publisher, except brief quotes used in reviews.

First Trade Paperback Edition Printing February 2008

Printed in United States of America

For comments or to contact the author via email: latifasanchez@tmail.com

ACKNOWLEDGEMENTS

First and foremost, I want to thank God for allowing me to struggle through certain situations so I could see the true meaning of love, friendship and family.

MANNY, what would I do without you? Where would I be without you? You have stuck by me for the past thirteen years, I would not have the strength and courage I do without YOUR love and support. We've come along ways from the nights in the mountains. When we were in the 11th grade, staying on the phone till three in the morning, knowing good and well we had to get up for school in the morning. I used to tell you something... I ALWAYS told you, I was going to marry you and we were going to have two kids. You thought I was joking, but I was dead serious. I knew then that you were going to be mine until the end of time, and look at us now! I know the nights get rough and you really want me to put the laptop down, I thank you for understanding the importance of me staying on my grind with this writing thing. You always believed in me. Probably because I used to write you ten page letters trying to convince you of how deep my love was for you (remember that)! You have always held me down & you continue to hold me down. If I had to choose between loving you and breathing, I would use my last breath to say, "I Love You"! Thank you so much for being my ROCK through thick and thin!!!!

ANTHONY & ANDRE know that everything I do is for you. Mommy is always here for you. And yes, Anthony you can grace the next cover as long as you do what Mommy asks of you. I know you feel there are times when the world is against you but you gotta be strong and remember that your parents ALWAYS have nothing but sheer love for you and I always got your back. Andre, you know you are definitely the apple of Mommy's heart, you have made this last pregnancy a tad bit easier by always being such a kind and loving child. I thank you for letting me know the difference between being 'fat' and being 'pregnant' (inside joke)! I thank you so much for seeing when I needed nothing but a small hug from you. I love you dearly.

Latifa Sanchez

FATHER, I want to thank you for all you have done for me and my family. You stepped up when you didn't really have to and I will always be extremely grateful to you for that. Sometimes I don't really understand the things you do and I often feel you are extremely hard on your children, but whenever I have needed things the most you always come through for me. Your support means so much to me!!!

MOM, through it all you stuck by me. You pushed me to be better and fought for me when I couldn't fight for myself. When I was young you taught me life lessons that have helped me to become a better wife, mother and person overall. I know you think I don't always listen, but I want you to know I hear everything you say to me. I thank you for showing me the true meaning of family. I love you so much. You are definitely my HERO! (p.s. you are such a kind and loving grandmother, my children would be helpless without you)

To my younger brother, **GREGORY** (excuse me Charles) and my younger sister, **ROSALIE** (excuse me Kinzena), ya'll are my hearts! I really don't know what else to say to you two. Greg: I can't believe how much you have matured over the last few months. I cherish all the quality time we have spent recently. It has definitely been my pleasure to show you as much family support as I could at the MATCH games, you know no matter where the game was we, the kids and I, were always there to cheer you on. Now, less thinking and more shooting... (just kidding). Zena: I want to thank you for being such a strong positive role model for Anthony and Andre. Whether you know it or not they look up to you and strive to be just as successful as you were in school. I don't know what I am going to do this fall without my baby sister or my lil brother around. I am so proud of the both of you. Continue to stay focused. You two keep me on my toes! I love you two so much and I am sure you both know by now there isn't anything I wouldn't do for you!

I must send a special shout out to **MS.TONI** of OOSA online book club. Sistergirl, you kept me up when I needed it. You pushed me when I needed to write. Thanks for the books and the love...

To my home girl, **ARITA**, ma I love you! You have ALWAYS been there for me, even when I was worried about showing you how vulnerable I was. I thank you so much for your support and your friendship; it means the world to me. Now do me a favor, "**GO OUT AND BUY THIS ONE!**"

ALICIA, I love you like you was my own sister! Know that if you ever need anything, I am always here for you. I thank you for taking care of my pride and joy, my baby girl everyday. I know in the beginning it wasn't easy because she was such a 'cry-cry' baby, but you soldiered up and cared for her like she was your own and I thank you from the bottom of my heart for that. Oh yeah, good looks on the cover, I see you doing the damn thang! Much love!

NIKKI.... Girl you are a trooper! Thank you for letting me use your name as a character and allowing me the freedom to write what I wanted. I know we don't always talk like we should but you should know that no matter what I always got your back! I hope you find some true happiness one of these days and let your baggage go!! I love you!

CHARISSE...I don't even know where to start with you. We girls, that's for sure. We done been through some real bull shit over the years, but we always manage to find one another and get things back on track! That's that true friendship...don't ever let anyone tell you anything different. I'm here for you always!

TONI & DANIELLE, we gonna have to talk because I know ya'll got some drama I can write about! Danielle thanks for stepping in when I needed you to and gracing this cover for me.

My big head cousin **DAWN**...girl do not change! Always stay true to yourself! I know most people don't understand you and think you're rude but tell them to do like Game, "Hate It or Love It". I can only ask one thing of you... GET FOCUSED! It's time to get cracking on them books, shawty. I'm out here making tracks for you, when you come along, the road will be much easier to travel. So stay focused… I always got your back. By the way, "Where's My Manuscript?"

TO MY ADOPTED SIBLINGS: **AMANDA, JORDAN, EJ** (EXCUSE ME EDWARD) AND **IMANI**… this is for you! Persistence and hard work pays off…ALWAYS! Keep that in mind as you head off to college and start to do the adult thing for real. I am so proud of you four for all the hard work you have put in over the years, continue to stay focused! If you ever need anything, don't hesitate to call me, I'm here for you fellow Bereans…..

AZEA, thanks for the poem, if you ever want to do a poetry book holla at me!

AYANA, stay focused on that court! Next year is your year to shine!! Make your family proud girl… Oh yeah, and stay off the damn floor!

I have to give a quick shout out to a new 'lil sister' I met this year…**CLAUDETTE**. I just wanted to take a moment to say thanks. I appreciate the poetry you laced for this book. Girl you are truly talented. Don't let it go to waste, get it together and let's do the damn thing for real! You know I am always here for you when you need me. Call me or text me… I got your back!

LYNETTE, its funny how God brings people into your life at just the right time. You are definitely the friend that gives me the fresh of breath air and I truly cherish that.
You definitely make the time at NEPA go a lot smoother if it weren't for you I would probably have gone insane by now. I know you will show this to John, so tell him there's his 2 seconds of fame! HA!

To my right hand, **NEKIA...MA, I AIN'T GOT NOTHING BUT LOVE FOR YOU!** No one knows it but you were the fire that got this whole "getting published" business started. You are definitely my sister from another mother and I love you dearly. I'm glad we reconnected! Now I know why I was lost all those years, because I didn't have my **SIS** in my corner. Well I'm here now and you ain't gonna be able to get rid of me. Thanks for being that listening ear when I needed to vent. Thanks for keeping me on the straight and narrow. Thanks so much for just being you! p.s. I guess we need to take that trip to the Coach store, maybe even my treat!

TO THE TWINS, CHEZLEY AND CHELSTON, I just want to send a special thank you to the two of you for stepping up and being there when I needed you in a crunch. I appreciate what you did!! Chezley, don't let it go to your head!! Just joking, I have much love for the both of you.

REE, I love you dearly. You're always there when I need you, no matter what. Thanks for being that aunt I can always go to even when I feel like I can't go to my moms.

To my #1 dawg for life.... **BIRDIE (EXCUSE ME SIMEON)** we grew up together, were practically raised as brother and sister and somehow we managed to fall off. You know you my nigga! I have nothing but crazy love for you. Sometimes we gotta let the past alone and hang up the grudges that we hold. I'm trying to; maybe you should do the same! You know what I'm talking about; we only got one life to live!! B, it's time for you to put that Fowler name on the map, let these people know we ain't nothing to mess with. My dreams are slowly but surely becoming a reality and I know your entertainment company will jump off too. We in here EARLY... I love you! Don't be afraid to call if you ever need anything. I always got your back, even though you a straight up knucklehead!!

To the FAM that didn't make this one, I got you on the next!

I'M OUTTA HERE......

Holla at ya Gurl!!

Latifa Sanchez

This Book is dedicated to my three children, Anthony, Andre and Alayna. Everything I do, I do for you!! I love you three dearly and thank God everyday for allowing me to be your mother.

SOMEONE

I want someone who adores me as if I was his mother,

So he treats me like a queen.

I want someone who is down for whatever so he treats me like one of his homies down the street.

I want someone who cares for me as though I was his sister, so no man is good enough for me.

Not even him...in my presence feels worthy.

I want someone who respects me as if I was his daddy.

See just like most men

A good girl is also hard to find.

So...he respects my soul, body, and my mind

I want someone who treats me like his brother.

Cause when I need help he's always there

Despite the needs of others.

I want someone that loves me so much

That we find ourselves addicted to one another's love for each other.

I guess like guns in the hood.

It's hard to live without it.

Latifa Sanchez

Like drugs to a drug addict

To have it feels so good.

But without it...without you

It's like my mind wont sleep. It's like my lungs won't breathe

And pain is all my heart will know.

If you leave me...If you go.

See

I'm searching for someone who does the things you do

I want someone who will at least remind me of you.

By Azea Mumford

Previously from Caught Up In Drama

Daryl led Amari out of the club and she was anxious to go somewhere private with him. Her heart was starting to beat rapidly at the thought of having him again. He always knew how to please her exactly how she needed to be pleased. They started walking to his car and she was more than ready to go with him.

"There's nothing I won't do, just to spend my life with you, I'll give my all to you... Promise that I will never lie to you boy" ~ the lyrics from Ciara's latest single came blaring through her Nextel i880 phone.

"Damn phone!" Amari cursed out loud.

Amari fumbled with her phone trying to get it out of the clip.

"Here let me help you with that," Daryl offered giving her a hand.

"Hello," she said after finally getting her phone free.

"Hey Baby, what's up?" asked Corey cheerfully.

Suddenly reality set in. Amari realized where she was and what she was about to do. She felt guilty and ashamed of herself.

She turned her back towards Daryl.

"Hey boo, what's going on?" she said trying to sound upbeat.

"Nothing, just here waiting for you to come home," he said honestly.

"Well, you don't have to wait too much longer, I'm getting ready to leave," Amari said looking Daryl in the eye finally.

Daryl couldn't help but show his disappointment. The loud sigh that escaped his lips let Amari know he wasn't happy to hear her say she was on her way home.

"Ok, I'll see ya when ya get here," Corey said before hanging up.

"So, I guess you are going home to him huh?" asked Daryl while fidgeting with his phone.

"I have to. He's my man," Amari said thinking about what might have happened between them if her phone hadn't rung.

They stood there once again in silence.

"Alright D, I'll see ya around," she said as though she was not just about to let him take her home.

"Peaches wait up," he called after her.

Slowly she stopped and turned to look at him.

"Please don't go," he pleaded.

"Daryl, please don't do this," she begged.

Amari didn't want him to get into having any feelings for her because at that moment her heart was telling her that she still had feelings for him. Her heart was telling her she was still very much in love with him and that no matter how much she tried to convince herself of her love for Corey, her love for Daryl was a helluva lot stronger.

"Don't do what? Don't tell you how I feel? Weren't you the one always preaching to me about honesty? I'm being honest right now and you can't take it. I want you. I love you," he nearly shouted.

Amari stepped back. She couldn't believe he just said what he said. She had waited so long to hear those words and now that he was finally saying them she wanted to jump in his arms and hold him tight. But she knew that was not realistic because she had to consider Corey and what they had together.

"Daryl, stop it. Let's be serious, you don't love me! You wanted to fuck me! And yes, I had a temporary memory lapse and was about to get down with you, but that has nothing to do with love! It has to do with alcohol and weed!" she yelled trying to cover her feelings for him.

"Amari, it's more than that and you know it. There is a connection between us still. There is a fire that we won't allow to burn out," he said looking at her.

"Whateva you say ain't shit going on between us," she said trying to convince herself.

"I felt the way you kissed me, you kissed me with passion and love, I can tell you still have feelings for me. Look me in the eyes and tell me honestly, you don't feel anything for me and I will leave you alone," he demanded.

"Daryl, I am not doing this with you. You can think whatever makes you happy but right now I am going home to my man," she said once again walking away to her truck.

"I love you!" he shouted.

"Daryl you don't love me. If you did we would still be together today. You abandoned me! You dissed me! You walked all over my heart, so don't think for a moment I am gonna give you the chance to ever do that to me again! We are finished, so just leave it the hell alone," she yelled back getting angry suddenly as she thought of how much he hurt her.

Amari really wanted him to think she was mad at him but the truth of the matter was; she was furious with herself. She was allowing herself to get caught up in Daryl again. The more she tried to fight it the deeper she fell in love with him.

She quickly walked to her truck. She couldn't get the door opened fast enough. She wanted to look back to see if Daryl was still standing there watching her, but her pride wouldn't let her do it. In her heart she knew the things he was saying were true, she did love him. She really did, but she couldn't hurt Corey like that. Corey had been too good to her for her to turn around and do some scandalous shit like that to him.

Her thoughts were interrupted when her phone started vibrating; alerting her she had a text message.

"He may have you physically but I will always have your heart! I will never give up on us! –Love Daryl"

CHAPTER ONE

Amari packed all of her belongings and headed for Clark Atlanta University with Corey following behind her. Corey moved into his dorm room at Morehouse College two weeks earlier, his roommate was a down to earth kid from Boston named Gregory Charles.

It was funny to hear Gregory Charles talk; he used the word 'son' so much she thought for sure it would drive her insane. Every one was his son! Gregory Charles was in school on a full academic scholarship from a charter school in Massachusetts, Media and Technology Charter High School (MATCH).

Corey and Gregory Charles hit it off immediately. Even though they'd only known each other for two brief weeks they acted as if they had known each other for years. Amari hoped that when she met her roommate they would hit it off half as well as they did. She had seen too many movies with horror stories of the worst roommates from hell.

Amari was really excited about meeting her new roommate. She really wanted to room with Xena but that unfortunately didn't happen for them, but at least they would be in the same building and no doubt in each other's room all the time. She thought about how crazy it would be if they ended up roommates. She didn't know her exact room number; she wouldn't find out until she reached the campus and got her room assignment. If they had ended up roommates she wouldn't have to put up the fake first time pretenses. She would be free to be herself and not have to worry about what her new roommate was thinking of her.

When they pulled up to the dormitory there were other students moving in as well. Corey and Amari climbed the two flights of stairs to the second floor both carrying bags in each hand. They searched the doors for room 204. Just their luck, it was at the other end of the hallway. The corridor was long and full of fresh meat bustle. The door to room 204 was closed, she was forced to put the bags down and dig into her Coach Hampton over night bag for the key she just received from the student affairs department. While she was fumbling around for the key she leaned on the door trying to get balanced and nearly fell on her face. The door was pushed open.

When she walked into the room one side of the room was extremely neat.

"Great, I'm going to be living with a damn neat freak," she thought to herself.

She opened the closet door and saw a row of multi colored Chuck Taylor sneakers lined up neatly on the bottom shelf. Amari couldn't help but to chuckle to herself.

"Hey Corey, my roommate seems to like Chuck's just as much as Xena," she said pointing to the neatly stacked sneakers.

"Damn, I ain't think there was another person in the "A" to like them ugly ass sneakers," he chuckled to himself.

Amari stayed in the room and began unpacking her bags while Corey went down to get the rest of her things.

"So what time are you coming to pick me up?" she heard Xena say.

She rushed to the hallway; Xena was standing right at the door talking on her cell phone, to Darvis no doubt.

"Xena, hey what are you doing here?" Amari asked excited to see her best friend.

Xena looked amazed; shocked almost. She glanced from Amari to the room door number.

"Is that your room?" Xena asked.

"Yeah," Amari said.

She started laughing instantly.

"Hey Darvis, let me call you right back," she said hanging up the phone without waiting for his response.

"Oh my God!" Xena exclaimed hugging Amari.

"We're roommates," Xena whispered in Amari's ear. They hugged tighter. They went inside the room quickly before people started thinking they were a little too friendly.

♫♫♫

Xena and Amari went out for the cheerleading squad. Tryouts were intense to say the least. They had to do all types of flips and jumps. They had to form periods and memorize about four cheers in about ten minutes. After it was all said and done they managed to survive and make the varsity squad. They were the only freshmen to do that. During cheerleading tryouts they started hanging out with the current captain, Keturah a.k.a. KeKe. Some of the other girls that didn't make the squad felt Xena and Amari only made the varsity squad because they were good friends with the captain.

♫♫♫

It was funny how two people could know each other for so long and come from the same part of town and yet grow so far apart. School had been coming along well for Amari. Xena and Amari were not only on the cheerleading squad but the dance squad as well. They had just about every class together and they chilled with each other as though they had known each other for an eternity instead of just one year.

Corey was good. He loved the college life. He was on the varsity football team; he was one of three freshmen. Yeah, he ended up having to repeat his freshmen year. When he was up north at college he spent so much time being fooled by that damn fraternity that his grades slipped and he ended up failing all of his subjects. Everything happened for a reason and he had definitely grown and matured since that time.

Amanda called today and gave Amari some very disturbing news about Daryl. She saw him a lot more than Amari did since they both attended the same college. It was a well known fact about the nature of Daryl's business. According to Amanda he was still heavy in the drug business but now he was dabbling in armed robbery as well. Daryl used to keep his business on a need to know only basis, lately he had been walking the campus and letting everyone know exactly what it was that he did. Everyone was fully aware about the gun he carried daily to school and his eagerness to rob or shoot whomever he felt was necessary.

For some odd reason Amari found this news to be very disturbing. She didn't want to believe Daryl could stoop to such a level but Amanda claimed she saw him in action on many occasions. Even though they were no longer together Amari still felt a strong bond between the two of them. It hurt her heart a little to know he was out living such a horrible life. She hoped and prayed for both of their sakes it would not end up killing him. Amari wasn't quite sure she would be able to deal with him not being in her life at all.

Corey and Amari would often rent a hotel room on the weekends, this was the only way they would be able to have time alone. The past weekend was their first together in about three weeks. After hours of passionate love making they both fell asleep, at three in the morning Amari's cell phone began to ring like crazy.

"Who the hell could be calling me at this hour?" she thought angrily to herself.

Corey stirred in the bed; Amari thought nothing of it when she heard him answer her cell phone.

"Mari here," Corey said angrily practically throwing the phone at her.

"And tell that nigga not to be calling you at this damn hour!" he added.

"That nigga, okay what nigga could he be talking about?" she questioned herself clearly confused.

"Hello," Amari said cautiously.

"Amari, it's Daryl, I need your help," he whispered.

"Oh my Lord, I can't believe Daryl is calling me at this hour. Damn Corey is probably lying right next to me heated beyond recognition," Amari thought silently to herself.

"Daryl it's late I'll call you later on," she tried to reason.

"Why do you need to speak to him later? Just go ahead and speak now while I'm here or are you two sneaking around doing some scandalous shit you have no business doing?" Corey shouted fully awake and clearly deep into Amari's conversation.

"Corey, it's not even like that, I don't even know why he is calling," Amari tried to reason with him as well.

"Daryl, what do you want? Please make it quick!" Amari demanded.

"I need you to bail me out," he half cried, half whispered.

"Bail you out!" She screamed confused.

"Yeah, I got arrested and my bail is $500.00, can you come and get me or not?" he asked with an attitude.

She sat on the phone speechless, realizing her hesitancy he spoke up.

"Amari please, I don't have anyone else to call. I tried to call Cease but he's not answering plus I will give you the money right back," he nearly cried.

She could not believe this boy was calling her to bail him out. What was worse was if she did go down and bail him out, she knew Corey would be highly upset with her. She didn't know what to say to him so she just sat on the phone with him silent as can be.

"Amari, I'm sure you probably need to talk it over with your man, but my time on the phone is up. Please come and get me. I'm down at Pre-Trial, next to the Greyhound Station downtown, you know right across the street from Magic City. If you don't come, I'll understand," he said hurriedly before his call was automatically terminated.

Just like that he was off the phone and she had a real dilemma on her hands. She placed her phone on the nightstand next to her and just looked at Corey who was now pretending to be asleep.

"Corey," Amari called out.

He stirred, turned and looked at her.

"Let me guess, you're going to go and bail him out?" he asked staring her dead in the eyes.

"If you don't want me to then I won't, what do you want me to do?" she asked honestly.

She didn't want to do anything that was going to upset Corey.

"You do whatever you want to do, I don't care!" he yelled turning his back to her again.

"Corey please don't act like that," Amari said trying to make things better between them.

He pulled the covers up high to his chin and began snoring within minutes. Amari managed to doze off around six in the morning, but when she awoke at eight Corey was gone. There was a note left on the nightstand that read, "Go bail your boy out, meet me at noon for lunch at Applebee's."

Even though he left that note, Amari still sensed there was some tension amongst them. She showered and dressed quickly and while she drove to the police station she called Xena and spoke with her about what she was minutes away from doing. Xena of course thought she was crazy; she said no matter what Daryl always managed to pull her back into him and his foolishness.

After Amari paid the bondsmen Daryl came out and he looked a total mess. He really looked rough; she couldn't remember a single time when she had ever seen him look so bad. He usually took great pride in his appearance. He had on extra baggy clothing and was in desperate need of a hair cut. When he saw Amari his whole face lit up.

"Amari, thank you," he said.

"Yep, don't ever call me for this bullshit again! This is the second damn time I have had to bail your dumb ass out; this is the last time I will bail you out of anywhere!"

He shook his head as if to say he understood, he then reached in his pocket and pulled out a wad of money, peeled off seven hundred dollar bills and handed it to her.

"Daryl, it was only five hundred remember," she said handing him two hundreds back.

"I know, keep that for your trouble," he said smiling while walking away.

Amari watched him walk towards the MARTA Garnett Station. She sat there in her truck pondering for a moment on whether or not to give him a ride; she decided that she might as well. Amari drove up to the MARTA station and rolled the window down, "I can drive you home," she said.

He jumped in real quick. The ride from downtown to Daryl's house in Lithonia was a silent one. The only noise came from Ashanti's CD, Foolish that was playing in Amari's CD player. Just as they were nearing his house he looked at her, "Amari, thank you. I know we've been through a lot and I did you wrong, but I want you to know I really do appreciate you coming out and helping me."

"Daryl, I've heard about what you have been doing with yourself and you really need to get your shit together. I helped you out today but I'm not going to do it again," Amari said trying to be stern with him.

"I know, thank you for helping me out this time," he said while climbing out of the truck.

He got out of the truck and walked into the house. Amari sat there for a moment just thinking about things and putting things into perspective. Her phone rang; it was Corey wondering if she planned on meeting him or if she was too busy with Daryl. Amari quickly told him she was on her way and made sure to tell him she loved him before they hung up the phone. She couldn't really blame Corey for being upset about Daryl's call, but sometimes she felt like Corey forgot she was in love with him. The fact that he was the one that she loved should have been assurance enough for him that she was not going anywhere.

♫♫♫

It was a big day for Corey. Representatives from the College Sports Information Directors Association were there, trying see if they were going to pick anyone from Morehouse's Maroon Tigers to be apart of the

Daktronics All Southeast Region football team, which recognized the best football players in the NCAA's Division II Southeast Region. On this particular day Corey's school, Morehouse College the Maroon Tigers happened to be playing their rival team, which happened to be Amari's school which was Clark Atlanta University the infamous red, black and gray Panthers.

Amari would be out there cheering for her school but on the inside she would undoubtedly definitely cheer for her man. He was having an exceptional season; there were rumors circulating that a NFL scout from the Atlanta Falcons would be there watching Corey as well. Corey was so excited, but at the same time you could tell just how nervous he was about the type of performance he would be able to put on athletically.

♫♫♫

Morehouse jumped out to a 13-point lead in the first quarter and never looked fearful, while holding the Panthers to a single field goal late in the second quarter. Quarterback Gregory Charles hit Corey in stride over the middle and he raced untouched into the end zone. The pitch-and-catch seemed to work just the way the duo talked about it in the tunnel prior to the game. Corey also saved his best for last, leading all rushers with 159 yards on 22 carries, to go along with three catches for 33 yards. It was his best performance in a Morehouse uniform.

Gregory Charles and Corey made one of the best plays, midway through the final quarter. After a handoff by Gregory Charles, Corey was tackled by three defenders at the line of scrimmage. But before submitting, Corey pitched the football to Gregory Charles who had trailed the play, and Gregory Charles was able to scamper into the end zone untouched. It was without a doubt the best game Corey had ever played.

♫♫♫

Amari's fellow cheerleaders were really depressed; this was a must win situation for Clark Atlanta's Panther's. She couldn't help but smile, this was a great game for Corey and Amari was happy for him. His ultimate goal in life was to become a professional football player. After his performance today, he was no doubt a s hoe in for the Daktronics All Southeast Region football team.

♫♫♫

After the game Amari ran across the field and gave Corey a big hug and kiss.

"Baby, you had such a great game!" she exclaimed.

He was beaming. They stood there for a moment just hugging and smiling at each other.

"Hey, since when did we start socializing with the competition?" asked a familiar voice.

That was Gregory Charles, Corey's roommate. They both stopped hugging for a minute and turned to see who was talking to them. When they both saw Gregory Charles they all fell out laughing.

"Hey Gregory Charles, what's up?" Amari said laughing.

She got a kick out of calling him that, she thought it was so hilarious that his full name was two last names.

"Not a damn thing son! Did you enjoy the game?" he questioned.

"Sure did, I saw that scout looking hard at my man," Amari stated with excitement.

"Of course, he's only the best in the entire Southeast Region; you know they will be trying to sign him hard! Oh yeah, before I forget son, there's a party tonight at Morris Brown College, ya'll down to go," asked Gregory Charles.

Corey and Amari looked at each other and in unison replied, "And ya know this man!"

They never missed a party. They always made time for the parties. In Amari's mind that's what college life was all about right, going to class during the day and then partying all night long. Corey and Gregory Charles needed to get back to the locker room before the coach came out looking for them. Amari and Corey said their goodbyes and promised to hook up later. Corey gave her a final kiss before he left and she walked away smiling.

When she got to her truck Xena was standing there with a frown on her face.

"Damn what's up with you?" Amari asked not thinking she would be that upset over losing the game.

"Where have you been? What took you so long?" Xena asked getting into the truck.

"I was congratulating Corey, why?" Amari asked.

She had the look like something was wrong with her.

"Damn girl you okay?" Amari asked while getting into the car.

"I think Darvis is cheating on me," Amari said throwing her head back to rest on the headrest. That didn't really shock Amari. Xena and Darvis had been down this road before. Amari looked over at Xena and Xena looked back at Amari with tears in her eyes.

"Hey, hey now, we will get through this if he did, tell me what happened," Amari demanded while handing her some tissue.

"I called him after the game and a female answered his cell phone," she began.

"Okay, and what did you say?" she asked.

"I was shocked! I was speechless and when I didn't say anything she hung up."

"Did you call back?"

"Yep, and she answered again, but this time I heard Darvis in the background asking her who was on the phone. I couldn't even say anything I just hung up the phone."

Damn now that's some fucked up shit! But what could she really expect out of him? The last time she caught him cheating he ran her ass over with his car! Darvis was Xena's man and all but Amari couldn't stand him for the life of her.

"Damn Xena, I'm sorry to hear Darvis has not changed his cheating ways, is there anything I could do?" Amari asked trying to comfort her.

Though Amari hated him, Xena was still her girl and she didn't want to see her all broken up over some bitch ass nigga!

"Nah, I just want to go home and go to bed," she said laying her head back again.

Amari drove Xena back to the dorm and after they both showered and changed out of their uniforms, they both decided to take a nap.

The ringing of the phone awakened Amari, "Hello," she answered groggily.

"Hey Mari, is Xena there?" asked Darvis; the nerve of him calling here like he didn't get caught again just hours ago.

Amari woke Xena up and she wasn't pleased. They stayed on the phone a good hour arguing. She confronted him about the strange female that answered his phone and just like every man he denied it again. Amari was proud of her girl though, she hung right in there talking with him and not taking any shit from him. Next thing Amari knew she had hung up the phone.

"That damn nigga!" she screamed, "I hate him!"

Xena was fired up!

"Xena what did he say?" Amari asked being nosey and curious about what excuse he would use.

"The usual male bull shit, he doesn't know what I'm talking about, yada…yada…yada," she said while cleaning her clothes off her bed.

"Xena, I was planning on going to this party over at MBC, you wanna roll with me?" Amari asked.

"Who's throwing a party over there?" she asked.

"I'm not sure, Corey's roommate Gregory Charles invited me," Amari said searching the closet for something to wear.

"You driving or you riding with Corey?" she asked looking at herself in the mirror.

"Riding with Corey but you know how twisted he likes to get so I'll probably end up driving home," Amari replied picking out a pair of red stilettos.

"Cool, yeah I'll go, anything to keep my mind off Darvis," she said headed into the shower again.

Amari opted for a red all over gold cat cami by Baby Phat along with a black Asian rose foil mini skirt. Xena opted for a denim jean skirt with a black tank top and her black chucks. When they left the dorm it was close to 10:30 p.m. Corey met them downstairs.

The party was off the hook. So many guys were checking out Xena, which really helped her to forget all about Darvis, even if it was only a momentary thing. Xena spent most of the night talking and dancing with one of Morris Brown's popular drum majors, Jordan.

When they reached back to the dorm room their answering machine was full to capacity with messages, surprisingly to Xena, from Darvis. Amari wasn't surprised at all; she knew just how guys thought. He was sorry right now only because he had not heard from her. He probably came by the dorm and realized they were not there and got hella nervous. He probably figured Amari had Xena in some party meeting a whole bunch of niggas. Yeah, he definitely guessed right.

Darvis really didn't want to be faithful but at the same time he didn't want Xena with any one else either.

That was how most men thought. They took what they had for granted, until someone else was interested in what they were not interested in. Did that just make any sense?

Xena was over there right now talking to Darvis. She was smiling awfully hard obviously he was saying everything she wanted to hear. Oh well, hopefully she would learn before she got her heart hurt any further. If not, then she would find out the hard way as most females did.

CHAPTER TWO

Damn did Amari call it or what? Xena and Darvis were back together and acting all happy and what not. Their so called happiness was driving Amari insane. Every time she turned around they were either on the phone together or he was dropping her off and they were just as cheesy as could be.

Meanwhile Jordan called the room like a mad man. Amari hadn't realized it but Jordan was feeling Xena something fierce. Amari was under the impression they simply had a good time at the party that night, but obviously he was hoping more would come out of their meeting. Hopefully for Jordan's sake Xena would see Darvis for what he really was and give Jordan a decent chance. But until then what could you do except roll with the punches.

♫♫♫

Corey and Amari argued constantly. All of their arguments were over the same thing…Daryl. Corey was still extremely convinced Daryl and Amari were secretly seeing each other. If by chance they happened to be in the same room or in the yard at the same time then he was convinced they planned it like that. Needless to say Corey and Amari had been doing anything and everything except getting along.

This particular evening Corey and Amari were supposed to go out but he got into one of his evil hatred moods and decided he couldn't stomach being in the same room as her; damn the nerve of him. You would think Daryl and Amari were sleeping together the way Corey acted. She was home alone enjoying the quiet time when Xena came into the dorm room upbeat and full of joy.

"Hey girl, what's up? Why you sitting in here in the dark like you in mourning or something?" she asked while flipping the lights on.

Amari's eyes squinted until they had time to adjust to the bright light.

"What up?" Amari uttered, secretly cursing Xena for taking away her quiet time.

"Keturah, Toni and I are going out, you want to join us?" she asked taking her denim jeans off and replacing it with a pair of tight baby blue Capri's.

Amari thought about it for a minute and wasn't sure if she was ready to go out or even felt like going out.

"Nah, Xena I'm straight," Amari said while curling back up in her bed.

"Come on Mari, it's no fun if you aren't there," she pleaded.

Xena never let up. She continued to badger Amari and pressured her to go out with them.

Finally after hearing Xena beg her over and over again Amari agreed. A big smile formed across Xena's face. Amari got up off the bed, took a quick shower and threw on a sky blue halter dress.

"Damn Mari you working the hell outta that dress, you gonna have niggas killing themselves just to get at you," she laughed.

The girls met up with Toni and Ke-Ke at The Palace. When they got there the music was bumping as it always was. Amari and Xena met up with Ke-Ke and Toni and started dancing and partying immediately. Amari needed a drink before she could do anything. She decided on a Bob Marley and started dancing in place. Two guys approached Amari quickly and propositioned her for a dance but she wasn't ready for that yet. She was enjoying herself without having to worry about keeping up with a dance partner.

"Mari, what up you coming out on the dance floor or what?" yelled Ke-Ke.

"Yeah, I'll be out there in a minute," Amari said gesturing towards her drink.

Ke-Ke brought her friend Toni with her tonight. She didn't know much about her other than what Ke-Ke had told her previously. Apparently they've known each other since they were in the third grade. They are tight as friends and that's a good thing because everyone needs that one tight friend. But as everyone does Toni has some serious skeletons in her closet.

According to Ke-Ke she has a real loser boyfriend that hits on her constantly. Amari couldn't understand that shit, never had. How anyone could allow someone to hit on them and think it was okay was beyond her. She had been at the bar for almost an hour now and she was having drink after drink. She started the night out with simple Bob Marley's; she soon graduated to Hennessy and Coke and then found herself doing shots of Hennessy. Feeling more than a little tipsy she decided to venture out onto the dance floor. She was having a good old time; momentarily she was able to forget all of her worries and troubles with Corey.

At the end of the night when Xena and Amari were going home she looked at her and smiled, "Thanks girl, I needed that."

"I know that's why I insisted you come along; don't you know by now I know you like the back of my hand?"

Both girls enjoyed a hearty laugh. When they got home they both changed their clothes quickly and curled up in their beds, watching television and nibbling on chips and dip. Moments into the Cosby show, they were both shocked when they heard a soft pound on their dorm room door; Xena got up and answered it quickly.

"Mari, its Ke-Ke and Toni," she said moving to the side so they could enter the dorm room.

Amari instantly sat up on the couch and looked at Toni whom you could instantly tell had been crying.

"Hey is everything okay?" Amari asked looking directly at Toni.

She took a crumpled tissue from her pocket and started crying again. Ke-Ke ushered her to the Sponge Bob chair and then went and sat on the futon next to Amari. The quiet was killing her.

"Mari, is it okay if Toni stays here tonight? She's going through some shit at her house with her boyfriend and my roommate is being a straight bitch right now," she offered as though Amari knew who her boyfriend was and all of the previous troubles that had disrupted their relationship.

"Yeah sure no problem," Amari said getting up to get her a pillow and a blanket.

"Toni is there anything I can get you?" Amari asked again.

Again she sat there quiet not saying a word. Xena and Amari looked at each other puzzled, not sure what they could say or do to make her feel better.

"When we got to her apartment, after we left the club, Tommy was in their bedroom with another female," Ke-Ke began.

"Damn that's fucked up!" Amari thought aloud remembering the heartache she felt when she learned of Daryl's indiscretions.

Ke-Ke went on to tell us how when Tommy saw Toni he didn't even seem remorseful for his behavior. She said he looked at Toni and asked her why she was home so early.

"Do you believe she looked at him and apologized to his ass for not calling first?" she asked the girls.

Amari's mouth dropped! She was shocked at his boldness and Toni's forgiving attitude.

"Whoever heard of such a thing, having to call your own house and tell your man you are on your way home, that's pure bullshit!" Ke-Ke yelled getting very upset over the situation again.

Xena and Amari sat in silence. Amari couldn't believe shit like this, unbelievable shit like this really happened. To her, to here a woman can have such low self esteem was unreal. They all sat there in disbelief at the thought of the craziness Toni actually went through.

When Ke-Ke left Xena and Amari sat on Amari's bed and just looked at each other still in shock. She could never imagine herself going through some bull shit, especially behind some man. Toni slept on the couch peacefully.

Amari slept like a baby. She didn't think about Corey or Daryl, she thought about no one in particular and it felt really good. When she got up the next morning she made it her duty to find out how Toni was feeling and if there was anything they could do to help her feel better.

"Toni, do you wanna talk?" Amari asked plopping down on the futon next to her.

She broke down.

"I love him! I can't understand why he continues to do this to me. How could he hurt me like this and not care? He's usually such a sweet and caring guy, but when he gets too drunk his whole demeanor changes," she sobbed.

Damn if someone could answer the million dollar question it would make life for women a whole lot easier.

"Toni, I don't have an answer to that question, all I can say is you will get through this. I'm sure right now it doesn't seem like it, but believe me when I say there is a brighter day."

Toni looked at Amari like she wanted to believe her but wasn't sure if she should. They sat there quiet both reflecting on their separate personal heartaches. Xena came into the room holding three plates of food she obviously picked up from Glady's Chicken & Waffles.

"Damn Xena, you knew just what was on my mind," Amari said thanking her for the food.

After breakfast they sat on the loveseat and watched, "You Got Served". Toni seemed to really start to warm up to the girls, she was laughing and cracking jokes with them. Halfway through the movie she glanced at the wall clock and nearly freaked the fuck out!

"Oh my God, its 4:00 pm, I have to get home or Tommy is going to kill me," she said in a panic.

Xena and Amari looked at each other puzzled. Toni grabbed her cell phone and called Ke-Ke immediately.

"Ke-Ke, hey can you give me a ride home?" she asked trying to calm her voice down.

"Ke-Ke please I need to be home by 4:30 pm," she whined into her cell phone. She shut her phone quickly and began pacing the room.

"Toni calm down I can take you home," Amari quickly offered. Amari saw a bit of hope glimmer in Toni's eyes.

"Can you, would you please?" she begged.

"No problem," Amari said getting up to throw her sweatpants and flip flops on.

She lived all the way on the other side of town and halfway to her house she was on edge and Amari was ready to strangle her. The whole ride she continuously badgered Amari to drive faster. And when she wasn't badgering her Toni was on the phone crying to Tommy about how sorry she was for not coming back home the previous night.

"Damn, how stupid is this chick?" Amari thought angrily to herself.

Xena was seated in the back almost at the end of her rope as well. She sat in the back and sucked her teeth continuously the whole ride. When they finally pulled up to Toni's apartment Tommy was standing at the front door with a bottle of Hennessey. Toni rushed out of the car without saying good bye or thank you.

"Damn ungrateful chick!" Amari muttered under her breath.

Xena came up front to sit and they watched as Toni ran to Tommy, kissed him on the cheek and continued to apologize. Tommy stared at her and then shoved her causing her to lose her footing and trip on the cement. They watched her fall and quickly get up and kiss Tommy on the cheek again.

That was the last that they saw of her before Tommy slammed the front door shut.

"Oh my God, Xena did you just see that shit? What the fuck is wrong with her? Why would she put up with that bull shit?" Amari questioned not talking with anyone specific.

When they got back to the apartment Darvis was waiting for Xena. That's another relationship that was in need of some serious help. She clearly was aware of the fact that he cheated yet she stayed with him anyways, why? It was just as bad as the abuse Toni was getting from Tommy.

Amari walked into the apartment and left Darvis and Xena outside talking. She stepped into her room and was engulfed with silence; a welcomed silence. It's what was needed, what she had been craving for. Corey hadn't bothered to call but she couldn't even worry about that at the moment. Corey would just have to get over his insecurities. He had to know and understand she loved him and wouldn't do anything to jeopardize that.

Amari wasn't in her room twenty minutes before her phone began ringing.

"Damn, I can never have a quiet moment to myself, someone always interrupts me, no matter what," she thought aloud to herself as she yanked the phone off the receiver.

It's Ke-Ke and she had the nerve to be all upset with Amari.

Damn girl, why don't you slow your role," Amari sighed into the phone.

"How could you take her back there? Do you have any idea what he's done to her this time?" she screamed.

Amari sat on her bed holding the phone in her left hand wondering what she had done to deserve so much drama in her life.

"Keturah look, I don't know what's going on with you and your crazy ass friend but at this point I really don't feel like hearing the fucking bull shit!" Amari said getting straight to the point and not caring if Ke-Ke's feelings were hurt.

She obviously didn't like hearing the tone of Amari's voice because the next thing she heard was the shrill of the dial tone. She couldn't help but smile. Maybe Keturah thought she was hurting Amari but in reality she was doing her a big favor. Finally, she was rid of everyone and able to lie in her bed in peace.

♫♫♫

"Greg, tell me that shit ain't fucked up? She hasn't bothered to pick up the phone and call me all day," Corey whined.

"Damn son why should she call you? She's probably sick of hearing all that whack bullshit you be spittin at her about that dumb ass nigga Daryl. Ya feel me son?" Gregory Charles said rationally.

Corey sat there quietly pondering over what his best friend just said to him. Was he really bugging and trying to make something out of nothing?

"Alright son, I'm bout to go hit the gym, I'll holla at you later," Gregory Charles said grabbing his gym bag.

Corey stayed behind and began looking through his memorabilia of Amari. He loved her so much and he really was missing her right now. Why he allowed his fear, his insecurity to overcome his whole being was beyond him. Damn, he could just kick himself for being so stupid; so petty and immature. Amari loved him and she knew first hand the effects of cheating, the pain it could cause, he didn't think she would ever put him through that.

As if he'd suddenly had an epiphany he jumped up off the bed, grabbed his keys and headed to Amari's. Driving over there he was nervous but knew that he needed to see her. He had to see her, to tell her how sorry he was. On the way over there he managed to somehow catch every red light which made his journey seem even longer. He pulled over and stopped at a Mobil gas station and picked up a sorry bouquet of roses. He couldn't just walk in empty handed, he needed something. When he pulled up to her dorm he spotted Darvis' car and sure enough him and Xena were sitting on the car lost in each other.

    He never fully understood why they spent so much time in the car parked in front of the dormitory. He couldn't understand why they wouldn't just go in the house, just as he had the thought; he remembered Amari's strong disgust towards the boy, ever since he tried to kill Xena with his car. She had it stuck in her brain that Darvis was out to hurt Xena and Amari couldn't have that, she refused to let anybody hurt her friend. Anyone that came near Xena with the intent of hurting her would definitely have to answer to Amari first, and little did people realize, she wasn't anything to fuck with!

    Corey walked slowly to the front door; still unsure of what he was going to say once he was face to face with her. He knocked on her door and prayed the words would somehow just come to him.

    "If it ain't the phone ringing then it's the damn door. Damn what the fuck, why can't I ever just have a moment of peace?" Amari thought angrily to herself as she got up out of her bed.

She stomped towards the door. When she swung the door open she was not expecting to see who was standing at the door.

A smile was dying to break free on her face; funny up until that very moment it never dawned on her just how much she was actually missing him. That was probably the reason for her cranky mood and not giving a damn attitude.

"Corey, what are you doing here?" Amari asked a bit confused.

He pulled some half dead roses from behind his back and handed them to her. She took them, glanced at them briefly and then placed them on the table. They stood for a moment in awkward silence.

"Do you think it'd be okay if I came in?" he asked.

She moved to the side and Corey slipped in. The smell of his cologne, his body slightly rubbing against hers sent chills down her spine. Not seeing him for a day had her feeling like she hadn't seen him in a month. Damn was she hooked or what? Corey made himself comfortable on her bed and waited for her to join him. She sat down beside him, again they both sat nervously through another moment of awkward silence.

"Amari, I love you," he finally managed to get out.

She smiled, "Corey, I know that already."

"Amari, I've been so stupid and I am really, really sorry," he managed to get out.

He turned towards her and she couldn't help but notice a single tear that was fighting its way down his cheek. She embraced him tightly and he allowed it all too just come out. He cried and confessed. He confessed how he was jealous of Daryl and the relationship they once had, he said he loved her and was just terrified of losing her.

Amari's heart went out instantly and they immediately began kissing. The next thing she knew she was feeling his hand find its way up her robe. He took two fingers and slid her thong over, allowing him full access. With no warning, the next thing she knew she was feeling his tongue diving deep within her.

"Oh my God!" she moaned over and over again. She wasn't sure she had ever felt pleasure as good as that.

He was down there licking her and sucking the life out of her chocha as if it were going out of style. She began to scream out his name. The louder she got, the harder he sucked. He took her to the mountaintop and back again. She lay on her bed feeling pleased. He hurriedly took off his clothes. He climbed on top of her and slowly entered her. The soft moans turned into loud cries of passion. Corey stopped and looked at her, "Are you okay?" he asked.

"No," she said easing him on his back so that she could climb on top and return the favor. They enjoyed countless hours of love making. When they were done they just laid next to each other, holding each other.

CHAPTER THREE

Amari's world crumpled right before her eyes. She did not even see or anticipate the upcoming blow. Now she found herself alone and unsure of how she was going to continue on in life without her lifeline. Her mother passed.

It was burying day. It was the hardest thing she ever had to do in her life. She was gone. That was the only thought that continuously ran through her head. This was her mother, her best friend, and her lifeline and now she was gone. She was dead and now Amari was convinced she too was dead on the inside. Amari dressed slowly and cautiously that morning. She wore the typical mourning attire, black skirt with a black blouse and blazer. She wore no make up only a light MAC lip gloss and she pulled her hair into a tight bun. She sat at her window and observed the rain pounding hard onto the ground just as her tears were pounding hard onto the windowsill.

When she reached the church with Corey she thought she would faint as soon as she viewed her mother's body. Looking at her just lying there still and lifeless ripped her up on the inside. This was not her mother. This was not the last picture of her she wanted to see.

Amari sat in the front pew of the church quiet and motionless. The people were starting to pour in and every time someone hugged her or tried to say something encouraging she felt her stomach turn and her heart ached more and more.

She was grateful to Corey for forcing her to go and see her in the hospital that time to make mends for the past. Since that visit their relationship went back to the pre drama days. The days of them being best friends and telling each other everything. Corey was sitting right next to her trying to comfort her, but she was definitely passed the point of comfort, there was nothing anyone could say that would make her feel better.

Xena, Amanda and Ke-Ke were there giving Amari as much support as she would allow. She saw Daryl and Cease walk in not to long ago, which didn't surprise her much; Daryl did know her mother. After all they did date for a couple of years and her mother absolutely adored

Daryl. If she could have seen the way he was going about his life now, she would be so disappointed.

The funeral started and she completely ignored the program. All she could think about was her mother's smile and the way she used to comb her hair and sit up all night with her gossiping about the life of a teenager and the stupid things they did for love.

Corey started nudging her hard in the leg, which pissed her off because she was in the middle of reliving some of the best memories she had of her mother.

"Mari, Nikki's here," he whispered.

She looked behind her and sure enough Nikki was sitting two pews behind her with her mother. That shocked Amari. She didn't expect to see her there today. Though they were friends for a couple of years and Nikki spent a lot of nights at Amari's house but the bottom line still remained they were no longer friends. In a way it touched her heart that she could put their differences aside by coming to the service and paying her respects. Nikki didn't look too healthy; she'd lost a lot of weight. Amari made a mental note to thank her after the service for her support.

The service was too long for Amari. She wasn't very comfortable crying in front of people and she felt like a total crying fit was about to occur. She whispered to Corey she needed to leave immediately. It was too much for her, it was overwhelming and she couldn't take it. She was crumbling and she was about to lose the little bit of control she had left.

Back outside of the church Corey and Amari sat quietly for a moment and then the tears began to fall and the loud sobs came not too long afterward. She couldn't stop; maybe she really didn't want to stop. This was the first time she was really able to let go and just accept the pain.

From the moment she received the call from her brother, she refused to accept the fact that she was gone, however, seeing her in that casket with no life left in her made her do nothing but accept it, she was never coming back.

Corey held her tight and let her know that it was okay for her to cry. He encouraged her to let it all out. He decided it would be best if she just went back to the house. He felt it would be too much for her to go to the burial site, but she needed to go. Seeing her body lifted into the ground would give her the last bit of conviction that she was really gone.

The burial was more than she thought it would be. She thought she could handle it but she couldn't and she really should have gone home as Corey had suggested. Once at the burial when they were lifting her body down into the ground something came over her and something inside of her decided she needed to be in there with her. Once you lose your mother was life really worth living? Amari didn't feel it was worth living for her. She tried to throw herself onto her mother's wooden casket. Corey and Daryl caught her just in the nick of time. She was depressed. She was miserable. She was lonely. She missed her mother; she needed her badly. She was mad at the world for taking her mother away from her.

After the funeral services for her mother were over everyone gathered at Momma Val's house. She really was like a second mother to Amari and if she hadn't been there through all of this to help, she didn't think she would have survived. She prepared a real nice meal for everyone and made her family feel welcomed in her house. Amari stayed in her room for awhile. Corey kept coming in and telling her that people wanted to see her to give their condolences. Amari really didn't think she was up to mingling with guests. Corey left only to come back five minutes later to say that Nikki really wanted to speak with her. Amari decided to speak to her only because she really wanted to thank her for coming.

When Nikki entered the room Amari quickly thought that maybe she had made a mistake. For a moment, only a split second, she felt like she may have hated her. Amari thought she still held a grudge but soon realized she didn't.

"Amari, I'm sorry," she began cautiously, 'for everything; your mother…and Daryl."

"Nikki, it's in the past."

"If it's in the past then why do we still act like enemies?" she asked honestly.

"We are not enemies I just chose not to speak to you because I was upset with you for what you did and I was hurting," Amari replied honestly.

"But you could talk to Daryl; why is it that I got the shit end of the stick?"

"You were my best friend. Daryl is a man and men cheat, but you were my friend and you were supposed to have my back not go behind it and fuck my man!"

"Amari, you had everything! I had nothing! I just wanted the life you had. I know what I did was wrong but I just felt at the time it was the only way for me to be happy, I mean really happy."

"And you were happy with Daryl?" Amari questioned.

Why Amari asked that question, she didn't really know, but something inside of Amari convinced her she needed to know the answer.

"I was happy with Daryl for a little while, he was never happy with me though. You were all he talked about. I lied and told him you cheated and got pregnant by someone else, but you were going to pass that baby off as his. He was devastated! He loved you so much. As much as I tried to change that, I couldn't. Even to this day he still has a deep love for you."

That didn't sit well with Amari. To hear someone say Daryl loved her made her instantly feel woozy.

Nikki and Amari talked for an hour and cleared the air. Amari could hear her mother in her ear telling her to forgive Nikki, and she did. She forgave her, they hugged and exchanged numbers and promised to keep in touch. She knew that their friendship would never be what it once was but at least they could begin to fix their relationship.

After Nikki and Amari had their heart to heart conversation, she decided to go out and mingle with the guests which came to pay their respects. Everyone there was really nice and really comforting. It was nice to see everyone all gathered together to bid farewell to her mother.

Amari's mother was gone and she didn't know how she was going to deal with it. But as her mother used to always tell her, 'God only gives you what you can handle' and 'Everything happens for a reason'. Though she did not know the reasoning behind forcing her to deal with the loss of her mother, if God believed she could handle it then obviously she was strong enough to deal with it. For now though she was definitely depressed and fighting hard to maintain and survive the pain of the loss of her mother, her best friend, her lifeline.

CHAPTER FOUR

Amari was so tired of hearing Corey and his countless accusations. The only thing he knew how to talk about was Daryl.

"Dammit already, Daryl and I were done!" she thought angrily to herself.

They spent so much of their time arguing about him, she had reached that point of feeling like she might as well be fucking with him; she was already getting blamed for it. Why should she even bother with the relationship? Losing her mother had left her with the 'whatever attitude'. These days she didn't really care much about anything. And at this point she really could care less if Corey was feeling insecure or not.

Last weekend they went to church with his family, as they have done every weekend since she started living there, and even in church he had the nerve to be talking about Daryl.

"You need to ask God for forgiveness," he'd said to her over and over again.

It seemed like Corey was making things up just to make it seem like a legitimate beef between the two of them. Corey did nothing more than crowd Amari; he knew she was trying to cope with the recent loss of her mother but still he got all in her face about the whole Daryl situation.

It would be a total lie if Amari tried to say she hadn't thought about Daryl. She thought about Daryl and whether or not she made the right choice by choosing to stay with Corey even though it was very clear Daryl wanted to get back together. Then she would think about Daryl's life and whether or not it would be any different right now if they were together or would he have still traveled his path of destruction. She had so many mixed thoughts in her head; she was not sure of what she thought or even truly felt for that matter.

Corey was constantly accusing Amari of being with Daryl that sometimes she honestly felt she might as well be with him. She knew she was better off with Corey. She was without a doubt in love with him; but she did still have a lot of love for Daryl at the same time.

Amari finally spoke to Xena; even though she missed her like crazy she still needed this time to be by herself, to mourn, and to regroup. It still hurt inside but things were starting to get better. Xena caught Amari up on all of the latest gossip going on around school. There wasn't really new gossip; things were pretty much the same as when she last attended. She did let her know that her and Darvis were still together, she also said Daryl called a few times looking for her. Amari felt that was kind of weird about him, he had her cell number yet he'd rather call somewhere knowing she wasn't there.

Corey and Amari were supposed to have some quiet quality time today, just the two of them. He was convinced they fought so much not only because she was cheating on him with Daryl but also because they never saw each other. Amari's thoughts were that she believed for some reason they were drifting apart. She couldn't put her finger exactly on why she felt this way, except that she was damn tired of all of his accusations and she was almost getting to the point where she felt he was just pushing her into Daryl's arms.

The loud knock at the door interrupted Amari's thoughts on the two men in her life.

"Come in," Amari yelled annoyed.

It was Lissa, no doubt coming to give her another pep talk. She was always sticking up for her brother no matter what, even when he was clearly wrong. She admired that about her though, that's what siblings were supposed to do. She often thought back to when her own brother deserted her.

"Hey Mari, how are you feeling?" she began.

"I'm doing okay, what's up?" she asked.

"Nothing, just checking on you, making sure you okay," Lissa said obviously dancing around something.

That's one thing that definitely bugged Amari about her though. She would come in her room clearly ready to defend her brother and his actions, instead of getting right to the point she would beat around the bush. They both sat there quietly smiling and staring at each other. Amari was just about to tell her to just say whatever she came to say when she began her long winded spiel.

Lissa went on and on about how much her brother loved her and how he was just concerned about where their relationship was going. He honestly felt that secretly Daryl and Amari had something going on.

"Lissa, how long am I supposed to deal with this? Every minute of every day that we speak, we speak about Daryl. That's bullshit! No matter how many times I try to tell him and show him that the only person I want is him; he always throws Daryl up in my face. Honestly I am tired of it. We hardly see each other because we both have extra shit going on at school and then we do see each other and all we do is fight. This whole situation is just bullshit!" Amari yelled trying to fight back the tears.

Lissa looked at Amari stunned.

"Are you planning on leaving my brother?" Lissa asked.

"No, I want to work things out but I can't make him feel secure, that's something he has to do on his own."

"Amari, if you really want to work things out then only the two of you can do that, I can't fix it for you," Lissa said as if Amari had asked her to fix it for her.

She needed to remember who approached who here.

"Lissa, I didn't ask you to fix anything, and it's not something I have to do, he has to do it for himself," Amari said quickly putting her back in her place.

"Let me ask you something, you don't think Corey should feel threatened?" Lissa asked seriously.

"Threatened of what, a non-existent problem? Whether or not you want to believe it like I said before Corey has to work this problem out on his own," Amari said looking at her, disgusted with her being there next to her at that moment.

Lissa was annoying Amari now; she had heard enough of her excuses. Amari simply told her this wasn't a conversation the two of them needed to have; it was ultimately between Corey and Amari. Lissa didn't seem to like that very much but whatever, Amari was not here to impress her or cater to her imaginary needs. After Lissa left the room Amari picked up the phone to call Corey.

"Hello," he answered out of breath.

"Hey," she said cautiously, not sure of what kind of mood he was in.

"Well I was wondering if you coming by the house today?" she asked.

"Nope, hadn't planned on it," he said abruptly.

"Corey are you okay? Is there something going on that you are not telling me about?" she asked.

"Nah, just a little busy, I'll call you later," and with that he hung up.

Amari sat on her bed dumbfounded as she realized Corey had just hung up on her. She was sure of it now; he had truly gone and lost his mind. Amari called right back and now the line was coincidentally busy. Amari thought maybe someone called so she tried to calm down for a minute and tried to call back twenty minutes later, still busy. At this point she was fuming! You could clearly see the smoke coming out of her ears. Amari called Xena to get her mind off Corey for a little while and they decided to go to the mall.

After a night of shopping with her girl, Amari decided to call Corey as soon as she reached the house. It was eleven o' clock at night and all she reached was his answering machine. Things were getting funny between them. A month or two ago and Corey would have never acted the way he is acting now.

♫♫♫

Amari sat and watched from a distance as Darvis climbed into his car. She still couldn't believe Xena had her sitting in this car with her stalking her so called boyfriend. For two nights now they've been watching Darvis like a hawk and he had done nothing suspicious. Why Xena insisted he was cheating again was beyond her. But once she had her mind made up there was no changing it, no matter how hard you tried to convince her other wise.

Darvis just climbed into his car and they were now following him down Paradise Road.

"Xena, come on tell me we are not going to spend the entire evening following him all over the city," she said irritated.

Xena was focused, eyes steady on the road. Darvis turned into Boston Market and picked up some food and then continued on his journey down Paradise Road. He kept going straight past Essex Street and he turned right onto Boston Street.

When they turned onto Boston Street Amari's stomach dropped. She wasn't sure why but she felt something bad was moments away from happening. When he made the next right onto Western Avenue her heart sank even lower than her stomach did. She stole a glance at Xena and she was already crying. Just as expected he stopped at the little white house with the chipped pink trim. The same house that had that oh so familiar navy blue Cadillac Seville with the license plate that read 'FOXY' parked in the driveway.

Xena parked at the side of the house and turned the car off. She opened the door, got out and started walking toward the front of the house. Amari got out too not sure how Xena was going to react once she was up close and personal with the bullshit. Xena and Amari stood near the driveway hid securely by a neighboring bush. They watched as Darvis stood standing at the door fidgeting with something in his pocket while he tried to hold the food steady with the other hand.

They both waited patiently to see who, even though they already had an idea, would open the door. The living room light switched on and then the front door opened. When Xena looked at who was standing at the door a wave of tears escaped her eyes and made their way down her cheeks and ultimately landed on her shirt.

Amanda stood at the door in a black lace teddy with a big smile on her face. Darvis stepped halfway into the door, leaned forward and hugged Amanda with one hand. Amanda took his face into her hands and kissed him gently on the cheek. At the sight of that Xena started throwing up. Damn! Amari was at a loss for words. She couldn't believe her girl had to go through this bullshit! After Xena threw up she must have felt relieved and rejuvenated. She marched up to the front door and started pounding on it.

"Xena, are you sure you want to do this?" Amari asked puzzled by her sudden boldness.

"Fuck yeah this is what I want to do! I want him to know I saw him here!" she screamed.

The door swung open and there stood Amanda wearing only a satin robe. When she opened the door she had a big smile on her face and when she saw us standing there her smile instantly turned into a frown.

"Xena, Mari, hey what's up?" she asked nervously.

"You tell me," responded Xena.

Amanda didn't know what to say she just stood silent probably trying to come up with a believable excuse in her head.

"Hey Danyale, what's taking you so long?" asked Darvis while walking from the back wearing only a pair heather gray Sean John jacquard monogram logo boxer briefs.

Xena became infuriated. She bought him those and now he was wearing them for another woman.

"Did he just say Danyale?" Amari questioned in her head trying to figure out what was going on. When Darvis saw Xena his face also turned into an instant frown.

"Xena, what are you doing here?" he questioned while looking at Amanda searching for answers.

Amanda shrugged her shoulders while trying not to bring too much attention to herself. Everyone stood there staring at each other not saying a word. A pair of bright headlights pulling into the driveway distracted everyone's attention.

A vibrant young girl came walking up to the front door oblivious to all that was transpiring around her. When she reached the door she smiled sweetly at Darvis, "hey boo", she said while trying to push her way through. Xena looked her up and down not quite sure what she was supposed to say or could say about the situation. Amari stood baffled at the scene that was unfolding before her eyes. Seeing that her girl wasn't going to speak up, she decided to speak up for her.

"Who the fuck are you?" Amari asked the newcomer.

"I'm Danyale," she said smiling.

Her pleasant disposition had Amari's mind boggled momentarily.

"Straight up, someone needs to speak up now and let us know what the fuck is really going on here!" Amari shouted, aiming her comment directly at Amanda and Darvis.

Amanda stood at the door with her head down with the look of shame written all over her face. Darvis advanced towards Xena, "let's talk privately," he whispered tugging on her arm.

"Why would you need to talk to her privately?" asked Danyale who was now beginning to feel the situation wasn't a pleasant one after all.

"Darvis who is she?" she asked again.

Darvis stood between the two of them not sure of what to say or who he should begin to beg. Momentarily, he stood paralyzed unsure of which one was worth the fight. Xena just stood there crying as though her whole world was over. Amari felt in her heart she definitely understood her pain at the moment. Amari knew first hand what it felt like to give someone your all just to have them shit on you in the end.

Amari broke the silence that had captured all of them, "Danyale, this is Darvis' girlfriend and you are?" she asked.

Danyale's eyes bugged out of her head as she turned to face Darvis quickly.

"What is she talking about Darvis, you have a girlfriend?" she asked puzzled.

"Damn Darvis, you wasn't even straight with your sideline ho, you had her thinking she was Ms. Thing! You real fucked up!" Amari said nudging him in his head.

Amari turned and looked at Amanda, "And don't think you're getting off easy, you're fucked up too bitch!"

"But I'm not fucking him," Amanda said in her defense.

"Nah, but you allowing him to fuck around on your girl, on your so called best friend, that's some straight up scandalous shit!" Amari yelled at her while giving her evil eyes.

Xena still seemed to be in a trance like state. She hadn't moved or uttered a word since Danyale walked up. She put her arm around her shoulders and helped her back to the car. She put her in and climbed into the driver side. Once they pulled off that street and reached closer to home, Xena broke down.

"How could he do this to me? Why would he do this to me?" she cried over and over again.

Amari had no real words for her other than he's a man, doing what men do. Amari told her that sometimes men get lost along the way, and they as women can only hope they will find their way back home. Xena didn't understand that anymore than Amari did.

♫♫♫

Amanda knew she was fucked up but she didn't know how else to go about handling her side business.

See Amanda was what you could call a 'madam'. She had about a dozen girls that worked for her, Danyale being one of them. When Darvis approached her about some side action she didn't know what to say to him.

At first she turned him down, but then he said he would pay top dollar and she just couldn't pass up that kind of money. He only wanted the best which is where she fucked up as well.

See Danyale was one of her more high class hoes. She didn't want to deal with anyone that had a girlfriend. So she made Darvis lie and tell Danyale he was not committed to anyone. Now the whole situation had gotten completely out of hand.

Xena was never supposed to find out and yet somehow she managed to. Amanda knew their friendship was over. The one true friend she had and now she too had managed to fuck that up!

♫♫♫

Amari and Xena were sitting in their dorm room. Amari was comfortable on her bed looking through a photo album of old pictures of Amari and Daryl. Amari wasn't sure exactly what made her want to look at them but something did. She was nearly tempted to shed a few tears at the fond memories the book held; but she wouldn't allow herself to do it. She had to remain strong.

She glanced over at Xena; she was curled up in her bed admiring a picture of her and Darvis.

"Xena, how you holding up over there?" Amari asked.

"I'm okay, just can't believe Amanda would do this to me. I mean I have a hard enough time keeping Darvis in line but to know she is in on it hurts so deep," Xena said placing the photo down.

"I know," was all Amari could think of saying.

CHAPTER FIVE

IT was Friday night and Xena and Amari were in the dorm chilling. Corey and Gregory Charles were out celebrating a recent winning streak with the rest of the team. While sitting there flipping through channels the phone rang unexpectedly.

"Hello," Amari answered.

"Hey girl, what's up?" Ke-Ke said sounding cheery.

"Hey Ke-Ke what's going on?" Amari asked.

"Nothing. I am just getting dressed to go to this hot party over on the Spellman Campus. I called to see if maybe you and Xena wanted to roll?"

"Who all is going?" Amari asked wondering if she was going to bring her crazy ass friend Toni along.

"I was gonna roll solo, that's why I called to see if ya'll was down to join me," she explained.

Seeing that they were not doing anything else Amari decided to tell her they would meet her over there. The girls showered and dressed quickly. Once at the party they looked around trying to spot Ke-Ke but saw her no where amongst the crowd.

Xena had definitely changed though; back in their high school days when they would go to a party Xena would fear the males so much she would hold up the wall all night long. Before Amari could even utter a word out of her mouth she was already on the dance floor having a good time. Amari was proud of her though; she came along way and really developed out of her shell.

After a few drinks Amari managed to loosen up and found herself on the dance floor enjoying a dance with some fine cutie that approached her. During a quick intermission on her part while at the bar grabbing a beverage she finally spotted Ke-Ke. She was having just as much fun as she was.

"Hey Amari, are you enjoying yourself?"

"I sure am," Amari said clearly out of breath.

"Alright go have fun, just make sure you holla at me before you head out."

The party was definitely off the hook and this was the best time Amari had in such a long time. She was definitely feeling tipsy she had a good four or five drinks. She needed to hurry and get herself home so she could pass out. Before they left they spoke to Ke-Ke and thanked her for inviting them.

Driving back to the dorm a bit tipsy Amari realized she was feeling a bit needy. She needed to see and feel Corey. A part of her was worried Corey wouldn't feel the same way.

She called Corey on her cell before reaching the dorm only to get his answering machine. It was damn near 4:30am and this nigga wasn't answering his damn phone. Instantly she got heated. This was that bullshit she had been dealing with for weeks now.

Amari was getting real tired of the dumb ass song and dance routine they were doing. They used to sneak away to the hotels on the weekends just so that they could spend some time alone, all of that stopped and she wasn't sure why.

By the time they finally reached the dorm she was worn the hell out. Xena and Amari crashed immediately upon arriving at their door. When Amari woke up in the early afternoon Xena was already gone and their message button was blinking red. When she pressed play she was surprised to hear Nikki's voice.

"Hey Mari, it's Nikki, I just called to make sure you were doing okay despite all that has happened. Give me a call whenever you get a chance, bye."

She hadn't talked to her since her mother's funeral. Amari decided to go ahead and return her call. They stayed on the phone for a good two hours just catching up on old times. Nikki informed her of some new guy she met at work and how he was so good to her, hopefully now she would find that happiness she had been searching for.

Amari promised Nikki she would attend her daughter's birthday party and with that they ended their conversation. When she got off the phone with Nikki she called Corey hoping to finally hear his voice instead she received his answering machine. She was so tired of speaking to the damn thing.

Amari sat down on her bed unsure of what to do next. She contemplated going to his dorm and awaiting his arrival but then she realized how desperate and pathetic that would make her seem. While she sat there trying to figure out the best approach to her problem the phone rang.

"Hello," she answered.

"Amari, what's up?" the caller sounder familiar yet strange in a way.

"Hello," she repeated.

"It's Daryl," the caller said.

"What do you want?" she questioned nastily.

Right now he was the source of all her troubles, so his call was definitely unwanted.

"Okay, so you don't want to talk, that's fine, I just called to say hello and to see if everything was good with you," he answered sincerely.

Amari was speechless.

"I'll see you around," he said quickly before hanging up the phone.

Okay, that was definitely weird. She hadn't seen or heard from Daryl since her mother's funeral and for him to call now out of the blue just to say hello bothered the hell out of her.

Ever since Nikki told Amari that Daryl loved her, her mind had been working over time. She thought about that statement all the time and it really had her messed up; to think he still loved her after all this time made her feel funny. Amari had no doubt in her mind if Nikki hadn't manipulated Daryl they would still be together. Did that mean she still loved Daryl or she still wanted to be with him, or was she just thinking about the past and how she felt then?

Right now she felt she loved Corey wholeheartedly. Or was Corey a mere replacement of Daryl? Did she simply repress her feelings for Daryl and make herself believe she didn't love Daryl anymore. This is what she went through every night; she fought with herself over who she truly had feelings for.

🎵🎵🎵

"C, man what's up? I met this fly ass shortie today," began Gregory Charles as he flopped down on his bed thinking about Shirayne.

"Yeah man, where you meet her?" asked Corey as he sat down at the desk and opened up his Psychology book to begin his studies.

"I saw her walking outta the Popeye's. She's thick as shit man!" smiled Gregory Charles remembering how curvaceous her body was.

"Yeah, what's her name?"

"Shirayne," smiled Gregory Charles.

Corey smiled.

"She rain huh," Corey repeated while laughing.

"Ahh come on man don't clown me. When you see her you'll understand exactly why I am tripping out over shortie!"

"Yeah, alright man I'm gonna have to see shortie for myself to be the judge."

"So what's good with you and Amari? Are ya'll okay? She's been calling here a lot," Gregory Charles noted.

"Yeah we cool," answered Corey as he turned around to start doing his homework.

Truth be told Corey didn't really know what was going on between the two of them. He knew he had met someone new himself and couldn't stop thinking about her. Her name was Lily and he met her at the club one night when the football team was out celebrating one of their many victories. The way she danced up on him made his manhood stand at attention and since that night he hadn't been able to get her out of his system.

Gregory Charles leaned back on his bed and began to daydream about Shirayne. He really wanted to call her but didn't want to seem too eager so he decided to lay low and give himself some time.

♫♫♫

"Damn, when the hell am I gonna get over her?" thought Daryl to himself.

All day he had been thinking about Amari and when they had been together. He still kicked himself for being stupid enough to let her slip away. He honestly loved her and didn't know how he was able to go this long without her.

The ring of his phone interrupted his thoughts. He quickly picked up the phone.

"Yeah," he answered.

A recorded voice came over letting him know he had a collect call from his right hand man. Daryl quickly pressed one to accept the call.

"What it do my nigga?" Daryl said excitedly.

"Same shit different day," replied Cease solemnly.

"My nigga how you holding up?" asked Daryl sensing how sad Cease sounded.

"I'm here!" replied Cease.

"I sent Riana down there yesterday to put some money on your books, did you get that?" asked Daryl making sure she went down there and handled her business.

"Yeah, I got that. Good looks!"

"No problem, you know you always got that."

"So what's popping off out there?"

"Nothing much, just doing me as always."

"Yeah, I hear that."

"Lately, I've been going fucking crazy behind Mari," confided Daryl.

"Yeah what's good with shortie? Ya'll finally stopped fucking around and got ya'll shit back together?" wondered Cease.

"Naw, she still with that crab ass nigga Corey."

"For real? I thought for sure she would have smartened up by now."

"Yeah me too. That dude can not make her happy!"

"So what you gonna do? Are you gonna sit by why she wit dude, or are you gonna make that move and get your wifey back?"

"I don't know man! I'm just gonna fall back for a few."

"Alright homey, I hear you on that. I guess you really don't wanna complicate shit anymore than it already is."

"Yo has Kat been up there?" asked Daryl out of nowhere trying to change the subject.

"Nah, she sent a couple of letters. She keeps saying she wants to come up here but doesn't want to run into Riana."

"Yeah, I feel her dawg, you know how psycho Riana can be!"

"I know dawg, I guess I can't really be mad at her, I just thought she woulda been here for a nigga! Have you heard any news on my case?" asked Cease switching the subject as abruptly as Daryl had earlier.

Daryl remained silent.

"Dawg, on some real shit, I gotta get up outta here! I'm not built for these walls! I'm dieing up in this shithole," Cease said sounding like he wanted to cry.

Daryl sat on the other end of the phone wanting to give him some words of encouragement. He hated to hear his boy sounding so defeated.

"Man, I talked to Attorney Weiner two days ago; he basically said his hands were tied. You gonna have to finish out them six months," answered Daryl truthfully.

DILEMMA

"Damn D man, I was really hoping to get outta here early."

"I know, I feel ya man, just keep your ground my nigga," Daryl said trying to give him some hope.

They each laid down on their beds and began to think.

Cease laid back and thought about what landed him behind these bars. Most would think he was locked up behind a gun or drug possession. However, that wasn't the case. He was locked up because he lost his temper and fucked Riana up. He could remember the day like it was yesterday.

He arrived at Riana's house, the house he paid for, not thinking anything. He walked right into the house not worrying himself with announcing his presence by ringing the doorbell or calling first.

The downstairs was completely quiet. He walked upstairs and found his daughter sleeping in her princess bed; he smiled at how peaceful she looked. He continued down the hallway, in pursuit of his son, when he didn't see him in his bedroom he preceded to the bathroom to take a leak. In an instant his whole world flipped upside down.

He saw his son lying face down in the bathtub full of water. He quickly ran to the tub and yanked his son out. He lay down on the tile and began to do CPR on him.

When he finally got him to breathe on his own he wrapped him up in a towel and headed straight to Riana's bedroom.

As he got closer to her door he became outraged as he heard her moans of pleasure. He busted through the door and became infuriated at Riana's naked body entangled with some strange man.

"Riana, what the fuck?" yelled Cease.

Riana jumped up in shock and tried to cover herself up.

"You lying up in here getting fucked while our son is drowning in the fucking bathtub!" he yelled.

Riana reached her arms out for her baby.

"Hell no, you ain't getting him," Cease yelled snatching the baby out of her reach.

"Cease whateva! Why don't you just take your kids and leave me the hell alone!" Riana yelled laying back down not giving a fuck.

Her lack of feelings for their son infuriated him even more. He began to see red and knew he was seconds away from losing his sanity. Without warning he snatched her naked body out of the bed and started pounding on her. When her body fell limp in his hands he let her go and spit on her. The man she was with, attempted to get outta the bed, one glance at Cease's glock quieted his ass down as well.

He picked up his son and then got his daughter out of the bed and headed straight to Daryl's house.

🎵🎵🎵

Amari wasn't sure what was going on with her and Corey. For the past two weeks he had been nothing but nice to her. He called her every day; they snuck off to the hotel to make love. This was the Corey she was used to. The one she fell in love with. Amari was happy, happier than she had been in a long while. She wanted things to stay this way forever, but she knew that his sudden change in behavior was only the calm before the storm.

🎵🎵🎵

It was the end of the basketball season and Amari really wasn't looking forward to going to the basketball game. She had no choice but to go, she already promised Corey she would support his man, and since Corey and Amari's relationship was so rocky she didn't want to do anything that would upset him. It just really made no sense to Amari. The team usually did well, but Gregory Charles always looked so timid on the court. He was always afraid to shoot. The first five or six games she attended, it just broke her heart to watch him out there and refuse to shoot the damn ball. In Amari's eyes, that's what basketball was all about right, shooting the ball into the hoop. But Corey had been talking Amari's ear off non stop about how much Gregory Charles had improved and how he wasn't afraid to let it be known he had some major skills on the b-ball court.

Currently as it stood, Gregory Charles was indeed a starter along with Sanchez, Mumford, Milt, and Trot. Where the hell these niggas got their names was beyond her, but whatever. Gregory Charles was the only normal named person.

So Xena and Amari dressed quickly and headed down to the gym for the last home game of the season before the playoffs. She spotted Corey immediately on the court shooting some hoops. Amari smiled admiring how sexy her man looked.

"Come on Mari, there are some seats right there," she pointed at two empty seats on the overcrowded bleachers.

Before they could even sit down comfortably the boys basketball team came zooming onto the court doing the ritual lap around the gym. Corey got situated right next to the coach as he prepared to get ready for the game as well. He wasn't on the team as an official player but as a consultant. He was the captain and leader of the team without actually playing.

She spotted Gregory Charles immediately and secretly

wished him luck. He looked different though. He had a certain swagga about himself she had never seen before.

The start of the game she was expecting to see him coward away from the ball, but at the jump ball he immediately went for it and scored the first two points of the game. He did a weird motion with his hands, sort of rubbing them together, as if to say, "Yeah, I touched that!" she smiled, admitting to herself this was definitely going to be a different type of game.

They went back and forth, trading baskets for baskets, Amari was thoroughly impressed with the caliber of confidence and assuredness Gregory Charles was playing with.

Suddenly from the crowd began the chant, "G-Money". She looked around wondering who the hell they were talking about.

"Mari, who the hell is G-Money?" Xena asked searching the gym.

"Hell, if I know," she said looking just as confused. Then suddenly, as their attention was briefly distracted, Gregory Charles got the ball and went for a three pointer. She was shocked and said to herself, "ooh he shouldn't have done that. But when it went in, she couldn't help but jump in excitement.

"That's what I'm talking about G-Money," a spectator yelled from the crowd.

Xena and Amari looked at each other in amazement, both realizing like idiots that G-Money was none other than shy guy Gregory Charles. Amari chuckled slightly to herself realizing Gregory Charles now had himself a little thug nickname.

🎵🎵🎵

It was 38 seconds left in the game and they were down three points. Xena and Amari watched with pure amazement in their eyes, at this point in the game Gregory Charles a.k.a G-Money had already pulled a triple double! The crowd was going bananas as they watched the seconds tick down off the clock. The ball was in the opponents hands with ten seconds left one of the players went up and was ready to dunk it and it was heavily tested by none other than G-Money himself. The crowd went wild! Corey was practically on the court cheering him on. The fierceness in G-Money's face let us all know he was not fucking around, he was here to win this game and he wasn't taking anything less than a win.
The ball was back in their hands, G-Money took the ball and started taking his time down the court, 5...4...3...he stopped at the three point line and shot the ball, 2...swoosh, he made it! The gym was in an uproar, the game was headed to over time.

🎵🎵🎵

"Damn Gregory Charles, you did your thing out

there tonight!" Amari complimented him as they were walking into Dave & Busters for the after game celebration.

They ended up winning that game in double overtime; it was the best basketball game the girls had ever attended.

"Thanks, I'm glad you could make it down, I know you wasn't really feeling the games since you thought I couldn't play and shit," he said teasing her.

"Yeah, my fault about that, I see you stepped your shit up big time," she laughed.

He smiled.

"But damn Gregory Charles what is up with this G-Money bullshit, I was hearing on the court today?" she asked being nosey.

"Oh, that, well that is just my alter ego, you know I just had to put that mask on and play my game, plus it's getting me much play with the ladies," he said laughing and giving Corey dap.

"Please, whatever nigga, these chicks still ain't gonna give your ass no play," she laughed giving Xena dap.

"Yeah, that's what you think, these chicks are coming at ya boy hard!"

"I bet, you betta watch yourself before you get yourself caught up with the wrong bitch out here, and that's some real shit!" Amari said getting serious with him.

"I know, you just looking out for your lil bro, right?" he said winking at Amari.

"Yeah, something like that," she said walking away from the two guys.

🎵🎵🎵

While at Dave & Buster's Gregory Charles got a very important phone call, it was Shirayne. He couldn't believe she'd called him. She was working and missed the game. He talked to her on the phone in a corner of the establishment. It was a bad time but he didn't want to let her off the phone. Finally after about five minutes of small talk, they made plans to go to the movies that following weekend.

Gregory Charles was excited about his upcoming date, he couldn't wait to spend some time alone with her and maybe get a relationship going with her. He couldn't believe how much he was feeling her.

CHAPTER SIX

Today was a really bad day for Amari. She took a final exam today in math and failed. She could not believe this; she hadn't failed anything in years, let alone math. She knew the source of this was all of this extra stress she was dealing with.

She still hadn't really spoken to Corey. She called him a couple of times and left messages but heard nothing in return. He hadn't even been to church which had his mother all upset. He called Amari briefly the other day; he said he was returning her call. That pissed Amari off something terrible. What did he mean he was returning her call? She was supposed to be his girlfriend, why was he returning her call instead of calling to talk to her? She was so angry she could barely speak with him. They sat on the phone in silence for a good ten minutes before he said he had to go do some homework. He didn't even talk to her, he had nothing to say.

Momma Val called and said they were having a celebration for Corey. Amari was completely confused.

"Celebration for what?" she asked.

Momma Val said the scout that was looking at him during the season wanted to sign him to Atlanta's Professional football team. Amari couldn't believe he was about to play football professionally and he never thought to call and share this news with her. Amari was hurt. She told his mother she had a lot of studying to do for the rest of her finals if she wanted to stay out of summer school, she ended the conversation by saying she would try to make it. Momma Val sounded upset but accepted her story nonetheless.

It was the middle of the afternoon and Amari found herself headed to the mall to relieve her stress.

Amari was walking through the mall when she spotted Nikki. Nikki looked really happy to see Amari. They decided to walk the mall together, the way they used to do back in the days.

They were in Macy's looking at the latest Rocawear line when all of a sudden Amari heard a horrifying gasp escape Nikki's mouth. Amari turned in the direction of her stare and there stood Corey kissing another female. Amari was stunned. She watched as he kissed and held her the same way he once did with her. Amari started shaking and thought for sure the tears would soon begin to fall from her eyes.

There he stood all hugged up and kissing some lady that looked to be at least in her early thirties. So that's what makes him happy? Amari really didn't want to but she walked towards his direction.

"Corey?" she questioned still wishing it really wasn't him.

He broke away from kissing her and looked Amari's way.

"Damn," was all he said.

"Damn! That is all you can say to me?"

"Amari, I didn't want you to find out this way."

"Really, so how did you want me to find out?"

"Look, I was just waiting for the right time to tell you."

"The right time? When do you think is the right time to tell me you are cheating on me?"

That was all she needed to say because the tears came down full throttle after that. Dammit, why did I have to start crying? She was in the middle of the store crying over some nigga and all he could say to her was damn!

"Mari, don't cry, I never meant to hurt you."

"Of course you didn't mean to hurt me. You just cheated, why would that hurt me?"

"Look, it's just something with me, you wouldn't understand," he said looking back at his new boo.

"How do you know? You never once gave me a chance to understand. Instead you just cheated and ignored me. And I really thought you were different and had genuine love for me. All this time you have been accusing me and you were the one cheating. Damn how stupid am I?" she muttered before running away.

"Amari, I do love you but we just can't be together," he shouted after her.

She turned around heated he would dare utter the word love to her.

"Fuck you! Fuck you! Fuck you! You don't love me; if you did you would not be cheating! If you weren't happy and felt she could make you happier then you should have been a man about your shit and told me instead of having me find out like this!" Amari screamed before practically running out of the mall.

Once she reached her car and was safely inside she nearly broke down. A moment later there was a bang on her window and she nearly jumped out of her seat. It was Nikki. She forgot she was in the mall with her. She rolled down her window not really wanting to talk to her.

Nikki looked at Amari and instantly Amari knew she could feel her pain.

"Amari are you okay? Do you need me to drive you home?" she asked with concern.

"Nah, I'll be okay, thanks for asking though. I will call you later okay?"

She nodded her head okay and then walked away. Amari sat there for a moment just thinking and reflecting on how her life ended up that way. Two boyfriends in her entire life and they both end up dogging her out the same damn way! Amari couldn't imagine what was wrong with her.

After driving around for hours Amari finally made it back to the dorm, distraught and full of tears. She absolutely did not know what to do or if there was anything she could do other than cry. She lied down and cried and just allowed the tears to flow out for hours upon hours.

About two hours later she heard the door creak open and the joyful voice of Xena talking on her cell phone.

"Jordan you are so crazy! All right let me shower and change and I'll meet you in an hour. All right cutie, yeah see ya soon. Hey Mari, you sleep?" she asked putting down her bag.

Amari wanted to pour her heart out to her but she couldn't bring herself to do it. So she lay there and faked sleep as Xena showered and dressed for her date.

Finally after an hour she was ready to leave. When she left Amari got up and walked down the hallway for a juice out of the machine. Amari's head was pounding due to all the tears she released in the past four to five hours. Once back in the room she lied down again and after a few minutes finally found some rest.

The annoying ringing of the phone abruptly interrupted Mari's sleep.

"Hello," Amari asked sluggishly.

"Mari, let me explain. Please just give me a minute," he begged hurriedly.

"Corey I have no interest in hearing anything you may have to say. You did what you wanted to do so leave me the hell alone. Obviously I wasn't making you happy. Now you can be happy with your new girlfriend, your older I guess more mature girlfriend!" Amari said before hanging up the phone.

Amari couldn't believe he had the nerve to call and ask her to listen and allow him to explain. What was there to explain? He cheated plain and simple, there was nothing more cut and dry then that. She wondered why this was happening to her. Amari couldn't understand why Corey would hurt her like this? She was falling apart. First Daryl cheated on her, but she just deduced that to him being a no good inconsiderate bastard! But now Corey, that was so unexpected. He seemed to really care for her; genuinely care about her. He loved her; at least she thought he loved her. He was a damn good boyfriend and he always took care of her. It seemed as if they were happy together.

He found happiness and now Amari found herself depressed and distraught because she had lost him. She couldn't understand why he wouldn't tell her if she was doing something wrong. He should have given her a chance to make things right? How was she going to live her life without him?

She lay down on her bed wanting nothing more than to fall asleep and never awake again. This was something more than she could handle. She couldn't hear the little voice in her head telling her she was stronger than this and to just brush it off, but she couldn't. She loved him and she didn't know what she was going to do without him.

🎵🎵🎵

Daryl lay on his bed tossing and turning. He finally got up out of the bed when he realized he wasn't going to be able to sleep. He couldn't quite put his finger on what was wrong with him but he knew it had something to do with Amari. He looked at the time and saw that it was four in the morning, there was no way he could call her at this hour, no he had to wait until a decent hour to call and find out if everything was okay with her. He tried to fall back asleep but couldn't. He went over to his stereo and pressed play, when he heard Nelly and Kelly's song, 'Dilemma', all of his feelings for Amari came flooding back. He loved her and he wanted to be with her so bad. Yeah, he dated other women but none of them came close in comparison with her. He couldn't help himself from thinking about her all the time. He really wished he didn't think about her so much, but there was nothing he could do about it. His heart made its choice and it was her he needed.

He wished daily she would call him and let him know she was feeling the same way. He needed to hear her say she still loved him and thought about him as much as he did her. Before the song was over he found himself crying. It had been so long since he had shed tears, he almost didn't know what to do with himself. His mother knocked softly on his door at the sounds of his sniffles.

"Daryl baby are you okay?" she whispered as she quietly entered his room.

"Yeah, mom I'm okay, go back to bed," he said trying to hide his face.

"It's Amari, isn't it?" she asked, knowing what the problem was without him uttering a word.

He looked at her suspiciously wondering how she knew what he was crying like a pussy about.

He shook his head yes.

She reached over and gave him a hug. He was momentarily taken aback at her show of emotion. He couldn't remember the last time his mother had hugged him or he wanted to be hugged by her. At the moment he needed that more than anything to help him to get all of the emotions out.

"Daryl, I can see how much you are hurting, but the person you need to show these emotions to is not me. How is she ever suppose to know what is going on inside that brain of yours unless you open up to her? You have to tell her how you feel or else you will always regret not giving your all at trying to get her back. You have to be willing to go through the fire for her. You have to be willing to do whatever it takes to get the one you love. That's what love is all about; sacrifices and commitments."

She hugged her son tightly, kissed him lightly on the forehead and then headed back to bed. Daryl knew what his mother was saying was right. He knew he needed to talk to Amari and let her know how he was feeling or else he would never have peace within himself and he would forever play the woulda, shoulda, coulda game when it came to her.

♫♫♫

Amari sat down at her desk completely unsure of herself. She started thinking heavily about Daryl. Her mind drifted back to when she found out Daryl cheated on her. The pain that shot through her heart at that moment was back with a vengeance. How did she find herself back in this position? How did she not know that once again she was being cheated on? Were there signs she missed or refused to see?

She reached into her desk drawer and pulled out a picture of her and Corey from last year's prom. They looked so happy but maybe she was the only happy one. After Corey watched her go through everything she went through with Daryl she never would have imagined he'd hurt her the same way.

She wanted to be angry at him but at this moment she couldn't. All she wanted was Corey back. She would do anything at that time to find out this was all a bad dream. She prayed endlessly that Corey would call her and tell her he made a big mistake and he never meant to hurt her. She loved Corey and she needed him in her life. She was convinced she couldn't make it through life without him by her side.

She took out a sheet of paper and decided to write Corey a letter. She hadn't decided whether or not she would actually give it to him but she needed to get her feelings out.

Corey,

Where can I begin? I never in a million years would have thought you could be capable of hurting me this way, to this magnitude. I loved you with every ounce of life in my body. I trusted you and gave you my all and it sickens me you could shit on me this way. I'm hurting baby but the fact still remains, I need you. I can't do this thing called life without you. I just...I...

She couldn't write anymore. The tears had come and her vision was becoming cloudy. She hated the fact that her love for Corey was making her one of those foolish stupid girls that would turn a blind eye to any indiscretion. She hated that she was already thinking about forgiving him. She hated that she felt she couldn't live without him.

♫♫♫

Amari sat in her dorm room not believing what she once again found herself dealing with. She couldn't believe she just caught Corey cheating on her. She felt that he of all people understood her and would never do something that would hurt her so viciously. She was more than heartbroken. Her entire world had been shattered.

Amari buried her head into her pillow and began crying. She couldn't hold back the tears. She was hurting so bad.

It wasn't until that moment that Amari identified with Charisse and the pain she felt when she found out the love of her life didn't feel the same way about her.

This story had been told so many times Amari thought for sure she'd be able to handle herself better if she were to ever find herself in this situation again. She wasn't sure how she'd be able to rebound from this. Her world as she knew it had unexpectedly been turned upside down and she wasn't sure she would be able to come back from this one.

Amari got up off her bed and walked over to her desk. She pulled out her favorite purple pen and her notepad and began writing a poem about Corey.

Writing was the only way Amari knew how to get all of her feelings out without having to worry about anyone interrupting her thoughts.

♫♫♫

Daryl sat down on his couch feeling he was in a lousy mood. He wasn't quite sure what was wrong with him but he was sure it had something to do with Amari. He was feeling fine and then within a split second his heart was hurting.

It was weird and unexplainable. He couldn't describe what he was feeling, but he knew she needed him.

He picked up the phone and decided to call her.

The phone rang three times then he was greeted by her voicemail. She sounded so happy so full of cheer.

"Hey you've reached Peaches, leave me a message. Just remember if you don't leave a message then you never called."

He smiled thinking about her.

"Hey Peaches, its Daryl, just calling to make sure everything was okay. You were on my mind heavily and my heart was telling me I should be worried, call me."

After Daryl left the message he hung up the phone and hoped she would call him back.

♪♪♪

The next morning Amari got up and re-read the poem she wrote about Corey. It still surprised her how accurately she could express her feelings with her pen.

The image of his and her body intertwined
The disheartening thought of her body
Replacing mine

Inevitable is the losing of my stability
Due to the reckless actions of both men
Hurting me constantly

Deception came twice baring a smile and a cunning heart
Both times deception cheated but I cannot blame it
For playing its part

Security is no longer my blanket

Latifa Sanchez

My emotions pushed out in the cold and
Forced to with stand it

Easy for men since they're on the outside looking in
I struggle to find my faults but maybe
My faults lie with them

CHAPTER SEVEN

It was Monday and Amari had to get up to go to class. She really didn't want to go to class because she was still trying to move on from losing the love of her life…again! However, she did need to go because she had already lost way too much class time due to the death of her mother.

She literally had to force herself out of bed this morning. Last night when Xena came home from her weekend with Jordan, as soon as she walked in Amari ran to her and hugged her.

"Mari are you okay?" she asked skeptical.

Amari let it all out. She was definitely her girl, her road dog, they cried together; literally. Xena was ready to go to his dorm room and attempt to kick his ass. Amari had nothing but love for her because of that. Xena had been good though, helping Amari out as much as she could and intercepting all of Corey and Gregory Charles' calls.

He was the one cheating yet he was calling Amari like a madman. It was not like he was calling to ask to get back with her, he was calling because he wanted Amari to know he did love her and didn't mean to hurt her, but he didn't want to be with her. What kind of bullshit was that?

Amari was dead smack in the middle of her Calculus class trying to focus on her exam. She had been sitting there daydreaming. She gave up on the final midway through because she had no clue as to any of the answers she was supposed to figure out. Hopefully the professor would have some pity on her and give at least a D for the semester.

After class she decided to go back to the dorm to get some rest. On her way back to the dorm she ran into Daryl.

"Hey girl, what's up?" he asked.

"Nothing, just chilling, trying to pass these damn finals," she answered.

As she talked to Daryl she noticed something different with his whole demeanor, somehow he seemed different. Hopefully, he was able to get his life back on track.

"Daryl I'll see you around okay?" she said trying to get away.

Amari didn't feel right talking to him; in her eyes he was the source of all of her problems with Corey. To say that she was depressed would be a definite understatement. All she thought about was Corey. Xena seemed to think Amari should give Corey another chance, listen to what he had to say, but what she didn't realize was that Corey never said he wanted to be with her, only that he couldn't be with her.

Since the night they went to the party with Ke-Ke they had all grown tighter. Amari considered her to be her second best friend, right behind Xena. When she spoke to Ke-Ke about the issue with Corey cheating she felt she should just leave Corey alone. Her advice made the most sense but it was the hardest to follow.

The next evening was the big celebration for Corey; Amari wished she could be there. Technically she could still go because Momma Val invited her. She didn't want to be there as a friend of the family, she wanted to be there as Corey's girlfriend, but she couldn't. He had chosen someone new for that role in his life.

"Hey Mari," Xena said sounding cheerful.

"Yeah," she replied in her usual dull state.

"You staying in tomorrow night?" she asked.

"Probably, why?" she responded.

"Well Corey invited me to his party and I think you should come with me?" she said.

Was this chick on drugs or something?

"Hell no I don't want to go, what are you crazy? Don't you think I have had my feelings hurt enough?"

"Come on Mari," she pleaded.

"NO!" she said adamantly while answering the knock at the door.

It was Ke-Ke; she knew she would be on her side.

"You will never believe what this girl wants me to do," Amari began.

"What?" asked Ke-Ke full of interest.

"She wants me to go with her to Corey's party," Amari laughed.

Ke-Ke sat there silently for a moment as if she was pondering something intense.

"You know that might not be such a bad idea," Ke-Ke said making herself comfortable on Amari's bed.

Okay these two chicks had definitely lost their minds and they claimed to be Amari's best friends. What would make them believe she could go to a party like that and not fall apart, especially if he was there with his new girlfriend?

"Mari, wait a minute and at least hear me out. Corey invited Xena and Corey's mother invited you which mean you are expected to attend. Now what you need to do is go to the mall and buy a banging form fitting dress, get your hair and nails refreshed and attend the party with Daryl as your escort. That right there is what you call serious payback. As hung up on Daryl as Corey is he will feel nothing but sheer pain when he sees the two of you together, the nigga will be straight heated!"

Her plan sounded devious and Amari wasn't sure if she was ready to be on those types of terms with Corey yet. Amari sat there for a moment just thinking trying to determine if she was ready to take things to the next level, the level of pain, heartache, and revenge.

"Well Mari, you down or what?" asked Ke-Ke.

"I don't know," she replied hesitantly.

"Mari, it sounds like a good plan, serves that nigga right for doing that fucked up shit to you!" argued Xena trying to convince her.

"I don't know you guys; I'll let you know in the morning."

"Fine, but I am calling you at six in the morning. If we are going to do this then we need to make moves early in the morning," explained Ke-Ke.

"Whatever," Amari replied.

"Alright with that said and done, I'll see you girls later," said Xena as she headed out on her date with Jordan.

Xena and Jordan had been together since the incident when they caught Darvis cheating again. Darvis called the room constantly and Amari couldn't have been happier for Xena since she had been able to hold her ground.

Ke-Ke stayed for another hour or so. The two friends watched television and gossiped. Ke-Ke spent much of the night trying to convince Amari to go along with her plan. When she finally left Amari couldn't have been happier, happy for the silence. Amari needed to be alone with her thoughts. She laid in bed and just contemplated whether or not she was ready to take things to that level with Corey. She watched other people do these same types of things and in the end the two people ended up hating each other she didn't want that to happen with Corey. By the time she fell asleep she decided she wasn't going to go through with Ke-Ke's plan, just didn't see it benefiting her in any way.

♪♪♪

She was fast asleep having a nice dream about Corey when they were together and in love when the phone interrupted her beautiful thoughts.

"Hello," she answered angrily.

"Can I speak to Amari?" a strange female voice replied.

"Who is this?" she asked annoyed.

"Lily," she replied.

"Lily? Who the hell is Lily and why was she calling at that time of morning," she thought angrily to herself confused and still half asleep.

"Damn, what did you say your name was again?" she asked still very confused and thinking she clearly dialed the wrong number.

"It's Lily bitch, Corey's girlfriend," she practically screamed.

That woke Amari up completely. She rose up out of the bed and looked at the clock on her nightstand; it read 3:00 am. No this bitch was not calling her crib at this time of the morning, on some bullshit!

"What the fuck are you calling me for?" Amari asked irritated.

"I called to let you know a few things, and I am only going to tell you this once, so make sure you hear me good. I want you to leave my man the hell alone. Don't call him, don't show up at his mother's house, and don't even approach him if you see him on campus. You are a thing of the past and I am his future, deal with it bitch! If I find out you have attempted communication with him I will hunt you down and kick your stupid ass! Don't fuck with me!" she blared.

All Amari heard following that was the dial tone. She was speechless and confused. She had half a mind to call Corey and give him a piece of her mind about his girlfriend calling her crib, but she decided against it. Instead she decided that Ke-Ke's plan would work perfectly. Fuck Corey and his feelings! She didn't want to hurt his feelings, that's why she wasn't trying to bring Daryl around him, if Corey was to see them together she knew it would fuck his head all up.

Even thought it was damn early she called Daryl. He clearly sounded asleep.

"Daryl, I didn't mean to wake you. Can you talk?" she whispered.

"Amari is that you?" he asked.

"Yeah."

"Damn, I do have company, but what's up? Are you okay?" he asked sounding concerned.

"Yeah, I'm straight; I just needed you to do me a favor."

"What is it?" he asked.

Quickly she explained the situation and as soon as she was done he agreed right away. Secretly she was relieved, she didn't know what she would have done if he had said he couldn't go. She would have probably broke down and cried. After he agreed, they said goodbye and he agreed to call her later once he bought something to wear for the occasion.

After talking with Daryl Amari felt at peace. She was still heated with Corey and the fact that his bitch called her crib trying to check her on some stupid shit. She smiled at the thought of seeing Corey's face when she walked in with Daryl.

CHAPTER EIGHT

This morning Ke-Ke and Amari went to the mall to shop for the perfect dress and after looking in about five stores they finally found it. It was a simple yet elegant, straight form fitting red dress, to match Amari's newly dyed red hair, with sequined spaghetti straps. She found a nice pair of clear sequined heels to match. Once they left the mall they went to the nail salon so that Amari could get a manicure as well as a pedicure, the feet had to look good as well. She had a hair appointment at 1:00 pm, so after their nail appointment they decided to get a bite to eat to pass some time.

Amari always hated going to the salon to get her hair done, it always took so long. Her hairdresser Tracy owned her own shop and she was a really good stylist but she had entirely too many clients, which made the wait for her a good hour or two. After sitting in T & T's Hair Care Salon for a good four hours she was finally done with a fresh new hair do.

Once back to the dorm she had to quickly shower and begin to get ready.
Ke-Ke was back at her dorm getting ready as well. Daryl called about 6:30 pm and asked if she was ready, unfortunately she wasn't. She needed at least another forty-five minutes. Ke-Ke and Xena were going to ride together along with Jordan, and then Daryl and Amari would ride in her car.

Finally after much preparation she was ready to go and she had to admit she looked damn good. She called Daryl's cell phone to see where he was, he said he'd been waiting in the lobby since he called her an hour ago; that made her feel really bad.

It still felt a little weird to be going to the party with Daryl as her date. When Daryl saw her exit the elevator his whole face lit up. He slowly walked over to her and took hold of her hands and just stood there admiring her. It unnerved her but it felt good to have someone look at her with such adoration in their eyes. She was getting nervous.

"So are you ready?" she asked breaking the silence.

"Nope, not yet, I want to admire you just a little bit more," he said smiling at her.

After two or more minutes of just admiring her they headed out the door and to her car.

"So am I your man tonight or just your escort to this corny ass party?" he asked smiling deviously.

She had to return the smile. He always liked to know where he stood before he did anything.

"Just my escort okay. Honestly, Daryl I am just trying to make Corey jealous." she said being completely honest. She didn't want him to think there was more to it than that.

"That's cool, so you really love this guy don't you?" he asked.

"Yeah," she said with a half smile.

The rest of the ride to Corey's parent's house was a silent one. When they got there she had to admit her nerves really began to settle in. Her stomach was doing flips and she thought at any moment she would bring up everything she had for lunch. She sat in the car for a moment hesitant about going inside and following through with her plan. Daryl must have sensed her hesitancy.

"Amari, come on let's just do this, you'll be okay, I promise," he said comforting her while holding open her door.

After taking a deep breath she got out of the car and started walking hand in hand with Daryl to the front door. She saw Ke-Ke's car, which also gave her some comfort knowing that her girl's were inside and no doubt had her back.

At the door she nervously rang the bell and her hands began to shake and sweat. Momma Val answered the door and was so excited to see her.

"Amari," she gasped, "I am so happy to see you. Xena said you wouldn't be able to make it."

"Hi, Momma Val," Amari said while leaning over and giving her a hug. "You remember my friend Daryl right?" she asked.

Momma Val nodded her head yes and ushered the couple in. They walked in and Daryl grasped her hand tighter. They walked around for a minute looking for Xena and Ke-Ke.

Xena and Ke-Ke were standing on the other side of the room talking to Lissa. Amari took Daryl by the arm and they walked over there together.

"Hey Lissa, what's up?" Amari said making her presence known.

Lissa looked at her and then her eyes roamed over to Daryl. The look of disgust was apparent on her face.

"Do you ever use your fucking head? Why the hell did you bring him here?" she tried to whisper to Amari.

Amari had to laugh at her.

"Lissa what are you talking about? I can bring whomever I choose."

"He's not welcome in this house," she said trying to keep her voice down, "Now get him outta here before Corey sees him."

"Your mother didn't seem to have an issue with him being here, so you and your brother shouldn't either," Amari said taking Daryl by the arm and leading him out to the makeshift dance floor.

"Damn she was upset," Daryl whispered to Amari.

"Yeah, I know but I'm sure her brother is going to be that much more upset," she said bringing Daryl closer to her.

Dancing this close to Daryl felt good, it felt almost natural. Amari was beginning to drift off into another world, when she suddenly heard her name being yelled. She lifted her head off of Daryl's shoulder and towards the direction of the commotion. Corey was charging down the stairs headed her way.

"Amari, let's talk," Corey nearly yelled.

"I have nothing to say to you," she responded.

"Amari, don't make me embarrass you out here, I said let's talk," he demanded.

"Yo dawg back up off her, she said she had nothing to say to you," Daryl said standing in between Corey and Amari.

"Nigga you don't know me, so I'd advise you to get the fuck outta my face," Corey said while giving Daryl a little push.

Out the corner of her eye, Amari saw just about the entire football team trying to make its way towards the middle of the room, their direction. She put her arm on Daryl's shoulder hoping to ease his temper.

"Daryl, its okay, I can handle this," she said giving him a quick peck on the lips.

The steam was boiling out of Corey, it was written all over his face.

"Fine, you want to talk, where?" she said giving Corey attitude.

"Upstairs, away from the crowd," he said gesturing towards the stairs.

"Daryl, I'll be right back," she said while making her way through the crowd and up the stairs.

When they reached the top of the stairs, Corey pushed her into his room and slammed the door.

"What the fuck do you think you are doing?" he began, "You know that he is no good for you."

Amari sat down on the bed and started touching up her make up.

"Do you hear me talking to you?" he shouted.

She looked up momentarily, "Of course I hear you talking, and I didn't think you were talking to me however, not in that tone at least."

"I'm sorry, let me talk more on your level, what the fuck are you doing slut, you sucking that nigga off now!" he said getting right in her face.

Amari got up from the bed ready to be done with him. She tried to push past him but he wouldn't allow it.

"Corey, move out of the way," she said.

"Nope, not until you tell me that you are fucking that nigga!"

"What does my sex life have to do with you? You don't want me remember? You wanted to be with Lily!" she said reminding him of his current girlfriend.

"Don't try to put the subject back on me; we are talking about you and your hoe like tendencies."

"I don't believe you are really sitting here calling me a hoe?" she said in disbelief.

"Well I am, because that is all that you are, a no good slut!"

"Corey, how can you say that?" she asked beginning to cry.

"I can say it because it's the truth; it just took me awhile to realize it. And yeah, I do have a girlfriend and she's ten times better than you," he said rudely.

"Yeah about your girlfriend, let her know that the next time she calls me I will whup that ass!" Amari said trying to stand tall even though on the inside she was near death.

In an instant Corey's whole demeanor changed. He violently pinned Amari against the wall and wouldn't let her go.

"Scream and I'll kill you," he said looking her in the eyes.

The tears began to flow heavily and she wanted them to stop.

Then suddenly, Corey had his mouth on hers, trying hard to get his tongue into her mouth.

"Corey stop it, what are you doing?" she cried.

"Don't act like you don't want it," he said slipping his hand under her dress.

She squirmed against the wall trying to get free, but his grip was too tight for her.

She watched as he unzipped his pants one handed. In an instant she saw pieces of her life flash before her eyes, "Oh my God, no, he's going to rape me!" she thought to herself.

"Stop squirming and acting like you don't want it, I know you miss this," he said trying to pull her panties down.

It was now or never, she kneed him as hard as she could to get him off of her. Amari tried to run for the door but tripped on some magazines that were thrown on the floor. Corey grabbed her from behind.

"Stupid bitch, what the fuck is wrong with you? I never loved you! You were just a good in house lay! Why else do you think I had my mom let your dumb pregnant ass stay here? I wanted to have easy access to the pussy! Fucking bitch, I hate you!" he said while slapping her hard across the face and spitting on her.

Amari looked at Corey astonished he could raise his hand to her and hit her forcefully. He must have shocked himself as well because he let her go. She fumbled with the door it would not open but the tears had already fallen. Finally it opened, she tore out of the room, and behind her she faintly heard Corey calling her.

Daryl was standing near the front door, she forcefully grabbed his hand and they left.

She was crying uncontrollably and her face had begun to swell.

"Just drive until I say stop, I should have never come here. Coming here was one of the biggest mistakes I could have ever made. How could I possibly think he loved me? Why would any guy love me?" she said while slumping down into her seat.

"Amari, don't talk like that, you know that none of that shit is true," he said.

"Oh yeah, then why is it that the only two boyfriends I have had cheated on me? Can you answer me that?" she asked him honestly, trying to find some insight on why this continued to happen to her.

"Amari, you're wonderful and any man would be happy to have you as their wifey," he said trying to encourage her.

"If that is so true, then why weren't you happy?" she asked.

"Whoa, where the hell did that come from," she thought to herself.

"I was happy," he uttered back.

"But yet you still cheated. I came to you and told you I was pregnant and you left me and denied our child, why?"

"What can I say men are stupid sometimes," he said trying to get off easily.

"That's a cop out and you know it," she said.

"Amari, please don't do this," he said looking at her.

"Don't do what? Daryl I loved you. You were my world. And you deserted me and you cheated with my best friend. Do you hear me? I loved you and I thought you loved me in return. I think about you all the time and how much you hurt me," she cried.

He turned toward her and put his arm around her, "I do love you, I never stopped loving you," he said.

That stopped her tears from flowing. She pulled away from his hug and looked at him in his eyes.

"What did you say?" she whispered.

"I'm still in love with you; I have known it for awhile. When you bailed me out that was all the validation I needed. Amari, you're special and I know you are hurting right now but I want you to know that there is someone out there that loves you. That person is me. I can't get you off my mind, I think about you all the time. I wish there was a way I could make it up to you for hurting you so bad."

She instantly fell into his arms and allowed him to hug and comfort her. An hour later and they were still driving. Daryl didn't once ask her what was wrong; he just drove as she asked him to do.

"He hit me and nearly raped me," she finally uttered.

Daryl swerved and had to grip the wheel with both hands to keep himself steady.

"Are you okay?" he asked.

"My face is swelling a bit," she said turning so he could see.

His eyes literally popped out of his head.

"A little bit, it looks like you have a baseball bat sticking out of your cheek," he said.

"It doesn't hurt as much as my heart does," she replied honestly.

"Oh Mari, I'm sorry," he said with concern.

When he finally stopped driving she noticed they were sitting in front of the dormitory, she didn't feel like going inside. She did not want to be alone tonight.

"Amari do you feel like going up or do you want to stay with me tonight?" he asked.

She sat for a minute debating on what she truly wanted to do. She might as well go with him. She was feeling lonely and was in definite need of some male companionship.

"Where will we go?" she asked.

"Back to my place," he said looking at her out of the corner of his eye.

"Okay then," she said.

It wasn't hard to see Daryl trying to suppress his grin.

♫♫♫

Corey sat in his room after watching Amari run out as though her life depended on it.

"Corey sat on his bed shaking his head. How the hell did I end up here?" he thought angrily to himself.

One minute he was happy and in love with Amari the next he was fucking Lily and trying to convince himself he loved her. Seeing Amari and Daryl tonight confirmed his inner true feelings...he still had a lot of love for Amari.

"Damn why am I so stupid?" he yelled.

"What are you so stupid about?" asked Lily appearing out of nowhere.

"Nothing," she said dismissing it.

She sat down on the bed next to Corey and began caressing his leg. She knew the fastest way to get him to forget about Amari was to give him some good head. She knelt down in front of him and was ready to go to work.

"Not now," Corey snapped getting off the bed.

Lily sat on the floor dumb founded. She couldn't believe he'd just turned down some head.

She watched him closely. He paced around the room mumbling to himself, it was almost as if he'd forgot she was in the room with him. He went to his closet and pulled out a shoe box. He took out a picture and started mumbling again. Then he shoved the picture back in the box and stormed out of the room.

Lily got up off the floor and went to the closet. She took out the same shoebox and started rummaging through it. Much to her dismay the shoebox was full of pictures and poems by Amari. She made herself comfortable on the floor of the closet as she began to read Amari's personal thoughts about Corey.

🎵🎵🎵

Lily couldn't believe how caught up Corey got when Amari came in with that Daryl character. She could already see she would have to keep a tight eye on him. She just couldn't get over the fact of how crazy he went when he saw them together. Them being together should not have caused such a reaction by him. Then for him to zone out on Lily the way he did when he was going through Amari's shit really had Lily bugging the fuck out.

"Shit!" she yelled.

As she sat plotting on how she was gonna get Corey's mind off Amari her phone rang unexpectedly.

"Hello," she yelled angrily.

"Yo Lil," shouted Andrea.

"What's good cuz?"

"Nothing just chilling down here at Barnacles, thought I'd let you know your boo was down here making a fool of himself. He's clearly drunk as can be," she said laughing.

"Dammit! Alright good looks I'm on my way," Lily said.

Lily got up off her couch heated she had to go get that nigga. He should have known better than to be out there acting a fool like that.

🎵🎵🎵

It was early the next morning and Amari was lying fully awake in Daryl's bed. Damn she couldn't believe she was here again. It was good though, she had to admit, the nigga done stepped up his sex game. But damn what the hell was she thinking?

She wished last night could have been just a mere blur, but it wasn't, it was all very clear. She still couldn't get over how wrong Corey treated her and the things he said to her. He hated her! He never loved her! What a mind blower. She was so crushed and hurt at that point. Her feelings were shot and her ego was done, how could she ever face the world again?

Daryl comforted Amari the only way he truly knew how. He deserved thanks though, he was there for her. He held her, he rocked her, and he wiped away her tears. She was impressed; he seemed absolutely sincere about his actions. He didn't act like he was only doing it to get into her panties.

Her cell phone rang non stop off the hook, it was no doubt her girls but she wasn't up for taking any calls. Daryl was lying next to her sound asleep. A big part of her wanted to sneak out of bed and go home, but that really wouldn't be right. It wasn't like he forced her to do anything she didn't want to do. But damn, how could she allow herself to fall back into Daryl's arms? She tried to make herself believe on many occasions that she was over him.

She tried to move an inch just so she could have some more room but as soon as she moved Daryl grabbed hold of her, he held her so tight you would have thought he was holding on for dear life. Convinced he would not let her get up for anything she finally dozed off.

Hours later she was awaken to the scent of pancakes and eggs. That was always Daryl's specialty. For some reason he always seemed to make the eggs just right. Damn it had been such a long time since she had his cooking. She was instantly reminded of the old days, the days when they were together and he would cook her breakfast. After breakfast they both just sat on the bed in silence.

For some reason there was a lot of tension between them. It was weird they just spent the night together and they were acting like they had issues with each other. Finally she spoke up.

"Daryl maybe I should be getting ready to go."

"Do you have to?" he whispered.

"It might be best, no feelings, no attachments remember?"

That was the pact they made last night before they dived into the hot passionate sex! Now after the fact it felt weird to get up and walk away.

"It's probably for the best," she said while gathering her things.

Amari was confident that leaving when she did was the right thing to do but it didn't feel right. Apart of her wanted to stay. Maybe she was in need of feeling loved by someone and at the moment Daryl was all she had. Even if he truly wasn't sincere about it, he sure made her feel that way. She drove home in a depressed stupor. Even though she tried to ignore last night's events, it was hard. All she could hear was Corey telling her he hated her and never loved her.

🎵🎵🎵

She finally sat down and had that talk with her girls, figured she couldn't hide from them anymore. Xena always her soldier cried with her when she recounted the events of what happened with Corey when they went upstairs. Ke-Ke instantly felt bad thinking that it was all her fault. Amari assured them both she would be fine. What she didn't tell them though was that she had spent the night with Daryl.

She wasn't yet sure how or why she allowed that to happen, so she knew there was no way for her to explain it to them. When Amari finally checked her messages there was a ton from Xena and Ke-Ke and even more from Corey.

What the hell was he calling her for? She didn't even bother to listen to them all, she just deleted them immediately. Now that she was single she noticed just how many cute guys there were on campus. How she ever missed them before was beyond her.

For the past couple of weeks Dave, a guy in her psychology class had been checking her out. She didn't really notice at first but Xena pointed it out to her.

When the semester first started he would sit way across the room, now he sat right next to her. Apart of her didn't even want him to approach her. One, she was not sure if she could even handle it, and two what if she turned him away the way she did Daryl and Corey. She was just not sure if her heart could take the rejection again. There was only about a week or so left of school then she wouldn't have to see him or be bothered by him until next semester.

He was definitely good looking but she really didn't want to set herself up for disappointment she had enough of that to last her a lifetime.

Amari felt it was weird to sit in class and to have him stare at her the way he did. Hopefully if she never looked his way then he would get the point. Since that terrible night with Corey she had not been much fun according to her friends. After class she went back to the dorm to get some much needed sleep. What her friends failed to realize was that she had been thinking heavily on what she was going to do when school ended.

She went back to the dorm to make some calls on where she could spend the summer. Anywhere but her parent's house and Corey's house would suit her just fine.

She even considered going to Boston to spend some time with her aunt. At least that would be somewhere for her to stay and she could get away from the drama for a little while.

Xena came home briefly wondering how Amari was feeling. Amari appreciated Xena and Ke-Ke for caring for her but it was getting a little out of hand now. But what could she do? After Xena left Amari decided to go grab a bite to eat.

When she returned to the room the message indicator on the phone was blinking. Not really wanting to be bothered she reluctantly listened to the messages. The first one was Xena telling her she was spending the night out with Darvis.

"Okay, Darvis, when did she start seeing him again?" she thought to herself.

The second message was from Momma Val asking when the last day of school was and would she be returning to the house.

The third message was from Corey, he really needed to talk to her. He sounded upset.

The fourth message was from Lily, she didn't want Amari returning to the Fowler house. Now wasn't that nice, she must look at Amari as a threat to her precious relationship. Fuck that bitch!

The fifth message shocked her a bit, it was from Daryl. At first it was silence and then in a hushed hesitant voice he said, 'I miss you'.

"He missed me? Wow, did I miss something that may have happen between us that would warrant him missing me?" she thought out loud.

"Amari, I haven't heard from you since the night of the party. I know you are doing okay, I have seen you a few times on campus. I didn't want to approach you though; I was trying to give you some space. School is coming to an end and I was wondering where you were going to for the summer. I was thinking maybe we could take a trip to Jamaica for a few weeks. Amari, I've been beating around the bush for a long time now, how else can I say this? Peaches, I love you. I am so in love with you. All I think about day and night is you. I feel incomplete because you are not apart of my life. Girl, you have to realize you are my air, I need you. Please give me a call."

Damn was he for real? Now he felt like Amari was his air? That was the tipping point for her; she realized she definitely had to get out of the city for the summer. She really could not deal with everything that was being thrown at her. She immediately called her aunt Theresa, explained the situation about Corey and not wanting to stay at his house for the summer break. She understood fully and said to just call her when she was able to book her flight.

The next day she went by the Fowler house and explained the situation to Momma Val. Momma Val refused to believe Corey had said and done such terrible things to her. That was his mother though, what could you really expect from her?

As soon as Amari walked back into the house she began having flashbacks of good times past. Up until that point she had allowed her mind to stop thinking of Corey. But now, today, being there again she realized just how much she missed him. She quickly packed what she would need. Momma Val was nice enough to allow her to keep her other belongings there as well.

Apart of Amari wanted to call Daryl and inform him she would be in Boston for the summer, but for some reason unknown to her she couldn't bring herself to make the call. She was afraid he would bring up the conversation of them and that wasn't something she could handle at the moment. She decided to stay at Xena's until Saturday when she would board the plane for Boston.

♫♫♫

What the hell was I thinking putting my hands on her and yelling at her like that? I don't know what came over me but seeing her there with Daryl just made my blood boil and I couldn't contain myself. I mean, what the fuck, we ain't been over but for a hot second and already she's laid up with that simple nigga! All that bull shit she was feeding me about loving me and being so hurt because of Lily and look at her, laid up with the next man.

"Dammit!" Corey yelled as he punched another hole in his wall.

He didn't know what was wrong with him. He couldn't stop thinking about Mari and Daryl together and he began to second guess himself. He wondered if he'd made a mistake by stepping out on her with Lily.

CHAPTER NINE

The plane just landed at Logan International Airport and already Amari felt like a big weight had been lifted from her chest. She got off the airplane and stood there for a moment just watching the hustle and bustle of the other passengers.

She walked slowly to the baggage claim area where she would meet her cousin Renee. By the time she got down there her luggage traveled the conveyor belt twice. She grabbed her bags and looked around hopeful for her cousin. Twenty minutes into her wait and she was tired of standing, she grabbed her luggage, found a seat and rested her legs.

An hour later and she was still sitting in the damn airport. On her way to the nearest payphone she was nearly knocked down by someone running through the airport.

"Damn, excuse me," she shouted at the person.

"My fault," the girl said as she turned towards Amari to apologize.

"Oh shit, Amari," Renee said laughing, walking towards her.

Amari could not help but laugh with her. After they got all of the laughter out of their system they hugged for a long moment. It was evident from the looks they were getting that passersby were unsure of what type of relationship they really had. It was not until that moment Amari had realized how much she missed her cousin, as well as her aunt Theresa. It had been five years now since they moved to Boston.

"Amari, girl it has been too long," she exclaimed as they climbed into her car.

"Nay girl, tell me about it, life has definitely been hectic lately," Amari began thinking back to her recent troubles.

"Yeah, I was thinking that something terrible must have happened to make you fly to Boston for the whole damn summer."

"Nay, everything is so out of hand, I almost feel as if I am about to go crazy," Amari said explaining to her everything that had happened beginning from when she was pregnant last year."

Renee just looked at Amari in awe; probably surprised she was even around to share the story. She did not say anything for a long while she just concentrated on the road.

Finally she spoke, "Amari while you are here I am going to make sure you have a good time, you will have no time to think about that Corey character," she smiled.

When the girls reached the house Amari expected a meal waiting for her, prepared by her loving aunt Theresa, who had slaved endlessly over the hot stove to make sure she had something warm and nourishing to eat. Boy was she wrong. When they reached the house it was silent and nothing was waiting on the stove for her. Amari was a little disappointed. Renee showed her to the guest bedroom and helped her fill the dresser draws with her belongings.

"Amari, I am supposed to go to my boyfriend's basketball game tonight, do you want to come along?" she asked.

"No," she said quickly not even giving the idea any thought.

"Damn, you ain't even gonna think about it?" she asked clearly annoyed.

"How you gonna have any fun and forget about them no good exes of yours if you stay bottled up in the house?" she asked honestly.

Amari thought about it for a moment and finally agreed to go with her. They left the house later that night and Theresa still hadn't come home. Renee later told Amari her mother usually worked double shifts during the week at the hospital.

At the game Amari was surprised to see just how many fine men Boston had to offer. She was not sure if she was really expecting ugly men or what but she knew she did not expect them to be that damn fine! She was too busy in her own world to have even noticed the amount of men that were checking her out until Renee brought it to her attention.

There was one man in particular who was standing on the sideline coaching a team of young boys. He was superfine! He was about 6'0", mocha colored with a tight fade, with gold rim glasses. He was sporting the latest Sean John fashion. He stood there as cool as could be; he had no idea she was watching him so hard. He was looking damn good to her; she was completely caught off guard by his good looks.

Amari slipped. She stared way too long and he noticed her, a big smile crept on his face. Shit, she was blushing. She quickly smiled back and then turned her attention back to the game. She tried to sneak looks at him every now and then.

After the game was over she began to drill Renee on the mystery man. Her answer depressed Amari; she claimed to know nothing about him. Amari's mood changed instantly, she went from being happy and giddy to feeling down and defeated. She was about two steps from being depressed. How could she feel this way over a total stranger? As if suddenly realizing she may never see him again she scanned the crowd frantically hoping to catch one last glimpse of him before they left. She had no such luck; he was nowhere to be found.

Amari sat on the bleachers alone while Renee spoke with her boyfriend. It was taking her forever and all she wanted to do at that point was go back to the house and crash.

By the time they finally reached the house she was four steps past exhausted all she wanted to do was shower and go to bed. After her shower as she was preparing for bed it suddenly hit her that she went just about a full day without thinking about Corey or Daryl.

She called Xena quickly and left her a message informing her she arrived safely and would call her later. She was so thankful and relieved when her head finally hit the pillow. Finally, she could get some much needed uninterrupted sleep.

The next couple of days she spent shopping and hanging out with Renee. They definitely were having a lot of fun together. The weekend crept up on her and she was quite sure Renee wanted to go out with her man, alone. She did not want her feeling like she had to take her everywhere she went for the next two months. So she planned on staying in so that she could have some alone time with her man.

They were sitting at the breakfast table enjoying cheese grits, scrambled eggs, and pancakes when the phone rang. Renee answered it and started smiling immediately. From the smile on her face she could tell she was on the phone with her man. Only a man can make a woman smile like that. Her whole face was glowing. Amari instantly remembered when her own face used to glow like that. Amari wondered if it would ever happen again for her. She got up from the kitchen table and went into the living room to give Renee some privacy.

Amari was sitting in the living room watching videos when Renee came in still smiling.

"Amari, you feel like going to the mall?" she asked.

"The mall, sure why not? But I am sure I have done enough shopping to last me an eternity," Amari commented.

"I'm sure but now we need to find some nice elegant dresses with shoes to match," Renee said still smiling.

"For what? I'm not going anywhere which requires me to wear an elegant dress," Amari replied.

"That was David and today is his parent's 30th wedding anniversary and they are having this black tie affair. He invited you and he even said he had a date for you," she said beaming with joy.

"Oh hell no!" she instantly protested.

"Renee, please I really don't feel like being bothered," she said getting irritated.

After listening to Renee beg for about ten minutes, Amari finally gave in. They left immediately for the mall in search of some elegant dresses. Amari could not believe she allowed Renee to talk her into going. When they got to the mall Renee did not have a problem finding a dress. Renee went Amari's normal route and bought a straight black dress with small spaghetti straps. The dress was cute but Amari wanted something that was gonna knock everyone off their feet.

When she walked into Cache she found her dream dress. It was a cherry red strapless dress that had beaded work around the top of the dress. The dress stopped just above the knees and definitely showed every curve that needed to be shown. Amari was hooked. The dress was absolutely spectacular, to die for. After that they went to search for shoes, she was bent on getting the perfect pair to accompany her dress. She ended up with a pair of cherry stilettos.

After they left the mall they headed straight to the nail salon. All of this shit Renee had her going through for this date, he better be good looking and he better not be stuck on himself. By the time they got back to the house Amari was still exhausted. It seemed like she just couldn't ever get enough sleep. She decided to take a nap before getting ready for the big gala. Sleep had never felt so good to her; she slept for hours and was suddenly awakened by the constant shaking of Renee.

"Damn, girl what is your problem?" Amari asked aggravated.

"Amari, its 6:30 we need to leave in thirty minutes," she practically screamed at her.

Damn where had the time gone. Sluggishly Amari dragged herself out of the bed and went to shower. After taking a quick shower she quickly dressed and combed her hair. She managed to get dressed in thirty minutes flat.

Once they got in the car was when Amari's nerves began to kick in. She did not know how to react to the situation at hand. What business did she have going out on a date as messed up as her head was? When they got to the function hall she really did not want to get out of the car. Renee kept trying to encourage her to go inside by saying that everything was cool, but the butterflies in her stomach just kept getting stronger and stronger.

She told Renee to go ahead and go inside, without her, reluctantly she did. She sat in the car trying to get up enough nerve to go inside. She couldn't understand why she was so nervous. As she sat there a man began walking towards the car. At first she paid him no attention until he began knocking on her window.

"Damn, he looked absolutely gorgeous in a tuxedo," she thought to herself.

She rolled down the window and he smiled.

"Hey," he said.

"Hi," she answered.

"You know it really sucks when your blind date won't even come in to meet you," he said.

He was the blind date? Damn, she had no clue. This was truly a great surprise. She climbed out of the car and was very impressed to see the full package up close and personal. That was definitely one helluva man! They walked in together and she was very happy. Renee came over and gave her a slight hug. Neither of them could stop smiling.

His name was Maurice and he was getting ready to be a freshman at Morehouse College. Imagine that, he was getting ready to move down to Atlanta. She was definitely happy. They danced most of the night and she was enjoying his company to the fullest. The way he held her close made her feel secure. She always had a problem with being too trusting; she wasn't trying to do that with him. Nor did she want to get her hopes up so she decided to just wait and see how things would play out on their own.

  The night was truly a breath of fresh air. When they weren't dancing they were sitting at the table talking. He was such a nice guy and every other word out his mouth was a compliment. She literally blushed for the entire evening. At the end of the night it was Maurice that brought her back to the house. They stayed in the car talking for about an hour. Finally at about one in the morning she went into the house smiling uncontrollably. She spent the rest of the night thinking about Maurice. She could not wait to see him again. At that moment she decided she would definitely be at Sunday's game just so she could see him again..

♫♫♫

  Daryl sat in his chromed Mercedes watching the streets. Once upon a time he would be out on these very corners slanging and hustling to get his dough. He had come along way. He had his whole operation set up and glued together tight. He had about 50 workers with 5 generals per territory. The workers reported directly to the generals and then the generals would do the pick up and drop off at secure locations. No one ever saw Daryl face to face, which was the way he liked it. He was no longer seen in the streets daily doing the dirt but everyone knew he was the one collecting the profits and everyone still feared him, or so he thought.

Daryl sped off as he watched before his eyes one of his workers get the beat down of his life. Once the assailants were done beating him to a pulp, they robbed him of his jewels, stash, and cash! Daryl hated to lose any type of money, so he began to follow the assailants. He watched as they jumped into a deep blue Dodge Caravan. The van sped off and Daryl decided to let them go without following them. If Cease were there he'd be sure to let Daryl know how much of a bitch he was acting.

He rolled back over to the corner where his worker was still laying on the ground. He picked up his cell phone and called his general that was in charge of that area and told him what was going on. Daryl raced back to his house to figure out what he was going to do about this situation. It was well known in the city what territory belonged to Daryl and what territory was still up for grabs. It was times like these when Daryl missed Cease. Cease was a hothead that rarely ever thought about the consequences of his actions. Daryl on the other hand, always thought about the consequences.

🎵🎵🎵

Daryl must have dozed off without realizing it. He looked at the clock and realized it was 2 am. If that was the case then why the hell was his doorbell ringing? He got outta bed, threw on a pair of sweatpants and went to answer the door. He was surprised when he saw Tyrone standing there covered in blood.

"What the fuck nigga?" Daryl said quickly ushering him inside.

"What the fuck are you talking about?" he asked tossing him a towel to clean himself up.

Tyrone began shaking his head.

"All dem niggas dead, Black from College Park, D-Bo from East Point, Crazy Lou from Decatur and Big Toney from Gwinnett County! Dawg all dem niggas is dead and your money and product is missing," finished Tyrone.

Daryl sat on his couch dumbfounded. He couldn't believe what he was hearing. Was this dude really sitting here telling him that his generals were all down for the count? Was he telling him someone had got to his fucking generals? What the fuck?

"Where's Mookie?" he asked of his last general.

"He's hiding out at his baby moms spot right now. Dat nigga is shook right now cuz he know niggas is coming for him next."

Daryl sat thinking. He knew he needed to send Mookie somewhere but wasn't sure where he could send him at this point.

"Check it, contact Mookie, and tell him to drive his fam out to Florida right now and then tomorrow I will have a flight ready for them to go either to Jamaica or Puerto Rico. Call up Tamika at Thrifty and get a rental for Mookie. Tomorrow I need you to meet with the workers and find out what the word is on the street. Meet me back here at 10 pm and we'll figure out what our next move should be," commanded Daryl.

"Alright my nigga," Tyrone said getting up and headed back out the front door.

Daryl got up and locked the door behind him.

"God dammit, what the fuck is going on?" he thought angrily to himself again as he headed upstairs to take a shower.

♫♫♫

"Alright Ty, please tell me you got some good news for me," Daryl said while eating his plate of Chinese food.

Ty sat down not sure how he was going to tell his man that these lil young niggas was straight out to get him. He paused and just stared at Daryl with a blank expression on his face.

"Ty man, just tell me what the fuck is going on!" Daryl yelled getting annoyed with all of the silence.

"There are these lil young cats from Bankhead that are tryna take over. Basically they did their homework and knew if they were gonna have a chance they had to start with taking you and yours out!"

"I get that. But these niggas ain't even try to get at me," Daryl said confused.

"Yeah, I know which is what's got me so fucked up! If they were trying to take over why these niggas ain't tried to get at you? The way shit went down I feel like they were working for someone, I just gotta put my ear to the streets to find out who," he stated to no one in particular.

They both sat in silence not sure what the next move should be. Daryl didn't want to seem vulnerable but something about the whole situation had his mind boggled.

♫♫♫

Corey sat on his bed feeling in a real shitty mood. Lily had been over earlier in the morning and all they could seem to do was fight. He wasn't even really sure why he was fighting with her but regardless they were fighting. Every second she got she would question him why he cared so much for Amari. Why couldn't she understand he spent a lot of time caring about Amari and wasn't sure he could just turn his feelings on and off for her the way Lily wanted him to.

He lay back on his bed and started thinking about Amari. He knew he hurt her the night of his party and he really didn't mean to hurt her but seeing her with Daryl just brought such a fire inside of him. The knock at his door brought him back to reality.

"Yeah, come in," he yelled sitting up on his bed.

"Hey Corey, what are you up to?" asked Lissa.

"Nothing, just relaxing," he said.

"Oh," she said getting herself comfortable on his bed.

"What's good with you?" he asked sensing she wanted to talk to him about something.

"Nothing, really," she said beating around the bush.

"Come on Lissa, I know you got something to say, so just say it."

"What's going on with you and Amari?" she blurted out.

"Nothing. I'm not even with her anymore, you know that already."

"Yeah but what happened the night of the party? I mean, she ran outta here pretty fast and then she came over and told mom she was leaving town, going to Boston."

"Boston?" he asked sounding confused.

"Yeah, I'm just curious to know what could have possibly happened between ya'll to make her bounce all the way up north."

"Lissa, I don't know what the hell be going through that girls head."

"Did you hit her?" she asked.

"Nah, not really."

"There's no 'nah, not really' either you did or you didn't!" she said starting to think maybe the stuff Amari told her mom was true.

"No!" he yelled lying.

She didn't believe him.

"Yeah whateva!" she screamed running out.

"Boston? Why the hell would she go up there?" he thought angrily to himself.

🎵🎵🎵

Lily sat in her car crying hysterically. She could feel she was losing Corey and she had no idea how to keep him. She couldn't believe he was acting this way over that dumb bitch Amari. He continues to deny he laid a hand on her but she saw the way Amari ran out of the party. Something happened upstairs in that room and it was more than just them talking.

Lily couldn't understand why Corey was so upset about Amari coming to the party with Daryl. He shouldn't care. He should be happy she had someone because then maybe she would leave them and their relationship alone. Even though Corey continued to tell her it was nothing, she knew better. All they did was fight and the only thing they fought about was Amari.

"Dammit, how the hell could I have let this happen?" she thought angrily to herself.

She knew when they first hooked up he wasn't over Amari, but she figured if she just continued to give him that banging ass pussy he'd soon forget about his little crush on that dumb ass bitch! Obviously she was wrong. Now she knows she's gotta step her game up if she planned on being with Corey for any lengthy amount of time.

🎵🎵🎵

Ever since Cease got locked up Daryl could feel he was losing his hold on his empire. Damn near his whole army was dead. Someone was going around knocking off all of his people and he didn't really know what to do. He knew he should really retaliate but he had no idea where to start.

This morning he got the best news ever. Cease would be home in less than 30 days. They were preparing for his release. Daryl couldn't wait to see his boy again.

He knew he would know exactly what to do about the current predicament Daryl found himself in.

CHAPTER TEN

Since Amari made the trip up north to Boston she barely had any time to think about her troubles from back home. She felt bad because she didn't have much time to speak with her home girls. She called Xena early that morning to see how she was doing and to find out if there was anything she was missing back home.

Xena answered the phone groggy, guess it was still too early for her. When she heard Amari's voice she made a loud screeching sound. The first thing Xena said was that Daryl had been calling her constantly to see when Amari would be back.

"Damn what is this nigga sweating me for?" she thought angrily to herself.

Other than that she really had no news to tell her. Everything was pretty much the same she said. She had not spoken to Ke-Ke much though; apparently she decided to go to Trinidad with her family for the summer. That meant Xena was back in ATL by herself. At the end of the conversation Xena made Amari promise to call Daryl and see what he wanted, she said he sounded a bit frantic.

Off the phone with Xena, Amari sat at the table for awhile just thinking about things. She started to think back to when Daryl and she were happy together. The countless days when he would come over and they would sit in her room just talking and watching videos. Or the late nights in the summer they would spend on the porch and before he left no matter what they always managed to have sex, right there on the porch. They didn't give a fuck about anybody or what anybody would say in regards to their actions. They were happy and in love and foolish!

The one thing that always stayed on her mind was the way he would take his hand and caress her face or the way he would move his tongue so sensually in her ear. Damn he always knew how to get her right to that point; the point where she would be close to tears and on the verge of shouting out his name for the world to hear. Her memories were rudely interrupted by the ring of the telephone.

"Hello," she answered, wishing her thoughts had not been interrupted.

"Hey Amari, its Maurice, what's up?" he asked sounding fine as could be.

He was the type of nigga that really did not need to look good; his looks were an added bonus. He just sounded so damn fine! It was a wonder she was able to contain herself around him.

"Hey Maurice, what's up?" she responded.

"Nothing much, I was wondering if you would like to go sightseeing with me? If you would allow me the pleasure of showing you around Beantown, and afterwards we could hit up some stores," he offered.

It was still early in the day but she had no plans for the day and she really did not feel like sitting in the house all day.

"Yeah, that's cool," she replied after deliberating silently in her head.

"Good, is twenty minutes enough time for you to get ready?" he asked.

"Yeah," Amari replied feeling a bit giddy at the thought of spending the day with him.

She quickly showered and got dressed. She opted for a pair of red Capri's, with a cream halter top and red and cream floral sandals. Maurice arrived on time. When she got in the car he sat there with a smile, probably not realizing that points were being deducted from him because she had to open her own door.

"What's up with you?" she asked as she slid into the passenger seat of his baby blue ford escort.

"The few times I have seen you, you were wearing the hell outta some Capri's!" he said smiling from ear to ear.

All she could do was laugh, that compliment gave him his recent loss of points back. They ended up going down to Fanueil Hall; personally she didn't see what all the hype was about. He wanted to show her some other historic spots in Boston, but she was more interested in going shopping.

He was doing most of the shopping, looking for clothes to bring down to Atlanta with him. They passed a couple of jewelry stores and she could not help but admire a beautiful heart bracelet. The bracelet was so pretty, so elegant; it was a diamond bracelet with miniature hearts surrounding it. She was definitely in love with the bracelet and she must have stared at it for a good give minutes.

Maurice and Amari had a really good time together. It was so refreshing being with him; almost like starting new because he knew nothing about her. After shopping he took her to Simco's, some famous hot dog place that was located on a bridge. The food there was actually really good, she had not expected it to be that good. At first she had a little bit of an attitude because he did not want to take her to a real sit down restaurant, but after having her first bite into the hot dog, she was in heaven and glad Maurice brought her there. At the end of the day, she was exhausted. She went home and went straight to bed without hearing Renee tell her Daryl called and it was important she got back to him right away.

🎵🎵🎵

"Girl, get up, you've been sleep long enough," boomed a vibrant and energetic Renee. Amari tried to ignore her, she tossed and turned and pulled the pillow over her head.

"I know you awake, I know you hear me talking to you, now get up I want to know what happened yesterday?" she demanded yanking the pillow from atop Amari's head and tossing it across the room.

Annoyed, she sat up in the bed and looked Renee in the eyes, Amari wanted Renee to know she was not happy about being awaken before her body was ready. She laughed.

"Renee, what do you want and why couldn't it wait until I got up?" Amari asked looking at the clock that read 7:00 am.

"Where were you yesterday?" she began.

"Out with Maurice," she replied wishing she would leave it at that.

"Out with Maurice huh, all day and damn near all night long?" she questioned like she did not believe the answers that were given her.

"Yep," Amari said sliding back down into the bed.

"Oh no, I am not done with you yet," she said pulling the covers down so Amari could not use them to hide from her.

"Renee, really what's the problem, why you acting like mother hen? I went out. Period. End of discussion," Amari said getting frustrated.

"Come on now cuz, now you know it ain't even like that, I just want to know if ya'll fucked or not," she laughed.

"Nay, you taking it a bit far, you know damn well I ain't give that nigga any!" Amari said appalled she would even suggest such a thing.

"Yeah, okay whatever," she said throwing the covers over Amari's head.

Grateful for the peace, Amari forced herself back to sleep only to be awaken a few minutes later by Renee throwing the telephone at her.

"Damn, this girl is really asking for an ass whooping," she thought angrily to herself.

"Hello," Amari said cursing under her breath.

"Hey, I didn't mean to wake you," he said sweetly.

Her eyes popped wide open and a big grin somehow formed on her tired face.

"That's okay, how did you sleep?" Amari asked.

"I slept okay, but I could not stop thinking about you," he admitted.

Thank you Jesus she was not alone. She knew just how he was feeling because she could not stop thinking about him either.

"Well I hope you were having good thoughts," she laughed.

"Nothing but the best," he replied.

The silence that followed was a sweet one, they were both thinking back to the thoughts they were having of each other.

"So did you have a good time yesterday?" he asked finally breaking the silence.

"Definitely," she said remembering briefly the events of the previous day.

"So can I expect you at tonight's game?" he asked hopeful.

"For sure," she replied with a smile at the thought of seeing him again.

"All right then, I'll see you tonight," he said.

"Okay," was her only reply before she quickly hung up the phone. After she hung up the phone Amari just laid in bed thinking about Maurice. She could feel herself falling for him even though she really did not want to. Maurice was just so sweet and sincere it was hard not to.

🎵🎵🎵

Xena sat in her room getting ready for her date with Jordan. She couldn't believe she had finally let Darvis go. It was hard but with the welcomed distraction of Jordan she was able to do it. She wasn't really sure how to handle being with him. He was the complete opposite of Darvis. He wasn't controlling or a womanizer. For once, Xena knew what it felt like to be extremely happy.

🎵🎵🎵

Renee was all on Amari's case about being late to the game. Amari couldn't understand the rush, but apparently Renee believed if she did not get to the game before it started then all of the chicken heads up in the gym would seem to think her man David was a free agent. Renee told Amari all types of stories about how she had to literally fight chicks that thought he was up for grabs. Okay, now that was some serious deep shit!

When they arrived at the gym the game was not due to start for another ten minutes. They walked into the gym and all eyes were instantly on them.

Renee leaned towards Amari, "You got all these niggas up in here checking you out!"

"How do you know they not checking you out?" Amari whispered back to her.

"Girl please, I am old news to these tired ass niggas, but you, nah you fresh meat," she said laughing.

Amari spotted Maurice across the gym warming up.

Renee scanned the entire gym for David and when she noticed he was not warming up with Maurice she became infuriated.

"I don't believe this shit!" she yelled storming back down the bleachers.

Amari sat still not sure what to make of the situation. She watched as Renee stormed over to Maurice, started doing a bunch of hand motions, Maurice shrugged his shoulders and she walked away. Amari kept her glare on Maurice and nearly wet her panties when he finally spotted her and threw her a kiss. She heard a few girls sitting near her say that the kiss was for them, but she knew it was meant entirely for her. Amari's attention was thwarted when she as well as the entire gym heard loud shouting and arguing going on right outside.

"Who the fuck is this bitch? What the fuck you think I am stupid or some shit?"

"Come on now, why you always gotta go there?" replied a laid back male voice.

When Amari realized it was Renee and David arguing she rushed up to see what was happening. David and Renee were standing right outside of the gym door arguing. An unfamiliar female stood in between them grimacing. It was not until Amari was right next to Renee that she noticed Renee was holding the girl by her long blond hair.

"And a fucking white bitch at that!" she yelled.

"Renee, you don't know what you're talking about," he yelled.

"So you not fucking her is that what you are telling me?" she said yanking the girl as she spoke.

David made subtle eye contact with the white girl, Renee didn't even notice it, but Amari quickly did.

"I am not fucking her! I don't even know her all like that," he concluded.

Amari never saw it coming. Renee slapped him hard across the face, so hard she left the imprint of her hand on his chocolate skin.

"You don't know her, yet I just caught you with your tongue deep down her fucking throat," she said yanking the girl harder.

"Renee, let's just go," Amari interjected.

Amari was beginning to feel extremely embarrassed, even if Renee wasn't. The whole gym was listening in on the drama.

"I'm not going anywhere till he admits he is fucking this nasty white skank ho!" she screamed.

David just stood there not willing to admit anything, typical of a man, fully aware he is indeed busted but will never tell the truth, will never admit the obvious.

"David I am waiting, and you know me, I will stand here all day and all night if I have to until you admit you are a fucking cheating ass muthafucka that just got caught AGAIN!" she yelled.

They all stood there for a good half an hour before the manager of the gym called the police to have Renee escorted from the premises. When the officers arrived they were not shocked to see Renee.

"Hey Renee, hey David," the cops sang in unison.

"Renee, you gotta let her go and Mike wants you off the premises," one of the cops said to Renee.

Renee stood her ground.

"Renee, come on please let's do this the easy way," the officer begged.

Amari stood by and watched in shock as the whole ordeal played itself out. Renee finally let go of the girl and turned and walked out of the door. Amari watched David turn to the white girl and kiss her on the cheek and ask her if she was okay, together they walked back into the gym. Maurice was standing at the door and gave me a sympathetic smile and a shrug of the shoulders, he mouthed the words, 'call me' before he headed back into the gym himself.

Amari felt like her mind was on overdrive. What the hell was all this shit about? Did this happen on the regular, is that why the officers knew Renee and David so well? Amari drove back to the house and Renee sat on the passenger side quiet for the entire trip. When they got to the house she went straight to her room, practically running.

"Amari what happened with Renee?" asked Aunt Theresa as she stood at the bottom of the stairs wondering what had her daughter so upset.

"I'm not really sure, some weird junk just went down at the gym," Amari said thinking back to the night's events.

"Well I guess I better go talk with her," she said beginning to climb the stairs.

"Aunt Theresa, maybe I should talk with her," Amari offered.

Amari knocked softly on the door and heard a muffled Renee crying. She opened the door without waiting for her to invite her in. Amari sat down on the bed next to her and put her arm around her, which only made her cry more.

"Renee, what's going on? What was all that shit about back at the gym?" Amari asked getting straight to the point.

She shook her head, "I am so fucking stupid! Do you realize how many times I have dealt with this shit, with him cheating? It seems like every other week I have to show my ass up at that damn gym! He is always fucking with me! Why does he fuck with me like this? Why can't he see how much I love him?" she sobbed.

Amari held her some more, feeling bad for her and herself at the same time. They spent the rest of the night talking about men and why they did the things they did. They both had their share of horrid relationship stories to share with each other. Amari thought she had it bad with her issues with both Daryl and Corey, boy was she wrong.

Renee seemed to fight on a regular basis just to prove her love to David. Amari told her she did not think what she was doing would solve any of her problems. There was no reason why anyone should feel the need to fight just to prove they loved someone. Amari asked Renee over and over again how she could allow David to disrespect her in such a way. She had no answer for that, she contends she was in love and felt this was what she must do to prove it. It's funny how a person can feel their life was so bad and then you listen to someone else's story and you feel your life really is not that bad after all.

Amari called Xena the next morning to tell her what happened the night before with her cousin Renee, Xena laughed her head off.

"Yo your cousin is straight gutta, she don't give a fuck!" she laughed. "Yo, we definitely need a chick like that to roll with us down here," she said laughing harder.

"Xena please, people like that live with constant drama, I'm trying to get rid of the drama I'm facing now," Amari whispered.

"So Mari, when are you coming back home, I'm bored as shit down here by myself. I don't have no one to go out with, no one to talk to, it's dead down here without you," she stated.

"Girl, I know you must be going out of your mind, but what up with Toni, why don't you chill with her?" Amari asked of Tee's friend.

"Nah, I'm good on that, that girl has crazy drama and I am not trying to get caught up," she stated.

"Have you talked to her though, is she doing okay?" Amari asked concerned that maybe something else had happened.

"Yeah, she called looking for you, I told her you were on vacation, and she said to call her when you got back in town."

"Damn, did she call today?" Amari asked getting worried.

"Nah, she called like two maybe three days ago," she said quietly.

Xena could feel that Amari was a moment away from blowing up on her for not informing her of this news earlier.

"Damn Xena, why didn't you tell me this when I spoke to you the other day?" she questioned.

"Chill out, I forgot okay," she said defensively.

"I don't know why you even concern yourself with that crazy ass chick, any chick that stays with a man that continuously beats her is fucking stupid!" Xena exclaimed.

"Xena, everyone has their own skeletons to deal with. I mean look at you and Darvis, he cheats like crazy yet you are still with him, no one is judging you for that," Amari said getting a bit annoyed by Xena's insensitivity.

"So what you choosing her over me, I can't believe you just said that shit to me," she said beginning to cry.

"Xena, you know what I am trying to say. You know how I feel about people judging people without really knowing them," Amari quickly apologized without even really saying the words, 'I'm sorry'.

"Yeah, whatever, look I gotta go," she said before quickly hanging up the phone.

"Damn, maybe I was a little hard on her," Amari thought to herself as she sat looking at the phone.

Amari made a mental note to call Xena back later after she had some time to cool off. She decided to give Toni a call to see what she needed.

"Toni, hey what's up, it's Amari," she said after hearing her softly say hello.

"Amari, hey when did you get back in town?" she asked.

"I'm not back yet, Xena just told me you called," she answered.

"Oh," she said sounding like her heart was heavy with sorrow.

"Toni, you okay, do you need something?" Amari asked.

"Yeah a new life," she said sarcastically.

"Toni, what happened?" she asked again.

"Same shit different day," she stated. "I just called because I needed to talk to someone and Ke-Ke is still in Trinidad," she said.

"Okay then, what's up?" Amari asked getting comfortable on the bed.

"Tommy's up to his usual ways. He was drinking heavily and then came home and took all of his frustrations out on me. He was like his boys saw me hugged up with some other nigga. I was like yo, they lying to you. Then he slapped me!" she cried.

One thing Xena said was true was that Toni was real stupid for staying with her punk of a boyfriend. But that was not for me to judge or speak on; people do all types of crazy things when they are in love.

"Toni, are you cool now or do you need to stay with Xena for a couple of days?" Amari asked.

"Nah, things are cool now," she said not sounding too happy about it.

"Are you sure, because Xena is in town and I can call her to come and pick you up," Amari offered.

"Nah, I'm good, thanks for the offer though," she said.

"Alright then, call Xena's cell phone if you need to go over there though," she said wanting to make sure she understood that the invitation was always open for her.

"Look, Tommy just got home so I better get off the phone, I'll talk to you later okay," she said hurriedly into the phone.

"Okay, bye," Amari said hanging up the phone.

At that moment Amari felt like her life wasn't that bad after all. Compared to Toni and Renee her life seemed like a walk through heaven.

🎵🎵🎵

"What the fuck?" yelled Daryl as he walked outside of his house.

This morning he got up early to go take care of some business, when he came outside his brand new Buckingham Blue Range Rover was trashed. All the windows were smashed and someone had spray painted, "Dead Man" on the hood of the truck. Daryl was heated!

He ran back inside and called Tyrone immediately.

"Dawg, get your ass over here right now," screamed Daryl into the phone.

"Cuz, what's good? What happened?" asked a sleepy Tyrone.

"Nigga I don't have time to talk, I said to get over here now!" he screamed before hanging up.

Daryl paced the floor in his living room the whole time he waited for Tyrone's arrival. Finally twenty minutes later, the doorbell ran signaling his arrival.

"It's open," he yelled.

Tyrone came bursting through the door.

"What the fuck happened to your ride?" he asked not believing what he saw.

"That's what the fuck I called you over here for. Did you see that shit? Someone has truly violated and I'm gonna have to deal with that nigga," he said going to the kitchen to get his nine out of his stash spot.

Tyrone wanted to calm him down. He hadn't seen that look in Daryl's eyes since they were freshmen in college.

"D man, let's think about this logically dawg," he said.

"Fuck logic! I been nice with these niggas and then they murked my whole crew. "Now those niggas wanna come and see me on my front step, it's on!" he screamed while grabbing the keys to his old school Honda Accord.

When Tyrone saw him headed to that car he knew Daryl meant business. Daryl only drove that car when he was about to put some work in.

CHAPTER ELEVEN

The next four weeks Amari spent heavily with Maurice. He was definitely a lot of fun to be with. Today was a big game for his team; they were playing their rival team. Amari arrived at the gym early with Renee.

Maurice and some other friends were on the court shooting hoops. When he saw her he smiled instantly, his whole face lit up which made Amari happy on the inside. Maurice and Amari had been together since the first night they met. They were on the phone constantly and spending a lot of time together.

She was getting excited about him moving to Atlanta. It was a blessing he didn't have a girlfriend as fine as he was. She walked over to him and he bent down to give her a kiss. He had the softest lips she had ever felt.

A lot of guys in the gym hated on Maurice at that moment; according to him just about all of them were feeling Amari. Imagine that, who would have thought such a thing. She definitely was not used to so much attention coming from guys.

"Baby you working the hell outta dem jeans," he commented with a smile while slapping her ass!

"Boy, if you don't stop doing that shit," she responded with a slight attitude.

Amari never appreciated that. She was not sure if men felt it was a sensuous touch but to her they always seemed to slap it to hard, making it more painful than anything else.

Renee and Amari went to sit down, when they noticed a strange guy staring hard at Amari.

"Damn Nay, is that nigga over there still staring at me?"

"You mean the one wearing the Paul Pierce jersey," she questioned.

"Yeah him," Amari answered.

"Yeah, he's still clocking you hard," she answered while laughing.

Renee and Amari sat there talking and gossiping about the various people in the gymnasium. Clearly out of nowhere the guy wearing the Paul Pierce jersey was standing right in front of them.

"Hey," he said with a bit of a devilish grin.

"Damn, what's up with you being all up in my space?" Amari asked while motioning to the invisible space in front of her.

He smiled.

She was not joking, she was dead serious. She did not appreciate him being so close to her. Amari searched the court trying to see if she could spot Maurice so she could motion for him to come and help her with the dirty old nigga standing before her.

Unfortunately for her, he was suddenly nowhere to be found.

"So Amari, you dating Maurice?" he questioned.

"It's none of your business!" she replied while turning her back to him.

He got really pissed at that point. He grabbed her shoulder and turned her back around. She sat there shocked and speechless momentarily not believing he put his hands on her. Renee gasped.

"Your little boyfriend will pay," was all he said before walking away from Amari.

She couldn't believe he literally put his hands on her and with such force. He literally bruised her shoulder. She couldn't even move. She wanted to move and go find Maurice and tell him what happened but she couldn't; it was as if she was temporarily paralyzed, frozen in space. She was so numb she never even realized it when Renee left to go and find Maurice. Moments later she was running back into the gym with Maurice and David on her heels.

"Amari are you okay?" asked Maurice.

He opened her up, up until that point she was not sure if she felt any pain or comprehended fully what really had just gone down. A single tear fell from her left eye and at the sight of the tear Maurice took her into his arms and held her tight for a quick moment.

Maurice rushed out of the gym in search of that nigga. Renee and Amari stayed inside; she was in shock and could not move. Renee sat next to her and urged her to get up so they could go and find out what was happening. She wanted to make sure David and Maurice were handling that nigga.

"Amari come on, we're gonna miss all of the action if we don't get out there now," she urged.

Reluctantly, Amari got up and started walking pointlessly towards the exit. When they walked outside there was a crowd of people hovering over two individuals. They both assumed it was Maurice and the stranger. They pushed themselves through the crowd and there was Maurice fighting.

At first she thought Maurice had a handle on him but that thought quickly ended. Maurice was being tossed and getting punched all over his body. Her heart was cringing at the thought of Maurice getting his ass kicked behind this bull shit. David must have been feeling the same way as Amari because he quickly jumped in and started helping Maurice out. When Maurice saw David had his back he got a sudden surge of energy and took control of the fight again. David backed out once he saw his boy had things under control.

"Damn Josh is getting his ass beat," an onlooker observed.

Josh lay limp on the ground and Maurice felt he'd had enough; he gave him one last kick and left him lying on the ground. Blood was squirting from different spots on Maurice's body and his clothes were ripped. He looked a mess! He walked slowly towards Amari and asked her if she was okay.

"Damn boo, I should be asking you that?" Amari replied.

He smiled. He put his arm around her and they started to walk away. They were almost to the car when a loud gun shot sounded too close for comfort. They all turned around and there was Josh standing less than five feet from them holding a gun pointed directly at Maurice's chest.

Maurice's first instinct was to stand in front of Amari, to shield her from harm. Amari's first instinct was to scream, David stepped up first.

"Yo, man what are you stupid or something, what the fuck you doing with that shit?" he asked.

Maurice stood still, sizing Josh up and never allowing his eyes to leave the gun.

"Am I stupid? Nah, I'm very sane and in less than a minute I'm gonna put a bullet through yo niggas heart!" he stated matter of factly.

Realizing this situation could possibly get very ugly Maurice turned towards Amari.

"Amari, I want you and Renee to go home," he whispered.

"I am not leaving you here," she replied feeling for a moment like the Bonnie to his Clyde. She was gonna ride with him and if need be die with him.

"Don't be stupid, I want you two to get out of here, now!" he commanded.

Amari feared for his life and her glassy eyes showed it all. The gathering of people had begun to disperse, they were basically the only ones left standing in the street.

Renee grabbed Amari's arm.

"Mari, come on let's go," she urged.

Amari looked at Maurice and could no longer hold the tears back, they came down full throttle. He bent over and kissed her gently on the cheek.

"I'll be over later okay?" he said.

She nodded her head in agreement because her throat was choked up and would not allow any words to come out.

Maurice then looked at Josh.

"Let the girls go and we can handle this ourselves like men," he demanded.

Josh not having a legitimate beef with the girls nodded his head okay. At the nod of his head, Renee practically dragged Amari to her car. When she turned back to look at Maurice and make sure he wanted her to leave, she saw that he too was holding a gun.

"Oh Lord, there is about to be a shoot out and Maurice is either gonna end up dead or seriously injured," she thought to herself.

Renee and Amari ran to the car and hopped in, by the time they made it to the corner; they heard the first round of gun shots. Amari's heart sank. Amari knew for sure Maurice was dead.

When they got back to her house she thought she was all cried out. Renee and Amari walked into the house and neither of them could say anything to Aunt Marie when she asked the girls what was wrong.

They went to Renee's room and just sat there in silence, both of them silently praying to God to keep Maurice and David out of harms way.

A knock at the door made them both jump.

Aunt Marie walked in, "Mari, your friend Xena is on the phone crying," she said handing her the cordless phone.

Amari jumped up to grab the phone from her.

"Hello," Amari said frantic, hoping and praying she wasn't calling her to tell her that someone had died.

"Mari, you'll never believe what he did," she cried into the phone.

Amari had bigger things to worry about and here Xena was crying, about to tell her how Darvis was cheating on her no doubt.

"Xena, I can't understand you when you are crying, you need to calm down and speak clearly. I can't help you if I don't know what the problem is," Amari replied calmly even though she was all torn up on the inside.

Amari could hear her crying and trying to calm herself down. It took her a few minutes but she was finally calm.

"Darvis got some senior in high school pregnant," she spit out in one breath before she commenced crying again.

Amari's jaw dropped to the ground; did she just say what she thought she said? She couldn't believe it, even for Darvis that was an all time low.

"Oh my God, Xena are you sure? Are you okay?" she asked momentarily forgetting her own troubles.

"Yeah," she sniffled.

"The bitch called here this morning and told me everything. How she's been sleeping with him and how she does things with him that he said I would never do how she is so in love with him and he loves her."

"Damn! So da bitch called your cell phone?" she confirmed.

"Yeah," Xena said while blowing her nose into the phone.

"And where is Darvis, have you spoken to him yet?"

"Now you know that nigga ain't gonna answer his phone," she said into the phone.

"That's cool, I'll handle that nigga when I get home, he should know better than to be pulling this bull shit!" Amari screamed, heated that Darvis had once again disrespected her best friend.

"Xena what happened to Jordan? I thought ya'll were kicking it and you had gotten over Darvis?" Amari asked getting confused on why Xena cared so much.

"On the real, we were kicking it and he's a really cool guy. But I slipped up and went to go see Darvis. I was yearning for him and this is the bullshit I walked into," she said beginning to cry again.

"But you still call yourself his girl?" Amari asked still confused.

"Yeah I guess I do. But still I ain't expect that nigga to have a fucking fiancé either," she said in her defense.

Amari was just as disappointed in Xena for allowing herself to be disrespected.

Renee sat next to Amari listening in on the drama back in Atlanta. Making it known she would fuck David up if another chick ever came calling talking about she's pregnant. They were both cracking jokes about fucking David up, trying to make Xena feel better.

🎵🎵🎵

Tyrone couldn't wait to get to Daryl's house. Through some investigation he was able to finally find out who had it out for him.

🎵🎵🎵

Daryl sat outside of the jail waiting patiently for Cease to come out. He couldn't believe his boy was finally getting out. He knew he would help him put an end to the bull shit that had been going on.

Cease practically ran to Daryl's Mercedes.

"D man, what's good?" Cease said jumping in the passenger seat.

Dilemma

"Nigga, shit so much has gone down since you were locked up," Daryl said.

"Yeah I heard the crew got murked, you find out who was behind that?" Cease asked getting straight down to business.

"Nah, not yet, but then someone came and trashed my new Range," Daryl said getting upset again.

"Get the fuck outta here! You know as soon as we find this nigga, he's dead!" Cease said with a serious face.

"Yeah I know," Daryl said not sure if he was capable of getting his hands dirty like that again.

When Daryl and Cease pulled up to Daryl's house, Tyrone was waiting outside.

"Damn D, I didn't know you were going to get this nigga today," Tyrone said while giving Cease pound.

"That's right muthafucka I'm back," Cease said grinning.

"Word. Cause right now muthafuckas need you," Tyrone began.

"What's good Ty?" Daryl asked plopping down on the couch.

"I found out who was behind the attack on you," Tyrone said waiting for a response.

Cease sat up immediately.

"Word, who?" Cease asked.

"This nigga named Darvis," Tyrone confided.

"Darvis?" Daryl asked saying the name out loud.

Daryl knew he knew that name but for a moment had a memory lapse and couldn't think of how.

"What the fuck this kid got a beef with D for?" asked Cease.

"Word on the street is that he's trying to get back at Amari," Tyrone said waiting for a response.

"D, Mari used to fuck with some cat named Darvis?" Cease asked confused.

"Nah, not to my knowledge. The only cat I know she fucked with was Corey."

"Where this cat from?" asked Cease.

"Decatur," replied Tyrone.

Then it hit Daryl.

"Oh shit! Xena fucks with this cat named Darvis. But I don't know what his beef with Amari is," he said putting things together.

"I'm not really sure how the story goes but I guess she called the cops on him," Tyrone said remembering what he heard when he was in the streets earlier.

"Oh shit, that's right. A couple years back he ran Xena over with his car and then Peaches called the cops on him. That shit is so old though, why that nigga tryna retaliate now?" Daryl asked.

"I don't know man, but he crossed the line. He fucking with real niggas and now it's time for his ass to die!" Cease said ending the conversation.

"True dat. Let me talk to Peaches first and see if some other shit popped off with dude," Daryl said picking up the phone to call her.

CHAPTER TWELVE

Today Maurice and Amari were both leaving for school. They had a full summer of romance. It was nice, real nice. They sat on the plane next to each other and talked the whole way about what Atlanta was like. He was excited! He had never left Boston before.

When they reached the airport he sat Amari down and said he needed to speak to her before they went any further. Hesitantly she sat down. He began by saying he had a good time with her in Boston, but now he was trying to find out if they had a future outside of Boston. She definitely was feeling him but she was not sure if she was ready to bring him into her world full of drama. He continued by saying he could feel himself beginning to fall in love with her.

Wow! Now that was a true shocker. Amari knew he was feeling her but she didn't think he was feeling her like that. Damn was he really ready to take it to the next level, the commitment level? Damn, she had no clue.

They both sat silent for a moment, and then out of nowhere he pulled out a long slender jewelry box. When he handed it to Amari she was shocked. Slowly she opened it and was shocked to see the diamond heart bracelet she had previously admired.

"Oh my goodness, Maurice, you bought this for me?" she asked in disbelief.

"Yes, I don't think you understand how special you are to me. I really want to be your man. I promise I will always treat you right," he pleaded.

How could she really say no to that? She turned and looked into his big brown eyes and noticed his eyes were pleading with her. Pleading with her to just say yes, and why not? He just might be the one to finally treat her right.

"Okay," she finally answered with a smile.

He looked at her and gave her a big hug.

"Amari, I'm so happy and I promise you I am going to make you just as happy."

They got up and retrieved their bags from the baggage claim and waited at the curb for Xena to arrive.

Finally a half hour later she showed up and she didn't look pleased when she saw them. When Amari got into the car Xena just stared at her and gave her dirty looks. When they reached Xena's house she jumped out of the car and said she'd talk to Amari later.

"Damn baby, I don't think your girl likes me too much."

"Oh well, she better get used to you," Amari said while slamming her foot down on the accelerator.

"I can't believe that girl had the nerve to get an attitude with me and for what, because I am with someone other than Daryl or Corey? She better grow the hell up!" Amari thought angrily to herself.

Amari dropped Maurice off at Morehouse and proceeded to Corey's house to grab some needed clothing. When she got there she didn't see Corey's truck in the driveway and was quite relieved. Hopefully, she would be able to go in and come out without running into him. Amari really didn't feel like seeing him or his girlfriend at that moment.

When she rung the doorbell Lissa answered the door. Great just what she needed; now she would have to stand there and listen to her mouth while she grabbed her things.

"Well, if isn't Miss Heartbreaker," commented Lissa upon seeing Amari.

What the hell was she talking about? Why would she call Amari 'Miss Heartbreaker' when her brother was the one that did all of the heartbreaking? That was so typical of her, the problem was never her precious brother, and it was always Amari's fault.

"Lissa, what are you talking about?" she asked still confused by her comment.

"I am talking about you and how you broke my brother's heart," she answered honestly.

That deserved a laugh. Amari just gave her a fake smile and proceeded into the house. She was searching the house for Momma Val. She saw her car in the driveway so she knew she was at home. Amari finally found her sitting in the kitchen with her youngest son, Rob. When she saw Amari a big smile appeared on her face. She outstretched her arms and gave her a big hug.

"Amari, dear how are you? I was waiting for you to return, I need to talk to you about a few things. Would you mind sitting down for a few minutes?" she smiled.

"Sure, no problem," Amari said while pulling a chair out to sit down.

"So this is it huh? This is where she tells me due to the circumstances and the fact that her son hates me I need to get out, permanently," Amari thought angrily to herself while bracing her heart for more heartache.

"Well let me start out by saying I don't quite understand what is going on with you and Corey, but I do empathize with you. I love you like you were my own, you know that, and I hate to see you and Corey in such pain. Hopefully you two will be able to work things out eventually. However, until then I am going to have to ask you to leave."

Momma Val said not quite able to look Amari in the eyes.

"Damn did I call it or what, and did she say Corey was in pain?" Amari thought to herself as she got up to go and start packing her belongings.

Momma Val must have sensed Amari's urgency.

"No need to bother packing your things they are already boxed up and they are sitting in my husband's truck."

Damn, she's no joke. When she said she wanted Amari out, she meant just that. Amari turned towards her as her eyes began to water with tears.

"Momma Val, thank you for everything you have done for me. I really appreciate it all," she said still trying to fight back the tears.

Momma Val looked at Amari and smiled. Damn she doesn't need to show her excitement just yet, Amari was still standing there in her presence. Amari grabbed her purse and started walking towards the front door. Just as she was about to open the door, she heard Momma Val call her name.

"You didn't really think I would put you out with no where to go did you?" she asked still smiling.

"Yeah, I mean, I am not really your child, you are not obligated to do anything for me," Amari answered.

She laughed.

"Child, quit being so hard on yourself. I am always going to be here for you. That's why my husband and I have leased an apartment for you; it's already furnished as well."

Amari wasn't sure she heard her correctly.

She looked at Amari, "don't I get a hug or some type of gratitude?"

Amari practically ran to her and gave her a hug as though she was a five year old child excited on Christmas morning.

"Momma Val thank you for doing this for me," she smiled happily.

"No problem, and please don't ever forget, I am always here for you no matter what you and Corey are going through."

She gave her the address, her keys and the phone number. She said her husband would drop off her things later. Before she left she gave her one last hug and then proceeded on her way to her new apartment. When she reached the apartment she was so shocked. It was beautiful; nice, big, spacious two bedroom apartment. The bedrooms were so big and she had a new bedroom set in her room. When she said the apartment was furnished she was not joking.

Briefly Amari forgot she was mad at Xena and called her up to share the good news, unfortunately all she reached was her voice mail. Next she called Ke-Ke and she too was not answering her phone. Damn where was everyone? She wanted to tell someone the news, so she decided to call up her man, Maurice.

He was at his dorm unpacking but said he would love to come over and check out the place. She drove to his campus and picked him up. Damn was her man fine! She watched as a group of freshmen girls tried to holla at him. He proudly walked up to her truck and gave her a big kiss when he got inside, making the girls extremely jealous.

When they reached back to the apartment Maurice asked her if he could have something to drink. Until that moment it had slipped her mind that she hadn't been to the grocery store yet.

"Yeah, let me just run to the store," she said while grabbing her purse and keys.

"What for, you have mad stuff in your fridge already," he said grabbing a can of Coca Cola.

What is he talking about? She went into the kitchen and looked in the refrigerator and sure enough it was packed with every type of food imaginable. Damn

Momma Val went all out. She went and sat next to Maurice on the couch and they were just chilling and having a good time. It felt weird to be there in her own apartment. She must have been exhausted from the plane ride home because within minutes she was fast asleep laying on Maurice's lap. Amari had no clue how long she was asleep only that she remembered hearing a loud commotion that awoke her instantly. When she lifted her head up, Maurice was still sitting beside her and Corey and Greg were standing in the doorway.

"Yo, you got to be fucking kidding me, who da fuck is dis nigga?" demanded Corey at once.

He had the nerve to be questioning Amari on who she was with. How dare he take such a tone with her and have such a big ass attitude with her when he was the one that cheated.

"Corey, what are you doing here?" she asked getting up off the couch.

She could feel Maurice begin to tense up at the mention of Corey's name.

"What am I doing here? What the fuck is he doing here?" Corey yelled.

"Corey why are you making such a big commotion about this, and does your bitch know where you are right now?" Amari shot back.

"Does she? How would she feel if she knew you were here questioning me on my business?"

"Don't worry about her?" he replied nastily.

"Don't worry about her, yet you can worry about who I am with, what fucking sense does that make?" she asked practically shoving her finger in his face.

He looked at Amari with pure anger in his eyes.

Amari stared him down right back, "like I said what are you doing here?"

"I came to drop off your things," he said lowering his voice.

"Then drop them off and be gone!" she said with much attitude.

"Who da fuck you talking to like that, don't try to act all big and bad just cause your little boyfriend is here! I'll fuck both of you up!" he yelled.

Okay, yeah this nigga was definitely on some ole buggin status. He's lost his mind for sure. The whole time Gregory Charles and Maurice just sat by quietly and allowed the two ex lovebirds to go back and forth. When Gregory Charles finally grew tired of their bickering, he spoke up.

"Corey come on let's just bring her things up and leave. Why are you arguing with her? You got yourself a bad ass chick back at da crib waiting on you," he said throwing salt to the already burning fire.

"Yeah, why are you bickering with me?" Amari taunted.

"Whatever bitch," he said before going downstairs to retrieve the boxes.

While they were downstairs Maurice looked at Amari and suggested it was time for him to leave.

"Come on now, don't let that nigga run you off, that's exactly what he is hoping for."

Corey and Gregory Charles came back upstairs after unloading the last box.

"Amari, let me holla at you in private for a minute," Corey said almost in a whisper.

"Damn, why is this nigga sweating me like this?" Amari thought to herself.

She allowed him to speak to her; they went into her bedroom to talk. When they went inside he closed the door and began pacing.

"Amari, what are you doing? Why do you have this nigga up in your crib like this?" he questioned.

"Corey, why did you have your dick all up in that bitch?" she shot back angrily.

Corey looked at Amari speechless for a moment.

"Look Corey last I checked you cheated on me, therefore relinquishing all rights you held to my personal business. You hate me remember, so just keep it moving!"

On that note Amari stormed out of the room. She wasn't in the mood to hear the bullshit! When she went back into the living room Gregory Charles and Maurice were sitting on the couch having a civilized conversation. God only knew what they were actually discussing. Amari went to the door and held it open hopefully they would catch the hint and get the hell out of her apartment.

When Corey finally came out of her bedroom his eyes looked a bit blood shot as though he was crying. When he reached the door he looked at Maurice and said with spite.

"Just to let you know, you fucking with a real nasty bitch!"

Amari couldn't do anything but slam the door behind him. She looked at Maurice and he looked really disturbed.

"Damn that was intense, but don't worry boo, I still love you," he said while giving her a really big bear hug.

What a day today had been for Amari, she was convinced that Corey was a true ass! After all that though she didn't feel like being bothered by anyone so she decided to drive Maurice home a bit earlier than expected. When she returned to her new apartment she showered and prepared for bed, she was absolutely exhausted. She lay down and though she was extremely tired she was having an extremely hard time falling asleep.

Amari's mind kept wandering to Corey. Today was the first time she had seen him since he told her he hated her. It was really weird, sort of because she was still upset with him for treating her how he did, but at the same time she missed him so much.

When she finally dozed off to sleep it was probably about two in the morning, which left her with only a few hours of sleep because she needed to get up early to register for classes.

CHAPTER THIRTEEN

What are you supposed to do when life throws you a terrible unexpected curve ball? When at the present moment everything is going great how do you prepare yourself to deal with a tragedy, a tragedy you see no way of getting out of? Granted, Amari has dealt with tragedies in the past but this one really hit her hard.

Nikki called Amari and told her she was in the hospital and would really appreciate it if Amari would come and keep her company for awhile. When Amari reached the hospital, Nikki was lying in the bed and all the life looked as though it had been drained from her body. She looked as though she was barely hanging on. Amari awkwardly stood at the doorway for a moment trying to collect her thoughts. She did not want to go to her bedside looking the way she did, she didn't want to depress her any further. When Amari stood next to

Nikki's bed and expressed her sympathies toward her she told Amari the most horrific news she had ever heard.

"Amari, I have pneumonia and just found out I am HIV positive," she muttered.

Amari stood there for a really long moment; her mind was racing with all types of thoughts.

"Nikki, how, what happened? Who did you get it from?" she questioned.

"I'm really not sure; I mean we all know I was a bit fast back in the day. But I have been contacting men I have been with and informed them of the situation so they could get themselves tested. You and Daryl should probably get tested as well, seeing the situation we had in high school."

Amari stood silent. Her mind began racing.

"Nikki just told me there may be a possibility I may have HIV. Damn, what if Daryl has it and I have slept with him at least twice after he was with her. Oh God!" she thought angrily to herself.

"Amari, I know this is bad, but I pray you and Daryl will be fine," she said still unable to look at her.

Amari wasn't sure if Nikki felt by saying that she should feel better about the situation now.

"Nikki, where is your mom, why isn't she here?" Amari asked not wanting to really think about the information she just shared.

"Well, she basically disowned me after she found out I was HIV positive. You know how that would destroy her social status. You know that's all she ever really cared about."

Damn that's cold. Amari was ready to run out of there after the news that she laid on her, but she didn't feel right leaving her alone. Amari silently prayed to God that when she took her test, it came back negative.

Amari sat down in the chair next to Nikki and they started talking. They talked about everything and she informed her of her new boyfriend. Nikki seemed sincerely happy for Amari, but quickly said she rather see Amari with Daryl, because he really loved her. Why everyone was so hooked on Daryl and Amari being together was beyond Amari. Regardless of what anyone had to say, Amari was enjoying the drama free relationship she found herself in with Maurice.

Amari sat with Nikki for two hours, they talked the whole time and then Nikki began to drift off. Amari watched her sleep peacefully until a man entered the room with a vase full of roses. Amari looked at him strange thinking maybe he had the wrong room.

"Hi, my name is Al, and you are?" he asked outstretching his hand to shake hers.

"Amari, who are you looking for?" she questioned.

"That's my wifey right there," he said pointing toward Nikki.

"Wifey," she thought strangely to herself.

"She must not have told you about me, but I have heard a lot of things about you."

"Oh yeah, like what?" she asked curiously.

"Just that you were the best friend she ever had and how much she regrets how she treated you."

Amari had to smile at that. Nikki and Amari were close but she just thought it was a thing of the past.

"So how are you doing?" he asked breaking her from a daydream.

"I'm good and you?" she lied.

Amari was falling apart on the inside; at that moment she could have been HIV positive and had no clue.

"No, really, how are you doing?" he asked again.

"I'm just trying to maintain right now. I mean to say that I am not mad at her or that I am not falling apart on the inside would be a bold faced lie," Amari stated surprised at her honesty.

"That's what's up? She told me what happened in high school and that was really fucked up but she has changed since then. She is not the way she was then."

Why Amari felt the need to play devil's advocate was beyond her, but she did.

"What makes you so sure she has changed?" she asked.

"Well for starters according to her when she was in high school she never used protection and now she makes me wear a condom each and every time, no matter what. She doesn't go partying every night; she is at home with her daughter and me. She's matured."

"Did you just say she never used protection in high school?"

"Yeah, I thought you knew that, you being her girl and all."

"I had no clue. I knew she slept with crazy guys but I always assumed she used protection."

Amari sat there completely devastated when she heard that; it seemed her chances of having a negative HIV diagnosis was surely creeping out the door.

"I have a question for you Al, and please keep it real. You sleep with her knowing she has what she has?" Amari began, "well, I guess technically you haven't known because you just found out," Amari finished.

"Actually, she has known for three months and yes I still sleep with her, we are just very careful," he answered.

"That's a bit risky don't you think?" she asked shocked at his answer.

"It's a risk I am willing to take because I love her, she completes me," he said smiling from ear to ear.

"A risk you're willing to take because you love her. You are willing to die in the name of love?" Amari asked now confused by his answers and way of thinking.

She was sure at that moment he did not know and fully understand the seriousness of the situation.

"Exactly."

"How does your family feel about this? Do you have any kids?" she asked still trying to understand his way of thinking.

"Yes, I do, I have two daughters and my family doesn't really know of her condition," he answered.

"Why is that, are you ashamed? And how do you think your girl's will feel when they learn Daddy died because he loved an HIV positive woman?"

"I am not ashamed of her but I know how my family is. My girls will understand."

"Don't be so foolish and selfish. They won't understand they will grow up to hate you because you chose a female over them. You are not being fair to them or your family," Amari said getting visibly upset.

"Why do you feel she does not deserve to be loved just like everyone else? If she didn't have HIV you wouldn't be concerned with my kids or family."

"That's where you are wrong. The fact you are choosing a female whether she is HIV positive or not over your children is what bugs me."

"Don't hate on us and our love because you can't find any of your own. There must be something wrong with you if all of your boyfriends end up cheating on you," he said feeling satisfied with himself.

That was cold and unnecessary. She stood up gathered her things and left.

Amari sat in her car for at least twenty minutes crying. What was she going to do now? HIV, what if she was positive? And how could Al say all those things to her, he didn't even know her. Maybe he was right though, maybe something was wrong with her? At that moment she was sure that sooner or later Maurice would cheat on her as well. She couldn't understand why God was putting her through this.

Amari drove out of the parking lot crying and unsure of where she was going. She really didn't feel like going home and being alone, she just couldn't deal with this type of news alone. She drove around for a few hours just crying and thinking about what she would do if her test returned positive. She knew she really needed to make an appointment to have the test done, but she was afraid; too afraid to make that phone call.

She stopped to grab something to eat and decided to make a phone call to Daryl, he deserved to know. She called his house first and received no answer; just the answering machine. Next, she called his cell phone and again she received the answering machine. Now she felt as though she was on a mission, literally she felt she would shrivel up and die if she didn't get a hold of him. Finally, she called Tyrone's phone and was relieved when he answered.

"Hey Ty, its Amari, have you seen Daryl?" she asked hurriedly.

"Amari, what's up? What you doing calling him?" he asked with an attitude.

She felt herself beginning to boil. Why did he feel the need to hassle her? She simply wanted him to tell her yes or no.

"Look Ty, I really need to speak to Daryl so have you seen him or not?" she asked again getting irritated.

"Yeah, hold on," he said before dropping the phone.

Damn, that's all he needed to say to begin with.

"Amari, he doesn't want to speak to you," he finally said after taking a long time to get back to the phone.

What? Why wouldn't Daryl want to speak to her? That made absolutely no sense.

"Ty please tell him it is important, it is a matter of life and death," she pleaded.

Again he placed her on hold. Moments later he returned on the phone and said Daryl said he didn't care and some other bullshit about life not running on her time and him not being able to wait around forever for her. And then she was left to ponder his response with the humming of the dial tone.

Amari sat in Wendy's parking lot and really began to cry. The boy wouldn't even speak to her. Why the fact he was so upset with her even bothered her was beyond her, but she just felt if anyone would always have her back and not get mad at her for silly reasons it would be him. After seeing his behavior she assumed she was wrong in thinking that.

Finally she decided it was time for her to go home and make that fatal appointment. On the drive home, her cell phone rang and she was hoping it would be Daryl, but instead it was Xena.

"Hey Mari, where are you?" she asked.

"On my way home, what's up?"

"Nothing really just haven't heard from you all day," she said sounding sad.

"Yeah, some shit went down today," Amari said reflecting on the days events.

"You okay?" Xena asked concerned for her friend.

"Honestly no, but I'll inform you of everything when I get home."

"Alright then, I'll see you when you get here."

When she got home Xena was sitting on the couch just watching television.

"Hey," Xena said as Amari walked through the door.

Damn life really sucked when both roommates were depressed at the same time. Xena never said anything to Amari about not having a good day but she could read it all in her face, she was having a terrible day.

"Xena, are you okay?" Amari asked out of concern for her best friend.

"Nope," she said beginning to cry.

"What happened?" Amari asked not sure if she really wanted to hear her story.

"Darvis happened, he is such an ass!" she sobbed.

"What happened this time?" she asked getting comfortable on the couch.

"The usual, he's cheating," she said in between sobs.

Why Xena continuously put herself through the torture was beyond Amari. She just did not think there was that much love in the world.

"Did you catch him or just a gut feeling?"

"The bitch walked in early this morning while we were in the middle of sex," she began.

"Damn, that's a hard way to find out," Amari thought to herself, wondering who the 'bitch' was this time.

"How did she walk in, did she have keys or something?"

"Yeah, she has keys, apparently they are engaged," she said suddenly crying out of control.

Amari's mouth dropped in pure shock at the sentence that left her mouth.

"Xena wait a minute, did you just say Darvis is engaged?" Amari asked in disbelief.

"Yup, when she walked in and caught us she started throwing a big tantrum talking about she can not believe she caught him cheating, AGAIN! I looked at her like she was stupid; I was like, 'hold up bitch, he ain't cheating with me, because he's my man'. That was when she politely held up her left hand for me to see the two carat fucking rock that was gently resting on her damn ring finger. I lost it at that point and ran out of there as fast as my legs would carry me," she said breaking down again.

"Why Mari, why would he do me like this?" she begged for an answer.

Amari looked at her best friend hurting and wanted so desperately to take her pain away, but she knew no matter what she said to her, her heart would still be broken and would never properly heal.

"Xena, I don't know what to say to you. I have no idea why he does what he does to you, other than the fact you keep forgiving him. When Daryl and Corey cheated on me, I asked myself those same questions. It was one of those unexplainable things of life that we have to deal with and move on from," Amari said trying to comfort her as best as she could.

"Hey, where were you all day, what's going on in your world?" she asked suddenly remembering that she too had issues that day.

"Nikki's in the hospital. She's HIV positive and thinks Daryl and I should get tested as well considering our past together."

Xena looked at Amari and then lowered her head and hugged me.

"You must be so upset."

"I am, but what upsets me even more is the fact that Daryl refuses to talk to me. I tried calling him to tell him but he won't answer the phone for me," she said thinking back to what Ty told her.

"Damn, what's up with that? He always answers when he knows it's you calling."

"I don't know, so what do you want to do now?" Amari asked feeling tired of sitting there moping about the problems they had recently been forced to deal with.

"I feel like getting twisted," admitted Xena.

"Yeah, might as well," Amari agreed.

The two friends spent the rest of the night just drinking their sorrows away. By the morning they were both regretting it. Amari called the doctor first and scheduled an appointment for later that day. Then she called Maurice and shared with him what was going on with her. He seemed okay; he let her know he was there for her and offered to go to the clinic with her. That was thoughtful of him but she rather go with Xena.

Amari tried calling Daryl again and still she only reached his answering machine. She was getting more than upset now; she was borderline furious with him.

♫♫♫

Her appointment was at 2:00pm and they were already late. She didn't do it intentionally even though her doctor felt as if she did. Before the doctor would send her upstairs for her blood work, she decided she needed to have a discussion with Amari on how she would allow herself to get caught up and end up possibly with HIV.

Amari decided this woman did not need to know all the details of her life so she just shook her head and agreed with whatever she said. She finished her lecture after about twenty minutes. Finally, she was allowed upstairs, after her blood work was done, the phlebotomist said she should receive a call within the week.

Okay, did she just say a week? Damn, this wasn't a test that results would be ready in a few hours? How was she supposed to go about her regular routine for the next week when she had this hanging over her head? She stormed out of the clinic with Xena fast on her heels.

"Mari, damn wait up," she yelled.

"What happened?"

"I have to wait a fucking week before I can get my results! A whole week of me waiting and wondering if fate has already determined the outcome of my life," Amari answered while beginning to cry.

Xena drove home and Amari went straight to bed. She was depressed, distraught, and a mental mess. She wanted to place the blame on someone, but she really couldn't, if Daryl was faithful and if Nikki never betrayed their friendship then maybe she wouldn't be in this predicament now. But then on the flip side of things, if she had had just practiced safe sex with Daryl, she definitely would not be in this predicament either.

When she awoke from her nap Xena and Ke-Ke were both sitting on the couch talking, she walked in and immediately the room was silenced.

"Damn, don't talk about me behind my back, say what you have to say," Amari said while sitting down on the love seat.

"Daryl is in the hospital, he has pneumonia," Xena said avoiding Amari's eyes.

At those words her heart literally stopped beating. This could not be happening. No, she refused to believe Daryl had pneumonia. Nikki had pneumonia and she was HIV positive. Did that mean that Daryl was too? If he was then her chances of having the virus just increased tremendously.

"What hospital?" she asked quickly.

"Dekalb General," replied Ke-Ke.

"You're not going down there are you?"

"Of course I am what do you think I'm going to do just sit here?" Amari said while rushing to put on a pair of sweats.

"Well at least let me drive you," offered Ke-Ke.

"Sure, whatever, let's just go now," she demanded.

When they reached the hospital she was already in tears. She already knew what was going to happen. She was going to go and see Daryl and he too was going to inform her that he was HIV positive and then at the end of the week she would get a call from the clinic telling her she too had been infected with the virus.

When she reached his room door she hesitated for a moment not sure if she was ready to do this. Ke-Ke gave her a slight nudge encouraging her to just go and find out what was going on. She opened the door and there lie Daryl as pale as could be. He looked a lot like Nikki; the life seemed to be gone from his whole body. He looked fragile.

"Hey," she whispered.

He opened his eyes and when he saw her he smiled, a big heartwarming smile.

Amari moved closer to the bed and sat on the edge of it.

"Daryl, what happened?" she asked.

"I'm not really sure, I fainted this morning and when I came to Ty drove me to the ER and after a few tests they told me I had walking pneumonia. I felt fine up until that point, other than a little cough," he reflected.

"Did you by chance have a HIV test?" she asked getting straight to the point.

"Why would I do that? I have no reason to believe I was HIV positive or ever exposed to it, or do I?" he questioned.

Amari sat silent not sure how to tell him the news Nikki gave her.

"Mari, what's going on?" he asked again.

"Nikki is in the hospital with pneumonia and she is HIV positive," she blurted out.

He looked at her and then just lowered his head.

"She has AIDS?" he asked in disbelief.

"She's HIV positive," Amari corrected him.

He continued to sit there.

"I took my test earlier today. That's why I was calling you like a lunatic yesterday. I needed to tell you."

He pressed the nurse's button on the remote control. A nurse popped her head in within five seconds, "yes, may I help you?" she asked.

"Yes, I need to take a HIV test," he stated straightforward, never making eye contact.

The nurse looked at Amari and then back at Daryl.

"Right away," she replied.

A doctor came in and asked Amari to leave. When she returned Daryl looked worse.

"Daryl are you okay?" she asked while poking her head in the door.

"No," he said near tears.

"Amari, can you come here?" he asked.

"What's up?" she said while positioning herself back onto the edge of the bed.

He smiled, "You came here when Ty called and I appreciate that."

"I had to make sure you were okay. I do still care about you, ya know."

RED FLAG! Hello, why did Amari just admit to caring about him? Did she subconsciously care about him still?

"I've been thinking about you a lot lately," he began. "I've expressed my feelings for you before in the past and they are still true. I love you and I want to be with you. I promise I will never hurt you again. I want to make you happy."

"Daryl are you asking me to go out with you again? Didn't we travel down this road already and obviously you weren't very satisfied with me if you felt the need to cheat. Besides I have a boyfriend."

"Leave him, he can't satisfy you or make you as happy as I can. Plus, I just dumped dis chick I was kicking it with cuz she wasn't you. I realize now I can't live without you."

Amari was at a definite loss of words. How was she supposed to answer that? What response could she give to that?

CHAPTER FOURTEEN

Damn these past two weeks have been a sheer blessing. Amari spent every free moment with Maurice and didn't have the time to think and allow her mind to wander. Maurice definitely kept her busy. They have been spending so much time together she briefly forgot she had a past.

Amari forgot, that is, until the morning she received a call from Dr. Smith's office. When she answered the phone early this morning she thought it was Maurice's daily good morning call, so she answered as seductively as possible.

When the nurse replied with an unsure hello, may I speak with Amari, Amari felt out of place.

"Speaking," Amari said hurriedly clearing her throat.

She identified herself as Pamela, Dr. Smith's assistant. She went on to say Dr. Smith needed her to come in to the clinic as soon as possible. Amari sat on her bed with her head in her hands and the tears falling down her face. Just like that she felt her world crashing down all around her. Spending all of her free time with Maurice it slipped her mind that she took a HIV test two weeks ago; and now the results were in. Believe it or not, Dr. Smith held her life's fate in her hands.

Would she die an early death or would she get to live her life out to its fullest thus one day conquering the American Dream? Amari couldn't remember hanging up the phone, getting dressed or driving to the clinic. Somehow though she was now sitting in the clinic's waiting room trying to wait as patiently as possible.

After twenty minutes she decided to call Daryl, she never did find out what kind of results he received. The phone rang three times before his voice mail automatically cut on, she left a brief message.

A wave of disappointment brushed over her body. At that moment she needed to speak to him, she needed him to say he wasn't infected with the virus. She wanted to call Nikki but felt bad she hadn't spoken to her since that day in the hospital.

Amari knew Maurice was home and would answer happily and would willingly sit on the phone with her offering as much moral support possible. But at that point she just didn't want him into this. She didn't want him apart of this. So she sat in the waiting room for forty-five minutes before her name was finally called.

Amari already knew what she was going to say but still she walked down the long corridor with Pamela. Yeah, she thought she had dodged enough life altering bullets and unfortunately this wouldn't be one of them. She would try to ease the news to her as easy as possible. When she finally reached her office, she wasn't there. Pamela told her to have a seat and Dr. Smith would be in shortly.

Again she was left alone; alone with her thoughts and fears. Twenty minutes into her wait, Dr. Smith came in apologizing profusely. She sat still with a fake smile plastered on her face. She rummaged through some files found the one she was searching for and said, "Oh yes," in a slumber type of voice.

Amari's stomach started doing flips and her hands were clammy. She tried to sit still but could not; she tossed and turned in her seat, fidgeting with everything imaginable.

She read the file over and then took off her glasses and placed them on the desk next to the phone. She stared at her for a moment, and then began yet another speech.

The only words Amari heard come out of her mouth were, "It's always so hard for me to give this type of news. I'm sorry to have to tell you this but your results came back positive for the HIV virus," she said looking at Amari.

On instant Amari fainted. She passed right out. Moments later when she awoke, she was surrounded by Dr. Smith and Pamela; they gave her a glass of water. After finishing the water they both helped her back into the chair.

Dr. Smith began talking again.

"Dr. Smith, excuse me but did you just say I was positive?" Amari asked incredulous.

She rechecked the file and confirmed Amari's thoughts with a yes and a sad pity smile. She offered her counseling services. Amari of course declined. She got up off the floor, grabbed her purse and proceeded to head for the door. Dr. Smith handed her an information booklet as well as about seven prescriptions she claimed she would need to take every day now. Amari practically ran out of the clinic.

How she ever made it home was beyond her. But when she did she vowed to never leave the house again. The phone rang continuously but she didn't wish to speak to anyone. She climbed right into the bed and pulled the covers up high over her head. She slept and cried for the better part of two days. She left her room only to use the bathroom. She couldn't even eat. She just couldn't believe the doctor was serious about her being positive.

How? Why? Had she done such awful things in her life to really deserve something of this nature? She already lost her child behind the scandal of her best friend and boyfriend; must she lose her life as well? Every time she allowed herself to think about it she just got depressed.

Maurice called but she couldn't bring herself to talk to him. On day three of her depression, Xena forced her way into her room.

"Mari, what is going on with you? I can't help you if I don't know what the problem is," she reasoned while positioning herself on Amari's bed.

Amari moved away from her, trying not to acknowledge her presence.

"Damn Mari, when's the last time you showered? This room stinks!" she said getting up and opening up the blinds and windows.

Xena turned and looked at Amari, annoyed she had yet to acknowledge her; she pulled the comforter from off of Amari hoping to get her up. She remained strong and ignored her still wishing she could just be left alone. Xena was quiet and Amari wondered if maybe she spotted the pamphlet or the prescriptions the doctor had given her that she had yet to fill.

"Mari, how long have you had these clothes on? Why haven't you bothered to take your sneakers off? Why are you sleeping fully dressed like that?" she yelled sitting down on the bed again.

Amari moved farther away from her and pulled the pillow over her head, she wasn't buying the sleeping act anymore but she felt she needed to do something because she just couldn't allow her to see her this way. Amari was always the strong one, the one that held their friendship and lives together.

Xena got off the bed and came around to the side Amari was laying on and pulled the pillow off her head.

"Amari, please talk to me. I thought we were girls, I expect more than this from you," she said with concern.

"All I want to do is help and if I can't help, then at least let me cry with you," she reasoned as a single tear fell from her face.

Amari glanced up at her with swollen red eyes.

"Mari, what happened?" she questioned again.

It was time she shared her destiny with her best friend in the whole world. Amari sat up in the bed and looked at Xena through tearful eyes. She wanted to tell her, she needed to share this news with someone. At the back of her mind she knew that sharing the information would undoubtedly help her, she felt ashamed to tell her this.

Xena sat in front of Amari fully aware something terrible, something life altering had occurred.

She held her hand, "Xena, I'm positive!" she finally managed to blurt out.

Her jaw dropped and the single tear turned into a flood of tears.

"HIV," she whispered.

Amari shook her head yes and hid her eyes from her sight.

"Amari, no are you sure?" she asked.

"Yeah, I had my appointment a couple of days ago and the doctor confirmed it," she said wiping away the sudden gush of tears that had erupted from her eyes.

They both sat silent, crying and holding each other. Xena managed to convince Amari she needed to get up and shower. When she got out of the shower she had prepared their favorite meal, barbecue chicken, baked macaroni and cheese, and corn on the cob. They both sat at the table and ate while catching up on the latest gossip around campus.

After they ate they sat down and watched television, it was while they were both immersed in MTV's reality show Making the Band when the phone rang unexpectedly.

Xena answered it and quickly handed the phone to Amari. Even though she really didn't feel up to talking to anyone she reluctantly took the phone from her.

"Hello," Amari answered.

"Amari, hey it's me. Where have you been?" asked Daryl.

A small smile formed on her face. For some reason she was extremely happy to hear his voice.

"Hey Daryl, what's up?" she answered.

"I've been trying to talk to you. Every time I call you I never seem to get an answer," he said.

She smiled. She didn't want to tell Daryl but she knew she needed to.

"Alright, so now you have me on the phone, what's up?" she asked.

"Well, I got my results the other day and they were negative," he said with a sigh of relief.

What the fuck? How could he cheat with an infected person and Amari end up the one that was infected? How could this be? Since she was infected she thought for sure he would be too. Just that quickly she transformed into the bitch from hell and no longer felt the need to talk to Daryl.

"Daryl, look I gotta go," she said quickly before hanging up the phone.

Amari hung up the phone and ran to her room. A few minutes later Xena was knocking on her door. Amari couldn't speak to her though. She was upset, depressed and angry. Amari was angry at the world; just that quickly she managed to slip right back into her depressive non-talking stage. She stayed bottled up in her room for the next five days. She accepted no calls and communicated with no one.

♫♫♫

It had been two weeks since she learned the news of her fatal demise. It was really hard for her to get up every morning and go on about her daily routine. She had attended a few classes and she tried to get her feet planted firmly back in the ground. She finally got up the nerve to tell Maurice what happened. She knew he felt uncomfortable so she did him the favor and broke up with him. That was one of he hardest things she ever had to do. She hadn't realized it until that moment but Maurice had really grown on her. She was secretly falling in love with him.

Before she hung up the phone with him he practically begged her to not leave him. He told her over and over again how much he loved her and knew they would be able to get pass this. She remained strong and assured him it was definitely for the best. When she hung up the phone she sat on the couch and practically cried her heart out. She was not sure how much pain and heartache her heart would be able to bear, but she definitely felt she was finally getting to the end of her rope.

Amari turned on the television and just as luck would have it the football game was on. She really didn't want to watch the game because she didn't want to see Corey, but him being third string and all, she didn't think she had that much to worry about.

She kept the game on secretly praying she wouldn't even catch a glimpse of him. Her prayer went unanswered, in the fourth quarter two quarterbacks were injured and Corey was called in to play.

Watching him run out onto the field melted her heart. Damn did he look good! She was in such awe watching him play she never realized the tears that had begun to fall at the sight of her ex-boyfriend; just the sight of him and her heart was breaking all over again.

It had been so long since she even thought about them and the time they spent together. However, seeing him out on the field made her realize the love never left, it simply hid itself within the depths of her soul. She ended up falling asleep daydreaming about Corey.

Amari hadn't realized she fell asleep until that shrill of the phone ringing woke her up.

"Hello," she answered groggily.

"Hi, I'm looking for Amari," a woman's voice replied.

"Speaking," she said while adjusting herself better on the couch.

"Hi Amari, this is Pamela from Dr. Smith's office, hold please and I will connect you," she said emotionless.

"Now why is this damn woman calling me?" she thought to herself.

Didn't she get the hint she really wanted nothing to do with her or her devastating test results? She stayed on the line regardless.

"Hi Amari, how are you?" she asked cheerfully.

"I feel like shit, how you expect me to feel?" she asked with an attitude.

"Right, well Amari I am really sorry about that, that's actually why I am calling you. Apparently there was a mix up within my office and I gave you another patient's test results by accident," she said apologetically.

"What?" Amari said while sitting up on the couch so she could hear her better.

"Amari, I am really sorry, after reviewing my files thoroughly though, it turns out I gave you the wrong results. Your results were negative for the HIV virus. I am truly sorry for any inconvenience and heartache this may have caused you," she said.

"So I'm straight? I'm not affected with anything?" she asked hurriedly.

"Yes, but I would encourage you to get tested again in six months just to make sure," she said.

"Thanks doc," Amari said quickly before hanging up.

After she hung up she sat there on the couch for a minute and just prayed to God for keeping her from the disease. Amari was definitely going out to party tonight. This called for an all night celebration.

Amari called up her girls and left descriptive messages about the evening's celebration. She showered and threw on some sexy partying clothes. She put on a black Baby Phat mini skirt, a black and hot pink Baby Phat halter top and she had on a pair of hot pink stilettos. She decided to wear her long hair down.

She stood back and admired herself in the full length mirror, she was definitely looking sweet! On her way out the door Ke-Ke called to make sure everything was okay, she told her to meet her at Club 112 and they would talk then.

When she got to the club the Terror Squad hit, "Lean Back" was blaring and the fellas were checking her out something fierce. She walked into the club and just breathed in the atmosphere.

"Thank you Lord" she whispered over and over to herself. Once she got farther into the club she spotted Daryl dancing tight as could be with some hoochie looking chick that was wearing a loud orange mini skirt that could barely cover her ass! She was determined not to allow that to affect her night of fun.

She proceeded onto the miniature dance floor, alone, and began dancing along to the latest Jay-Z song that was playing. She wasn't even on the dance floor two minutes before she was approached by a not so tall cutie.

He stood about 5'4" and wore braids to the middle of his back. He stood before her wearing the latest Sean John fashion and a new pair of Timbs. His face was as smooth as a baby's bottom and his big hazel eyes pleaded with her to allow him to join her on the dance floor. She quickly agreed.

She was blinded looking at only Ricardo, her new dancing partner. She found out later that evening he was Puerto Rican and spoke Spanish fluently. Wow, imagine that, never in her entire life had she seen a man look as gorgeous or be so well dressed as Ricardo. She was definitely hoping to see more of this one.

When she finally spotted her girl's standing at the bar, she felt elated. She couldn't wait to share her news with them. She walked towards the bar and Daryl tried to stop her in her path, she didn't even bother to stop she simply put her hand up and said not now. He stood there confused but she kept on going, trying to reach her girls as quickly as possible.

When she finally reached the bar after pushing her way through the crowd of people, Xena was standing alone. She walked up behind her and squeezed herself in between her and the guy standing next to her.

"Hey girl!" she practically screamed to be heard over the crowd.

She smiled, "Amari, are you okay?" she asked concerned.

"Better than ever," she said while filling her in on her good news.

Her whole face lit up and she reached over to give her a big hug. They sat there for a long moment hugging and comforting each other, once she felt the tear threaten to fall from her eyes she pulled away from her and ordered drinks for the both of them. They both sat there enjoying their drinks and observing the environment around them. She was so lost in her world and her thoughts she didn't even hear Ke-Ke sneak up behind them.

"Hey Amari, girl you are wearing the hell outta that outfit! How many niggas already tried to holla at you?" she asked laughing.

"I know they just knocking down the doors to get to you," she commented with a smile.

Amari had to laugh at her; she always knew what to say to get you to crack a smile.

"Girl please, I have been dancing with the same nigga all night. This fine ass Puerto Rican named Ricardo. Girl the nigga is FINE!" she smiled reminiscing about their time on the dance floor.

"Well damn where is this cutie? Let me at least catch a glimpse of him," she laughed while looking around the club in search of a sexy Puerto Rican man.

"Oh by the way, Daryl stopped me and asked me if I could get you to speak to him privately for about five minutes," Ke-Ke whispered so only Amari could hear her.

The thought of him wanting to speak to her made her stop for a moment; to think Daryl was actually concerned with her and wanted to speak to her unnerved her. She was determined to stand her ground though and her ground was that she had no time for Daryl and anything he thought he needed to say to her.

After Amari finished her drink and kicking it with her girls, she went in search of Ricardo, she wanted to make sure they exchanged numbers before she left the club. It was already two in the morning and she had to get up for class in a few short hours. When she finally spotted him he was on the dance floor booty shaking with the same hoochie mama she saw Daryl with earlier. She didn't want to throw salt on his game so she just walked right past him towards the restrooms even though she would not dare use a restroom at a night club.

She went into the bathroom and fronted like she needed to use it. The sight of a night club bathroom always disgusted her. The bathrooms usually only had one working stall with one sink and a cloudy 8x9 mirror. They were usually over packed with hood rats in there gossiping about some nigga they were trying to get to notice them. She made her 'front' in there as brief as possible and practically went running out the bathroom door; just her luck she ran out of the bathroom and straight into the arms of Ricardo.

"You're cute, you know that?" he questioned.

"Why you say that?" she asked puzzled.

"You know I watched you walk right past me. If you wanted to speak to me you could have easily saved me from having to dance with the female version of Shaq," he smirked.

She laughed.

"Yeah okay, I was looking for you, I just wanted to tell you goodbye and that it was really nice to meet you and dance with you," she said like she was all proper and what not.

"Goodbye huh, without even as much as a hug and a phone number? Oh come on, I thought for sure I would get at least that," he said looking Amari in her eyes while running his fingers through her hair.

"And what made you think you were worthy of my phone number?" she asked trying not to allow herself to get emotionally attached by his sweet words and seductive gestures.

"I just thought we connected and I really am trying to get to know you better," he smiled.

"Okay then I will give you my digits," Amari said while taking out her candy apple red lipstick.

Amari then rolled up his shirt sleeve and wrote her name and number on the inside of his arm. He blushed the whole time she was writing. The whole three minutes she stood there flirting with her new friend she had no idea that to the left and right of her Corey and Daryl were staring hard at her, clocking her every move. The both of them were feeling angry and envious. They were feeling anger towards Amari for ignoring their repeated attempts at communications with them and they were envious of Ricardo because she gave him the chance to speak to her and she was flirting and laughing with him and secretly Daryl and Corey both missed having that with Amari.

CHAPTER SIXTEEN

Amari spent so much time and energy on dealing with all of the bullshit she had allowed herself to slip within her studies. Once again she found herself having to work extra just to be able to finish the semester with passing marks. Ever since that night at the club she felt so refreshed, so alive, so full of energy. Amari wasn't sure if the news of her not having HIV did it but she felt great!

Ricardo was someone she was able to just have fun with. She was not really looking to get into anything serious at that moment and thankfully he understood that. He didn't pressure her to do anything he seemed to understand and be quite content with the extent of their relationship.

To be free with no worries was such a relief, such a blessing. Even though Ricardo and Amari weren't officially dating they did tend to go out every now and then. She considered it something fun to do. It was also weird to her to be able to go out and have no commitments. Xena and Ke-Ke continuously told her how good of a man Ricardo was and how she better not let him slip away. To Amari it was not so much as slipping away as it was the fact that she really didn't need to be in a relationship at that moment. She fully understood the need of her just having some time to herself. Some time so that she could just take a breath and relax.

Her girls didn't see things like that, they felt she should take what she could get when she could get it, bottom line. She knew they meant well but sometimes she felt they were just saying that because they were lonely and wishing they had someone to share their time with.

♫♫♫

Amari watched Corey's game on Sunday and nearly broke down and cried. About a month back the starting quarterback was injured and they put Corey in; for the past four weeks he had been the starting quarterback. It still surprised Amari how well Corey did at quarterback, in high school and college he played running back. He had been doing really well and the football community had quickly fallen in love with him.

On this particular Sunday he rushed for 101 yards and passed for 300, with three touchdowns in his pocket, on the last play of the third quarter he went in for a quarterback sneak and was doubled tackled hard. The referee threw both hands in the air signaling a touchdown and the crowd went crazy. Slowly the crowd began to quiet down; Corey was still lying on the ground. On instant Amari knew he was hurt, she could feel it in her bones. She watched in shock, horror and concern as the trainers marched out onto the field and tended to him. Still there was no voluntary movement on his part. He lay there as still as could be. The crowd was completely silent now. The other players from both teams stood by idly watching and praying he would be okay. The two linebackers that tackled him sat on the bench on the sideline holding their heads in their hands wishing, hoping and praying they had not fatally hurt the star quarterback. In their heads they were thinking all they wanted to do was stop the run, not stop the player.

After a few seconds of still non movement the EMT workers made their way onto the field with their stretcher. Carefully they loaded Corey's limp body onto it. Xena and Ke-Ke sat on each side of Amari and held her. Ricardo sat on the loveseat feeling mixed emotions. He felt bad Corey was hurt but at the same time he wished the feelings she obviously still harbored for Corey she had for him.

As the stretcher wheeled Corey out the crowd remained silent. And then they paused for a commercial break. And that was when her phone began to ring off the hook. Everyone was calling hoping to be the first to inform Amari of Corey's unfortunate accident. The last two calls touched her heart.

Maurice called first. Amari hadn't spoken to Maurice since the day she called him and dumped him. She hurt him so bad who would have thought he would call her to try to comfort her. But he did, and she was grateful.

"Amari, hey were you watching the game?" he asked.

"Yeah, I saw it," she replied through sobs.

"Are you okay? Do you need anything?" he offered.

"Nah, I'm good, just waiting to hear them announce what's going on with Corey," she said still crying.

"So other than that you're doing okay right?" he asked again.

She took a deep breath.

"Yeah, I'm okay," she answered.

There was a moment of silence. In that moment she could tell Maurice wanted to say more but probably felt this was not the proper time for any other type of conversation. Or maybe it was the time but he was just scared. Scared to open up and tell her how he was really feeling and what emotions he was trying to deal with. They quickly hung up the phone both wishing they had said more.

Her next call was from Daryl.

"Amari, hey I just saw what happened are you okay?" he blurted out, barely giving her the chance to say hello.

"Yeah, I'm alright, I'm just waiting to hear what kind of condition he is in," she answered.

"Damn, that nigga took a hard hit but he's a soldier he'll be okay," he offered trying to make her feel better.

"Amari you don't sound too good," he commented.

For some reason she just broke down. She wasn't sure why but she just busted into tears. She was hurting and she was not sure if at that moment she even realized just how much she was worried about Corey or just how much she loved him. She didn't remember saying goodbye to Daryl, but all she heard was the dial tone. She hung up the phone carefully. She sat back down on the couch and Xena looked at Amari stunned and wondered what happened. She just shook her head no because she didn't know what happened.

The commercial break was finally over and the game was back on but they had yet to announce any news on Corey's condition.

The doorbell rang, Ricardo got up to answer it and once again drama was popping off.

"Amari, it's for you," Ricardo said with an attitude.

She looked towards the door and there stood Daryl.

She got up off the couch and went to the door.

"Daryl, what are you doing here?" she asked confused.

"You didn't sound good on the phone. I was worried about you," he said leaning against the door frame.

"I'm fine," she said.

"I didn't mean to cause anything, didn't know you had company," he apologized.

They both stood there staring at each other.

"Amari, come quick they are talking about Corey," yelled Ke-Ke.

Daryl and Amari both ran back to the living room and turned the volume up to its maximum.

"We have just spoken to the head coach and unfortunately we have terrible news, regarding Corey Fowler. As you know he was taken off the field earlier via stretcher. He has been taken to

Atlanta Memorial where he has already undergone a variety of tests and has since fallen into a coma. Our thoughts and prayers go out to his family, friends and the entire football team."

And then they took another commercial break.

Amari sat on the couch numb. Immediately Daryl hugged her and all of the tears began to flow. Xena and Ke-Ke sat nearby and cried silently to themselves. She was out of control. She began to heave and shake. Corey was in a coma. What if he never came out of it or what if he just didn't make it all together? What would she do if he were no longer around? Daryl held her tight and comforted her just how she needed to be comforted. She was so wrapped up in her own thing she never noticed when Ricardo got up to leave.

"Amari, do you want me to call Mrs. Fowler and see if I can find out anything else?" asked Xena.

Xena took Amari's silence for a yes and made the call. Amari faintly heard her talking to Mrs. Fowler but she couldn't make out what was being said.

"Amari, Mrs. Fowler said she was getting ready to call you, said she's on her way to the hospital, she'll call you once she knows more about his condition," Xena said while handing Amari a tissue.

They all sat by quietly, the television was on mute. They watched the rest of the team try to finish what Corey had started, it was amazing to Amari the team didn't allow the devastating news of Corey stop them or distract them from accomplishing their ultimate goal which was to win the game.

She spent the rest of the night crying. By around eight in the evening Daryl tucked her into bed. She fell fast asleep. She had no idea Daryl stayed by her side until the phone rang late in the night. It was Momma Val. She sounded like she was trying hard to keep herself together but wasn't succeeding at it. When Daryl first handed Amari the phone and she said hello, Momma Val sounded confused.

"Amari is that you?" she asked.

"Yes it's me," she answered softly.

"Oh but who just answered your phone?" she inquired.

"Daryl," she replied honestly, not sure exactly why she was concerning herself with who was answering her phone.

"Oh," she replied even softer.

"So how's Corey?" she asked getting back to the subject at hand.

"Corey is in a coma," she began, "the hit he took could have been fatal, should have been fatal. He has a nasty head injury. We are hoping he will pull out of this with no brain damage," she said sniffling.

Amari couldn't believe what she was hearing. She didn't want Momma Val to hear her crying so she rushed herself off the phone. Momma Val promised to keep her posted and she was grateful for that. She lay back down and cried long and hard into her pillow. Daryl stayed with Amari for the rest of the night holding her and comforting her.

The next morning Amari willed herself up to get ready for class. When she got to her psychology class everyone was talking about Corey, it took everything she had and then some to remain strong and not break down and cry. She skipped her next two classes and went home to bed. She slept for a good two hours got up and felt a bit refreshed. She called Momma Val and she said nothing had changed. When Xena came home she asked her about going to see Corey, she said she didn't think it would be a good idea.

Daryl came by later in the evening after he was finished with classes and practice. He bought her dinner and she was grateful, she just wasn't up to eating. Again, he spent the night comforting her. When she awoke in the middle of the night with nightmares he was right there to hold her and wipe away the tears.

Day two of Corey's coma she thought she would lose her mind for sure. When she awoke Daryl was sleeping peacefully in the rocking chair. He looked exhausted even though he was sleeping. She crept around quietly not wanting to wake him. Her first class and only class of the day was not until mid afternoon. She decided to get up and watch some television before she showered and got ready for class. When she turned the television on the news was reporting the unfortunate hit the pro football, Corey Fowler took in Sunday's game. Apparently they had an exclusive interview with one of the linebackers that tackled Corey that day, thus sending him into a coma. The man looked hurt. He looked like he was suffering some serious pain and going through some serious guilt due to the seriousness of Corey's situation.

"Hey Amari, I didn't even hear you get up," Daryl uttered.

He woke up groggy and was standing in the entranceway to the living room rubbing his eyes.

"Yeah, I have been up for awhile but I didn't want to wake you up," she said while patting the empty couch next to her, inviting him to sit with her.

He followed suit and sat down next to her. She curled up next to him allowing him to take his big arms and wrap them around her frail body. She had lost so much weight over the past few months that it was ridiculous. He held her close and tight it was just what she needed at that moment.

They both sat there briefly just enjoying the time together. It was just as if they were still together.

"So are you going to class today?" he asked out of the blue.

"I'm going to try to go. I am not sure how long I will be able to stay though," she replied honestly.

They sat there for awhile like that not saying a word. The silence was deafening but they both had a lot of things on their mind. She eventually fell asleep in his arms, it felt so right. It felt like this was where she was meant to be. She must admit that after all this time, strange as it may seem, she still had a lot of love for Daryl. She thought for as long as she lived she would always hold a special place in her heart for him. After all he was her first love.

♫♫♫

The class was taking forever. The professor was standing up there lecturing on some ridiculous shit, some shit she had no use for. At that moment she felt there were more pressing issues than this lecture. When she felt the buzz of her cell phone going off she couldn't have been more relieved. Quietly she took out her phone and said, "Hello," the number read private.

"Amari, its Lissa, are you busy?"

What was Corey's sister doing calling her? Please God, do not let the reason for her call be anything negative about Corey. She whispered hold on and grabbed her things as quickly and as quietly as possible. Once outside the lecture hall she said hello in her regular voice.

"Lissa are you still there?" she asked.

"Yeah, what took you so long?" she asked with an attitude.

"I had to get out of class," she replied back.

"Oh well let me get straight to the point. I thought you loved my brother!" she began angrily.

"I do," Amari said unsure of why she was bringing this up at that point and time.

"Then why haven't you been around to see him?" she asked.

That was a damn good question. Maybe Amari was scared, scared of what he may look like and the fact he wouldn't be able to hear her, killed her.

"I just wanted to give the family their time. We are not even together, I didn't want to just come barging in there," she tried to reason.

"Besides I didn't want to get his girlfriend all upset and I figured seeing me there would do just that."

"Please that bitch ain't been down here her damn self. I just figured if he heard some familiar voices it would wake him up. Do you think you could come down here and sit with him for a little while?" she finally asked.

Amari allowed her mind to mill over her request for a brief moment and finally agreed to go and visit her brother. Amari told Lissa she would meet her at the hospital in an hour. When she got back to the apartment she called Xena to see if she was free to go with her. She had a lab she couldn't miss. Ke-Ke was at work and Daryl had practice. Daryl was willing to skip but she didn't want him to because then he wouldn't be able to play that weekend.

So she made the trip down to the hospital alone. When she pulled up to the hospital she didn't know what to do. She sat in her car and just thought about previous days when they were together and happy. She contemplated turning around and driving back home, however, something inside of her willed her to get out of the car and follow through with what she set out to do. She walked cautiously through the hospital until she reached Corey's room; she braced herself before entering his room so she wouldn't be shocked by his presence. She thought she braced herself but nothing in the world could have prepared her for what she was about to see or the emotions that would erupt from within her because of it.

Amari opened the door and found Corey lying on the bed lifeless. He had all types of tubes running all through his body and his head was wrapped tight with white gauze. She inched closer to the bed and stood next to his lifeless body. She was at a definite loss of words. She held his hand and nearly broke down. She decided to pull up a chair.

"Corey, its Amari, please let me know if you can hear me?" she begged.

Nothing, he just laid there and said nothing and made no indication he would be waking up anytime soon. She sat there for a good thirty minutes just watching him and pleading with him and God to just show her a sign. She needed some type of sign to let her know he would pull through. At some point she must have fallen asleep she was awaken by a constant nudging. When she opened her eyes, Momma Val and Lissa were standing over her. She stood up immediately and began apologizing.

"Amari, please you do not have to apologize. It might be good for Corey to hear your voice. Who knows it might just be the key to waking him up," Momma Val stated while gently rubbing Corey's head.

After she stood there rubbing his head for a few minutes she then leaned over towards Amari and gave her a hug, "I've missed you," she whispered in Amari's ear.

She smiled. If Amari was being honest with herself she would admit she too missed her and the rest of her family as well. Corey's doctor came in right before she was getting ready to leave and said they wanted to take him off the life support to see if he would breathe on his own. Momma Val was leery about it and said she would need to wait until her husband arrived before making such a decision. When the doctor walked out, Corey's girlfriend, Lily walked into the room and that was when Amari regretted coming to the hospital. She glared at Amari with evil eyes when she saw her seated next to Corey. She walked in and kissed Momma Val and spoke to Lissa. Then she went around to the opposite side of Corey's bed and kissed him gently on the forehead. Then she turned her attention towards Amari.

"What the hell are you doing here?" Lily asked angrily.

Amari refused to argue with Lily at the damn hospital. Amari got up gathered her things and said goodbye. On her way out of the door she heard Lissa telling Lily she was out of her place and that Corey really loved Amari and not her. Amari couldn't suppress the smile that instantly formed on her face.

When she got back to her apartment, she flopped down on the bed and had a really good, much needed cry. Amari realized at that moment how much she missed Corey. She needed Corey. Somewhere during her cry she must have fallen asleep she didn't really remember, she just remembered feeling groggy and hearing the phone ringing, obnoxiously.

"Amari, hey are you okay?" asked Daryl over the phone.

"Yeah, I'm good, what's up with you? Are you coming through tonight?"

Why she asked him that was beyond her but she was beginning to get used to seeing him and being with him every night. She needed to see him and just feel his arms around her.

"Of course, you know if you need me then I am there, no matter what. We've got a team meeting in twenty minutes, I'll be over after that, I was just checking to see if you needed anything before I came through," he said.

"Nah, I'm straight, just having you here with me is all I need."

Amari was not sure where this sudden sweetness towards Daryl was coming from.

She could hear him smiling through the phone.

"Okay then I'll see you when I get there, you sure you're okay right?" he asked again.

"Yeah, I just can't wait to see you," she said again.

"Okay then I'll try to get there as quickly as possible," he said before hanging up.

Amari sat on her bed still holding the phone unsure of why the conversation with Daryl was the way it was. Something strange had definitely come over her. She didn't understand why she had this sudden compassion and love for Daryl. She decided to take a shower and put her pajamas on before Daryl arrived. After she showered the phone rang and she figured it was just Daryl calling to tell her he wouldn't be able to come through.

"Hello," she answered.

"Amari," the female voice replied.

"Yeah," she said wondering who this female was calling her.

"It's Lily. I thought I told you to stay the hell away from my man! What were you doing at the hospital today?" she began.

Amari hung up right in her face. She didn't want to hear her bull shit. She was tired of it all already. She lay in her bed thinking about Corey and hoping he would come out of the coma and be okay. That was the only thing she was praying for. Her thoughts were interrupted by the constant nagging of the buzzer.

Daryl stood at her door holding a dozen red roses. She was shocked.

"Daryl, what's all this?" she asked in disbelief, gesturing towards the roses.

"A guy was selling them at the gas station. I saw them and instantly thought about you," he smiled.

Her hormones were probably all out of whack at that moment because that cheesy line had her all into him at that moment. It was like they were freshmen in high school again and they just began dating. Daryl entered the apartment and went straight to her bedroom while she found the vase to put the flowers in.

By the time she was finished with the flowers Daryl was already on the bed comfortably flipping through channels.

"Damn you look comfortable," she observed.

He sat up quickly.

"I'm sorry," he apologized.

"Nah, no problem, I'm just messing with you," she said while climbing onto the bed.

Amari lay down next to Daryl and snuggled up next to him. They lay together for about an hour before something strange happened. Daryl was trying to get comfortable and his hand accidentally grazed her left breast. The touch of his hand sent chills through out her whole body. Daryl quickly apologized.

"Amari, I didn't mean to do that."

She climbed on top of him and said as seductively as possible, "don't apologize, its okay."

She looked into his eyes and saw a glint of hope in his eyes. She leaned close and gave him a soft kiss on the lips. He was shocked. She felt his whole body tense up underneath her. Wanting to loosen him up a bit, she began to shower him with sweet sensuous kisses from top to bottom. She started at his neck and worked her way down. His body began to loosen up. With one swift movement Daryl flipped her onto her backside and began returning the favor. It felt so good to feel his lips roam all over her bare body. She was laying there enjoying the feel of his moist lips smother her body with kisses. They were enjoying themselves when the damn phone rang.

Damn, she hated it when that shit happened. She apologized quickly to Daryl and reached across the bed and grabbed the cordless.

"Hello," she answered quickly with an apparent annoyance.

"Hey," a soft male voice replied.

"Who's this?" she asked.

"Damn shortie you forgot me already?" asked the voice again.

She sat up a little and demanded to know who the mysterious caller was. She watched Daryl out of the corner of her eye and he seemed to be getting annoyed as well. The caller was silent.

"Hello," she yelled into the phone.

"It's Ricardo, but I don't even feel like talking to you anymore," he began to say something that was sounding bit on the downside.

"Good, because now is not a good time for me," she said before hanging up the phone.

By this time Daryl was off of her completely and lying down next to her with his back turned.

"Damn, is the mood ruined?" she asked while reaching under the covers and grabbing him and thus making his manhood rise.

Before they took things too much further she made Daryl put on a condom. He didn't seem too happy about it at first but he finally agreed. They enjoyed each other for the rest of the night taking a break only to use the bathroom. She forgot how good sex with Daryl was. He was definitely the best sex she had ever had. When they finally fell asleep it was early in the morning, time for waking up. When she finally awoke she was a bit shocked yet happy to see Daryl lying beside her. Amari put on her bathrobe and went to take a shower. In the shower she allowed the steamy hot water to penetrate her body. It felt so good. After her shower and after throwing on a quick sweat suit she went to make some breakfast.

Ke-Ke and Xena were sitting at the kitchen table no doubt talking shit about Amari.

"Hey girls," she said while grabbing some eggs out of the refrigerator.

"So, I noticed Daryl's car sitting outside, again," began Xena.

"Anything I should know about?" she asked.

"Nope," Amari said trying to suppress her smile.

"Okay, but at least tell us this, are you guys together or not?" she asked.

Amari looked at her oddly unsure of what that had to do with anything.

"And that has what to do with what?" she asked bluntly.

"It has nothing to do with anything I just see how close the two of you have grown over the last couple of days and we don't want to see you get hurt," explained Ke-Ke.

Amari chuckled at that comment that was just their polite way of trying to be all up in her business.

"Girl, I don't want to see me get hurt! Believe me I am not trying to rush into anything, I am taking it very slow and step by step," Amari explained thinking back to the previous night with Daryl.

Last night was definitely something special and yet something unexpected. It still shocked Amari how much she wanted him and how at that moment she felt as if she couldn't live without him. She felt so strongly that she needed him, as if she would die without a taste of him.

Last night the only thought she had was of Daryl. It was funny you can be with someone again and suddenly things seem to have never changed. Last night felt like they were still dating. The way he held her and explored her body was with such tenderness and softness. They made love all night long and she swore he took her to the heaven and stars each time. Daryl left awhile ago, he needed to get to practice and she too had class.

She called Lissa earlier to check on Corey and she said nothing had changed. She also informed Amari that now Lily was up there 24/7 trying to act like she was all concerned. Amari found it so funny to hear Lissa talk bad about Lily when not too long ago she was all for the relationship between Corey and Lily. People were funny like that, on the outside and at first meeting people look good but then when you have had a chance to really get to know them and find out what they were really like you wish you had never accepted them to begin with.

Amari went to class feeling a bit better than she had for the past few days. She was able to stay for the entire class. Xena two wayed her during class and said she wanted to go shopping after class. Amari had to admit she wasn't paying much attention in class but at least she managed to stay for the entire lecture. After class she met Xena, Ke-Ke and Toni at the Science building and they headed off to the mall.

While they were shopping Amari's cell phone rang. She answered it without even checking the caller id.

"Hello," she said laughing a bit.

Ke-Ke just busted her ass! She was wearing these black boots that had a pretty high heel and she could hardly walk straight. Instead of concentrating on her walking she was too busy flirting with this cutie that was walking by and her foot gave way and she ended up flat on her ass!

Xena, Toni and Amari couldn't stop laughing.

"Hello," she said again trying to suppress her laughter.

"Hey boo," replied Daryl on the other end.

Amari quickly straightened up and got serious.

"Daryl, hey how ya doing?" she asked smiling.

"A lot better now that I am hearing your voice," he said.

"How sweet," she replied.

"So what's up with you?" he asked.

"Nothing just at the mall with the girls," she replied.

"Yeah, you buying anything sexy?" he asked.

"Wasn't planning on it, do I have a reason to?"

"Actually yeah, I was hoping we could go out to dinner tonight?" he suggested.

"Dinner huh, that sounds like a date to me, why Daryl are you asking me out on a date?" she teased.

The phone was silent.

Amari stood there hoping and praying he would say yes. She wanted this to be a date. The girls stood around her hanging on to each and every word and secretly hoping this would be an official date as well.

"Amari, I would love for this to be an official date, if that's okay with you?" he questioned.

Amari couldn't stop the smile from spreading on her face.

"Sure Daryl, what time should I be ready?" she asked not wanting to seem too anxious.

"Is seven good for you?" he asked.

"Yeah," she said still trying to suppress her excitement.

When she hung up the phone the four girls screamed. Why the sudden excitement over Daryl was beyond Amari. But excitement was all she felt. They began their hunt for a sexy dress. Daryl's favorite color was blue so she was looking for a sexy blue dress. After four stores she thought she would never find a dress. She ended up buying a pair of tight fitting Baby Phat navy blue pants and a navy blue Baby Phat halter top with a pair of baby blue leather stiletto boots.

By the time she reached home she had exactly one hour before Daryl was due to pick her up she was running ragged. Amari was trying to get everything done in time. When she stepped out the shower was when she heard the doorbell ring.

"Damn it, he would be on time!" she muttered to herself while she tried to hurry up and get dressed.

As she was zipping up her boots there was a soft knock on her door.

"Yeah," Amari screamed.

"Mari, it's Toni, Daryl said he was gonna go and get some gas and he'd be right back," she yelled.

Amari took a sigh of relief.

"Good, that gives me like fifteen more minutes," she thought to herself.

When Daryl returned ten minutes later she was ready to go and feeling damn good about the nights events. Daryl stood at the doorway of the apartment just admiring her.

"Daryl, let's go, we're gonna be late aren't we?" she asked.

His constant staring was making her nervous.

"Yeah okay, I just can't get over how damn good you look tonight. You make me want to say fuck the reservation and let's go back to the bedroom," he whispered in her ear.

Ke-Ke, Toni and Xena all sat on the couch smiling and watching them as if they were proud parents of a daughter's first date. Amari looked at Daryl and gave him a kiss on the lips.

"There will be plenty of time for that later," she smiled.

The couple said their good byes and headed out the door.

CHAPTER SEVENTEEN

Amari decided to get a part time job so she would have extra money. She figured it was time for her to stop asking Momma Val for cash whenever she needed it. She looked around for months and was continuously turned down. She ended up working at an office supply store which she hated.

All of the people she worked with were older and married with kids; she felt so out of placing working there. There was no one there she could relate with. She didn't speak to anyone casually; she went to work, did her job and left when her shift was over. After working there for a few months she started talking to the guy who ran the office supply department. He was this real cool white guy. He literally had Amari cracking up whenever they worked the same shift.

He wasn't all snobby acting like everyone else that worked there. He was just that type of person that didn't give a shit about anything or anybody. He hated working there just about as much as Amari did. They would sit at work and straight talk about all of the other people that worked there. How they all felt they were better than the next person. There was this one chick that worked up there that just thought that everything revolved around her. She always seemed to be kissing the boss's ass! It was as if she was his little spy, she would tell him everything that went on when he was not at work.

♫♫♫

Damn, it was eight o'clock already? Amari had to hurry up and get to work before she was late. If she was late Jerry would have her ass! She quickly threw on her red work shirt, grabbed her name tag off the kitchen table and headed off to work. Today was no different from any other day, she hated her job, she dreaded going to it. But she needed the cash so she had to do what needed to be done.

When she reached work Jay was standing at the register ringing. The sight of Jay ringing always made her chuckle. Here you have a sales associate that was not used to ringing getting thrown in the trenches. It always happened to him. He always somehow managed to get stuck ringing. She rushed to the back, punched in and hurried back up front to relieve Jay of having to ring.

"Hey Jay, what's up?" she said while making her register available for customers.

"Yo, everything is up, we'll talk later though," he said while looking around making sure no one could hear him.

Alright he definitely had her interest piqued. She was curious to know what juicy news he had to share with her.

She was standing at register two ringing in customers when Samantha called her over to the service desk. After she cleared out her line she walked over to the service desk.

"Sam, what's up?" she asked.

"I'm gonna have you working the service desk today, your lunch is at 11:30 a.m.," she barked as though she were the boss.

That's the shit about her that always made Amari so mad! She felt like she was the boss at times, always barking out orders as if she had to do what she said. "What if she didn't want lunch at 11:30 a.m. the least she could do was ask Amari what time she wanted to take lunch," she thought angrily to herself.

She stood at the service desk for four hours by herself, ringing in every customer that walked into the store. At one point she must have had at least ten people in line, she called for back up about five times, you think Sam ever came out to help her. No, every day she did that shit! As soon as she got in she went running off to her office, talking about she had all this work to do.

"Fuck your office work!" Amari thought angrily to herself as she walked towards the back of the store to punch out for lunch.

Jay was standing at the managers door laughing.

"What the hell is so funny?" she asked with an attitude.

"Damn what's up with you, Sam getting on your nerves or something?" he asked knowing quite well that she was about two minutes from telling the manager she was done working for his bullshit store.

Amari didn't even answer him she just grabbed her purse and headed out the door. Jay followed her. As soon as the store door closed behind them Jay could no longer contain his excitement.

"Yo, guess what happened?" he taunted following her to Boston Market.

"Jay, I don't feel like playing guessing games with you," she snapped.

"Okay, cool I see you are all mad at the world so I will just tell you. Sam fucked Jerry!" he exclaimed.

Amari stopped walking and turned to look at Jay to see if he was just pulling her chain. He had that I'm serious devious grin plastered on his face.

"Are you for real?" she asked shocked.

He shook his head yeah. She couldn't believe it.

"I knew it," she screamed.

"Didn't I always say those two were a little too close to just be co-workers? The way she's always fucking all under him and writing those twenty page letters," Amari smiled.

"That's wild!" she commented.

"It doesn't end there," he said as if the next bit of info would make Amari feel even happier.

"Alright, then what else happened?" she asked intrigued.

"How about his girlfriend found out and she is supposed to be out looking for Sam. I overheard Jerry on the phone telling her if she comes up here with any shit he'd call the police on her," he laughed.

"Okay, that definitely tops the cake! Are you telling me there is some big ass woman out there looking for Sam's tiny ass? Oh I would fucking pay to see that fight go down," Amari laughed while ordering her food.

After they got their food, Jay and Amari walked back to the store and sat in the break room eating and laughing.

After Amari's lunch was over she was definitely in a better mood. No wonder she was been hiding in her office all day and Jerry in his. BK came in around one wanting to know why Sam was in such a bad mood. Amari wanted to share the news with him but he was management and management wasn't privy to such gossip.

When Amari got off work, Xena and Amari went shopping. She spent the whole shopping trip informing her of all the gossip going on at work. They had a good laugh. When they got home their answering machine was overflowing messages the majority of them from Toni.

"Damn, I wonder why Toni was calling there like a mad woman." she thought out loud to herself.

"I don't know but call her back and make sure that she's alright," offered Xena while curling up on the couch with the remote.

Amari grabbed a drink out of the fridge and made a call to Daryl to see how he was doing.

"Hey girl I haven't heard from you all day, where you been?" he questioned.

"I had to work today," she said softly.

"Word, how was it? Did you quit today or are you saving it for another day?" he asked sarcastically.

"Oh, so you got jokes?" she questioned.

Amari then filled him in on what was going on at work. He didn't seem to find the humor in it as Xena and Amari did. He promised to come by when he got off work. She sat for a moment, why was she procrastinating in calling Toni back she didn't know. But something just didn't feel right about all of the calls. She decided to just get it over with and to see what drama was going on this time.

Toni's phone rang seven times before the answering machine kicked in. Amari left her a quick message. An hour later Xena and Amari were on the couch watching Charmed when the phone rang. Amari grabbed it and checked the caller id; it read Toni's number so she answered it.

"Hey girl," Amari said.

The phone was silent.

"Hello," she said again.

The phone was still silent. She muted the television trying to see if she could hear anything. There was nothing but breathing. She could definitely hear someone straining to breath.

"Hello," she yelled into the phone.

The phone went dead. Amari didn't really know what to do. The uneasy feeling she was feeling earlier just found its way back up her stomach.

"Xena, come on we need to go check on Toni," Amari said grabbing her purse and keys.

"Why what happened?" Xena asked slipping on her flip flops as she pulled the door shut behind her.

"I'm not sure but she just called and didn't say anything. I could hear breathing but no one answered me when I said hello," Amari informed her.

In the car Amari became frantic. She threw her cell phone at Xena and told her to call Ke-Ke and Daryl and have them meet them at Toni's house. Amari's gut feeling was telling her something bad had gone down.

After getting a speeding ticket they finally made it to Toni's house. Her car was parked in its usual spot in front of her house, but Tommy's hunter green Honda Accord was nowhere in sight. Amari saw that as a good sign at least he was no longer at the house. Standing on the steps Amari rang the bell hoping Toni would answer the door. She didn't. She rang and rang the bell and no one ever came to open the door. Xena and Amari stood facing each other both pondering what they should do next. Xena leaned on the door and the door creaked open.

They both looked at each other scared of what they might find inside. Xena grabbed Amari's hand as they began to walk into the house.

"Toni, are you in here?" Amari yelled.

They checked the living room first and found nothing. They searched the whole house and it was empty. They both sat down on the couch trying to think, trying to figure the whole situation out. The banging at the front door made them both jump off the couch. Amari walked towards the front of the apartment to see who was there. Thankfully, it was Daryl. Amari opened the door and hugged him tightly. He held her.

"Mari, what's up, what happened?" he asked puzzled.

Amari shook her head.

"I don't know," she said quietly.

Slowly she told him what she was thinking. Amari explained to him about the messages from earlier and then the last phone call. He looked just as puzzled as she felt.

"Did you try calling her cell phone?" he asked.

"No, but her cell phone is sitting on her dresser," commented Xena.

Amari walked towards the patio and opened the blinds and screamed instantly. Daryl rushed over and questioned her on what happened. She couldn't even speak all she could do was point. On the patio lay Tommy covered in blood. His whole body was bloody; he lay there limp with the phone in his hand. Amari couldn't help but cry. She cried hysterically.

Ke-Ke must have walked in while she was crying because all of a sudden she was standing next to her crying just as hard as she was. Xena came over to see how Tommy's body lay on the concrete nearly lifeless.

The time the EMT workers spent there and the endless questions the detectives asked seemed to never happen. The only thing she could remember was that somehow Ke-Ke and Amari ended up sitting outside Tommy's father's house prepared, ready and willing to kill him and whoever else got in their way. Ke-Ke was convinced that Tommy's family knew what happened.

Ke-Ke took her boyfriend's gun and they were now sitting in her car in front of the house waiting for him to show up. No words were spoken. When they left Toni's house they both knew what needed to be done.

Amari's phone rang endlessly and she knew it was no one but Daryl calling to find out where she was. Amari was sure by now Xena had cracked and told him what the two girls were up to.

They sat in the car silent. No music, no talking, no nothing but concentration and anger. Her phone continued to ring. Damn what was taking Tommy's peeps so long to get here? Amari could tell Ke-Ke was fed up with Amari's cell phone constantly ringing.

Ke-Ke yanked it out of Amari's bag and answered it.

"What?" she yelled.

"Oh hi, I'm sorry, hold on one minute," she said handing Amari the phone.

"Hello," Amari said.

"Amari, hi, I'm glad I caught you," began Momma Val.

"Yeah, is everything okay?" she asked, hoping she wasn't calling to tell her something else happened with Corey.

"Well Corey came out of the coma earlier, and he has been pleading everyone to call you. He's drifting in and out and every time he comes around he asks about you. I was wondering if you could come down here?" she finally blurted out.

"Come down there and do what?" Amari asked confused.

"I need you to come down here and talk to my son, I need you to convince him to fight, to stay with us," she pleaded.

"How am I supposed to do that?" Amari asked confused.

"The doctor seems to think if he saw you and talked with you, heard your voice, it would be enough to keep him conscious."

"Can it wait? I am in the middle of something important right now," she responded.

"Amari, my son's life depends on this; I need you at this hospital right now! As much as my family has done for you this is the least you could do," she demanded.

Amari sat for the moment thinking.

"Amari, are you still there?" she asked.

"Yeah, I'll see what I can do okay?" Amari said hanging up quickly not giving her anymore chances to try to guilt her into coming down to the hospital.

"What happened?" asked Ke-Ke.

Amari told her what Momma Val told me.

Ke-Ke looked at Amari.

"So what are you going to do?" she asked.

"I don't know, you think I should go?" she asked her hoping she would be able to give her some serious advice.

"Mari, it seems this boy's life lies in your hands, say you don't go, if he was to slip back into the coma and never recover would you be able to live with yourself?" she asked honestly.

Amari thought about it and she knew what she was saying was the truth. She knew she needed to go and do what she could to help him out medically but at this point so much shit was going on and she could feel herself starting to lose control. In her mind she knew she couldn't deal with this shit anymore.

♪♪♪

Nikki lay in the hospital bed alone. No one sat by her bedside, no one sent her flowers, no one called to check up on her from time to time. She was alone in this world.

Her mother had long since taken custody of her daughter and Al was long gone as well. How could she be so stupid and blind? She wanted to believe he loved her, needed to believe he loved her because no one else did. She had spent so much time and energy looking for love.

At first he was good to her. Then slowly he started staying out late which eventually turnd into not coming home. She invaded his privacy and started going through his cell phone calling back unfamiliar numbers trying to see if a male or female would answer.

When a female would answer she would grill her trying to find out if Al was cheating. When she finally found a female's voice that didn't seem to care about her feelings and told her straight up that she was Al's girl she just about lost her mind. Instead of leaving him though she stuck with him hoping he'd see what he had and stop taking her for granted. Day in and day out she listened to his web of lies and wondered when the day would come when he would be able to be honest and upfront with her.

She tried to leave him but something kept pulling her to him, something unfamiliar kept her attached to Al and all of his lies and deceit. She wondered what it would take for her to be able to finally say she could not deal with his shit anymore and mean it.

It was the night before their anniversary and he once again decided he was going to stay the night out. She crept over to his mother's house and saw his beat up Camry sitting out front. She peeped in the basement window where he slept and saw him laying in bed. The lights were out but the television was on. She felt relieved that he was in fact at home in bed alone. She sat on the grass and just watched him for awhile, watched him sleep peacefully and chastised herself for thinking the worst of him.

A slight movement caught her eye. For a moment there it looked like maybe he wasn't in bed alone. Nonsense she thought to herself. Al reached across the bed and turned the lamp on. Nikki almost fell through the window. He had a chick laid up in the bed with him. What the fuck is this shit? The chick got out of bed wearing only a tee shirt and opened the door. She watched Al as he lay in the bed flipping channels and rolling a blunt while he awaited the return of his friend.

Moments later she reentered the bedroom and shut the door. She stood in front of the bed and pulled her tee shirt over her head. She stood in front of the bed in all her nudity posing for Al and he was definitely enjoying it. She then climbed onto the bed slowly and went straight for his penis. She performed oral sex on him and that was when Nikki decided she had seen enough.

She walked up to the front door not caring about the time and started banging loudly on it. Al's brother answered the door and instantly told Nikki that Al was sleeping. After arguing with him for ten minutes she pushed her way into the house. She marched down the stairs to the basement to confront Al. She barged through the door and started yelling.

"Al what the fuck are you doing?" she yelled.

"I was about to get my nut off until you so rudely interrupted me," he said not giving a fuck anymore.

Nikki stood there shocked at his comment.

"Al how could you?" she began to cry.

Al paid her no attention, he was too busy trying to enjoy the female that was trying hard to swallow his penis despite the fact that Nikki was still standing in the room with them.

Nikki became infuriated. She yanked the chick off the bed by her tacky weave. She went flying across the room. Nikki never in her life felt such a rage such a hatred towards a person before. She grabbed the lamp off the night table and threw it at Al's head; luckily for him it only grazed his head.

Nikki didn't remember much of anything else. She remembered the police coming and handcuffing her. They arrested her and she spent two nights in jail. Monday morning when she went to court Al informed the court he wasn't interested in pressing charges. They gave Nikki a court date for three months from the date. She hated herself for how she allowed herself to behave. She hadn't seen Al since that day.

A week after the incident she got really sick. She came down with a severe case of pneumonia. She'd been hospitalized for the past two months.

Now she lied here still alone and tired. Nikki was tired of the world and all of its pain. She has been fighting her destiny for years now, now it was time for her to succumb. She took out a pen and paper and wrote a letter to the one person she needed forgiveness from, Amari.

Amari, I don't know where to begin or what I should say to you. I do know I need to say some things to you. I have apologized before but I feel the need to do it again. I am deeply sorry for all of the pain I have caused you. I want you to know I wish I hadn't done the things I did to you. You were the only true friend I have ever had. I hope that one day you find true happiness, the kind you had with Daryl in high school…you deserve it! My time on this earth is coming to an end; I feel it in my heart. I can't say I am not happy about that because I am. I just can't survive here anymore. I can't deal with pain. Amari, I hope that one day you will be able to forgive me for all of the terrible things I have done to you. I must say goodbye to you my friend, may we meet again someday…

Nikki

She folded the paper in two and wrote Amari's name on the outside. She placed the paper on the nightstand beside her. She took the picture of her daughter off the nightstand and laid it on her chest. She laid her head back on the pillow, closed her eyes and succumbed. She succumbed to the deep sleep that was calling her, that had been calling her for months. She slept and felt peaceful. Peace had finally found her and she could not have been happier.

🎵🎵🎵

Amari sat at Corey's bedside not sure of what she was supposed to say. Everyone was standing around her hanging on her every word to Corey.

"Why don't we give them some privacy?" suggested Lissa.

"Yeah, I think that's a good idea," agreed Ke-Ke.

"Why would they need privacy?" asked Momma Val, "just talk to him already," she said.

"Ma!" exclaimed Lissa.

Even though she didn't want to she agreed to let Amari have some quiet time with Corey.

When they left the room she just sat there looking at Corey. How he managed to always pull her back into his life was beyond her. Did they really have a special bond?

"Okay Corey you wanted me here, so I'm here, what do you want?" she asked talking out loud.

He lay there motionless. She sat quietly with her hands in her lap.

"I have my own life now so why did you want me here? Don't try to pull me back in, I want no part of it, so if that's your plan you can just give it up," she warned.

Amari rambled on and on about things that held no importance. She grabbed his hand and held it for a minute.

"Corey," she whispered wishing he would just wake up.

She sat with her head bowed while she held his hand. Suddenly she felt a squeeze, she looked up and Corey was looking at her smiling.

"Oh my God, Corey?" Amari questioned in disbelief.

"Hey," he whispered.

She smiled at him. At that moment she felt an abundance of joy, it felt really good to see Corey open his eyes.

They both sat there looking and smiling at each other. He motioned for her to come closer. She got up out of the chair and leaned over him. At first he just smelled her. Amari looked at him like he had definitely lost his mind.

"I miss you," he whispered.

Amari leaned back and looked at him.

"Corey," she began.

He put his finger to her mouth to stop her from speaking.

"I love you," he uttered.

"You're my air," he said.

Amari's hand began to get clammy and her throat felt like someone had stuffed a towel in it. She couldn't breathe and was beginning to feel nauseous. She stumbled around looking for the chair so she could sit down. After she was able to catch her breath, she looked at Corey who gave her those eyes that just said, "I need you, I want no one but you, I love you."

"Corey I have moved on," she said slowly.

His eyes showed pain and heartache.

"I haven't," he admitted.

"But what about Lily?" she asked confused.

"She's a distraction, she's a lily, you, you're a rose! I need you," he cried.

Her heart was caving in; she was moments away from telling him she loved him too, that he was her air. But she couldn't. He hurt her. And Daryl had been so good to her and she loved him. The room seemed to be closing in on her. She felt like she was suffocating.

"Look Corey, I'm going to get your mom she has been so worried about you, okay?" Amari asked while walking towards the door.

"Just promise me you will come back and see me, please?" he begged.

"Fine," she said while practically running out the room.

"Amari, what happened?" asked Momma Val when she came out of the room.

"He's awake," she said while walking past everyone.

Ke-Ke followed her. She didn't stop until she was safely behind the wheel of her car. She rested her head on the head rest and allowed the tears to flow freely.

"Mari, you okay?" asked Ke-Ke when she finally made it to the car.

She shook her head no. She hugged her. Amari told Ke-Ke what Corey said and she looked at her in shock.

"You love him, why can't you accept that?" she asked.

"What about Daryl?" she said.

"Maybe Daryl was your distraction, did you ever think about that? Or maybe you are holding onto the feelings that you used to have for him," she said.

At that moment Amari didn't know what was what anymore. The only thing she was certain about was that life was never smooth for her. How can one person go through so much? She went home that night and lay in bed alone trying to think of everything that was going on.

Tommy was dead and Toni was missing.

Daryl was at home thinking everything was right between them. Corey was lying in the hospital hoping they could get back together. Lily was somewhere thinking everything was right between her and Corey. Amari was utterly confused. Who should she choose? What if she chose the wrong man and ended up regretting her decision for the rest of her life? She finally managed to doze off somewhere around four in the morning, only to have to wake up at seven to get ready for work.

♫♫♫

Amari's alarm clock was buzzing and she dreaded to get up that morning. Her body was so tired and weary from all of the drama. She managed to force herself up and luckily made it work on time.

"Hey Amari, what's going on?" asked Sam when she walked through the door.

She gave her a simple head nod. The head nod said it all.

"Don't fuck with me today; I am not in the mood."

Amari walked to the back, punched in and walked right back to the front. She was close to calling in today but felt that working would be a helpful distraction. About four hours into her shift, a tall husky woman walked in wanting to know if Sam was working today. Amari thought nothing of it and told her yeah, she would page her for her.

When Sam walked out from the office she never saw the blow coming to her head. Amari stood shocked for a moment then remembered the drama from the other day and realized it was Jerry's girlfriend.

She paged Jay and a manager to the front immediately. She didn't even try to help her out. Amari was in such a shitty mood, she felt that Sam had to learn to fight her own battles. His girlfriend had Sam on the floor and was just stomping her pale frail body into the ground. When Jay and Mike reached the front, Jay was shocked to find Sam getting her ass whipped so violently.

He went to help her immediately. Jay and Mike pulled Jerry's girlfriend off Sam and instantly Amari felt bad. Sam lay there bloody and hurting. She walked over to Sam and tried to help her up off the ground. She was floating in and out of consciousness. Amari immediately dialed 911.

♫♫♫

Working at the office supply store was definitely full of adventures. Jay wasn't your typical worker at the store. He was one of the few cool down to earth people that she worked with. He didn't seem to care much about anyone's feelings he simply told it how it was and if his words happened to hurt your feelings than that was just a price he was willing to pay.

Jay was different from the rest though. Even though he liked to put on a tough act, she knew there were deep dark secrets that were making his life miserable.

When she at her register Jay liked to tease her and say he was going to hang himself right at the front of the store during her shift so she could witness it. To hear him say such things put a bit of fright into her. She had dealt with enough death to know that it was nothing to be taken lightly.

♫♫♫

When she got to work she prayed that Jay was in a much better mood because she really did not like to hear him talk about death that way. She had been at work maybe three full hours and already Jay was talking about killing himself.

"Amari, today is the day, I hope you're ready," he said while walking past her to help a customer.

Amari tried to act like she thought as lighthearted as him, she brushed off his comment as if it were a mere joke.

The day was dragging along. There were hardly any customers left in the store. The manager came up to the front of the store looking desperately for Jay.

"Amari, have you seen him?" he asked.

She shook her head no, the last time she saw Jay was when he walked past her and claimed that today would be his last. The manager began running around frantically looking for him. After about 30 minutes Jay walked back into the store with half closed blood shot eyes. Amari looked at him suspiciously and he winked at her telling her not to say anything. The manager returned to the front of the store and asked again if she had seen him. She apologized profusely and informed him she forgot he told her that he was going to lunch; the manager looked at her with suspicious eyes and then stalked off towards the back of the store.

♫♫♫

Mondays were always the hardest days for Amari to get up and go to work. Today was no different. She forced herself to get up out of the bed and go to work. Something felt odd about the day, she just had no energy to get up and do what she needed to do. She was already running behind schedule and felt like calling in sick, but she knew that on Friday when her paycheck was deducted nine hours she would be highly upset.

Amari forced herself out of her apartment and tried to have a decent attitude about it. When she reached work the parking lot was filled with police cars, ambulances, and two fire trucks. A rush of panic filled her body.

She rushed into the building to see what happened, all the while praying that no one was seriously injured. When she walked in Sam was at the front of the store crying hysterically.

"What happened?" she asked.

Sam couldn't speak; she could barely breathe on her own thinking about what she saw. She walked over to the service desk where BK stood quietly answering the frivolous questions of the detectives. She stood next to him trying to overhear anything; any type of valuable information that would tell her what was going on.

She searched around frantically looking for Jay, he'd give her answers, she was sure of it. She walked to the back of the store towards the break room and ran right into Mike, one of the assistant managers.

"Oh Mike, I'm sorry," Amari said while bending over to pick up the papers she made him drop.

She looked him in the eyes and saw that he too had been crying.

"Mike, what's going on here? What happened?" she asked hoping he'd give her some answers.

"Jay hung himself in the men's bathroom," he said softly.

Amari stood there still, in shock. She didn't think she heard him correctly.

"Did you just say what I think you said?" she questioned, hoping he'd tell her she heard him wrong.

"Jay's dead," he offered the final blow, not wanting her to mistake his words.

Amari instantly felt nauseous and stepped back to lean on the wall to steady herself. She didn't want to believe Jay had finally made good on his promise to her.

"Amari, why don't you go ahead and go back home, we're not going to open today," he said while patting her on her back.

Amari grabbed her purse off the ground and headed back out the door. Somehow her body knew when she stepped foot in her house because as soon as she did the entire vile rose up in her throat and she threw up everywhere.

"Damn, what's all the commotion?" asked Xena coming out of her room in her pajamas.

Xena saw Amari curled up on the floor and came to her side immediately.

"Mari, what happened? Are you okay?" she asked nervously not sure exactly what was going on.

"It's Jay, he committed suicide today," she said hurling again.

Xena looked around confused.

"Who the fuck is Jay?" she asked.

I was sickened by Xena's lack of respect for the dead. Amari slowly steadied herself to stand up.

"Jay is, excuse me, was this guy from work I was cool with. I told you about him a million times," she said annoyed walking to her room to grab a towel so she could take a quick shower.

Xena pondered her words for a moment trying to remember in her brain who she was talking about.

"Oh the cool ass white boy?" she asked suddenly remembering him.

Amari shook her head yes and kept walking, shutting the bathroom door behind her.

CHAPTER EIGHTEEN

Amari's life was always so rough and filled with so much turmoil! She couldn't understand why nothing could ever go smoothly for her? Somehow, someway drama always managed to find itself into her life. Damn, when will it ever end? She was at the point now where she didn't know what to do. She didn't know how to handle the things that had been put on her plate. She could feel herself breaking, crashing into the madness.

Nikki was dead! She left a note for Amari explaining why she did the things she did and asked for her forgiveness. Her death hit Amari pretty hard.

Tommy was dead! Toni was missing. The cops had been searching for Toni but always managed to come up empty handed.

Ke-Ke was passionate about finding Toni before the Atlanta Police Department could. They had all come to the conclusion that Toni had most likely snapped in a fit of rage. None of the girls could blame her considering how much abuse she had endured from Tommy in the past.

Corey had been awake and conveniently had a memory loss that had got a lot of things fucked up. He suddenly didn't know, remember, or seem to want to remember Lily. In his mind the last relationship he was in was with Amari. His family wanted her to pretend they were still together, they felt doing this would speed up his recovery process.

And then there was Daryl. Amari loved Daryl. She truly loved him. They had become closer and had been spending a lot of time together. She didn't want to hurt him. He was good to her and they were genuinely happy.

Amari had no idea what she was supposed to do? How would she ever get through this? She was sitting on her bed looking at her reflection in the mirror. What if she just ended it all now? What if she removed herself from all of this pain and misery and went to visit with Charisse and her mom? She could join them and receive eternal happiness.

She lied down on the bed and fell asleep contemplating how she would end her life.

***

"Xena, do you think we should tell Daryl what's going on? Mari needs help. I can feel it, she is gonna crack," stated Ke-Ke.

"Ke-Ke, I'm not sure. Amari will be heated if we go running off at the mouth," replied Xena.

"Xena, I know but Amari is in trouble, she has got too much to handle and she can't handle it all. She is gonna end up having a nervous breakdown if we don't do something," reasoned Ke-Ke.

Ke-Ke didn't wait for Xena's reply. She picked up her cell phone and dialed Daryl's number.

"Hey Daryl, its Ke-Ke," she said quickly while watching Xena.

"What's going on girl?" he asked wondering why she was calling.

"We need to talk about Mari, can you come over here?" she asked.

"Yeah of course, I'm on my way," he said hanging up.

It took Daryl about five minutes to get to Ke-Ke's house. He walked into the house and sat on the couch without saying a word.

Ke-Ke and Xena looked at each other both not knowing what to say.

"Look you said you needed to talk. I can't help you help her if I don't know what is going on. I know whatever it is that she doesn't want me to know about it and she'll most likely have a huge fit when she finds out that her two best friends have opened up and shared her business, but this is the only way," he reasoned.

Xena having been Amari's friend the longest knew exactly the consequences she would be facing if she opened up and told Daryl everything that was going on. She couldn't see herself betraying her friend like that.

Ke-Ke cleared her throat and without hesitation told Daryl everything he needed to know.

Daryl sat dumbfounded not believing what he was hearing. How could Amari be going through all of this and he hadn't noticed anything. He became angry within himself for not being there for her when she needed him.

He jumped up and dashed out the door. Feeling that he was angry and may get violent Ke-Ke and Xena followed him. Neither of them was surprised when they ended up at Mari's apartment.

They watched as Daryl ran up the stairs and used his key to enter. They were not far behind him. As they entered the house in the distant they could hear Daryl calling Amari's name repeatedly.

They ran to her bedroom and were shocked to find Amari laid out on the bed with an empty bottle of Vicodin beside her.

Xena began to cry first. She couldn't help herself, thoughts of Charisse committing suicide began to dance within her head.

Ke-Ke stood numb not believing what she was seeing. She refused to believe her best friend was dead. How could she lose two best friends within a matter of weeks?

Daryl stood closest to Amari. He reached his hand out wanting to touch her, to feel her, but not wanting to believe her lifeless body was no longer alive. The three stood speechless and motionless for more than five minutes, it took a stranger to stumble onto the scene before 911 was dialed.

Maurice was stopping by because he missed Amari immensely. He couldn't stand to be away from her, it was killing him inside. He had a weird feeling she needed him so he decided to stop by. When he reached her apartment and found her front door wide open an alarm went off in his head. Grabbing the metal bat she kept in the front closet, he began to inspect the house. Upon entering her room, he saw three shadows and thought she had been raped. He entered the room with a vengeance and was shocked beyond words to see Daryl,

Xena and Ke-Ke standing around her lifeless body lying on the bed.

"What the hell is going on in here?" he demanded.

His demands went unanswered.

He picked up the Winnie the Pooh telephone that sat on her nightstand and immediately called 911, within moments the sirens could be heard from down the street.

♫♫♫

"Who would dare take me out of my new life? Why did they have to save me? Could they not see I did not wish to be saved?" these were the thoughts racing through Amari's head.

Here they were sitting in her room watching her, feeling sorry for her. She didn't want pity. She wanted peace! For years everyone had been coming to Amari to solve their problems and to put her into their personal drama! She was sick of it! She wanted to have peace and she almost had it until those same people came and 'saved' her!

Amari was trying to play like she was sleeping, but it wasn't really working. Daryl was there talking to her, begging her to not stop fighting. She felt bad that she wanted to leave him but what other choice did she really have?

A knock at the door interrupted her thoughts and Daryl's pleading.

Corey was wheeled in followed by his mother. Momma Val was shocked to see Daryl sitting next to her bed holding her hand.

"Excuse me young man, what are you doing here?" she questioned.

"I just wanted to make sure she was okay," he replied barely making eye contact.

Amari slowly opened her eyes and squeezed Daryl's hand as he stood up and prepared to leave. Shocked, he looked at her and smiled a huge smile. She wanted to let him know she was still his girlfriend; she was still his life. The connection they had was so unbreakable, he understood her instantly and felt at ease as he was leaving.

Momma Val wheeled Corey closer to the bed. He grabbed Amari's hand and started to caress it.

"Hi," she whispered.

Corey smiled.

"Oh Mari, I was really worried about you. What made you try to take your life, I thought we were happy," he stated, still not believing she was lying in the hospital bed behind a suicide wrap.

How could she ever explain to him she was just under too much pressure? Amari had to act like his girlfriend while at the same time not miss a beat with her real boyfriend. Tommy and Nikki were dead and that shit was really eating her up on the inside. She had finally found her breaking point; she just couldn't take all the drama.

Amari shrugged her shoulders allowing him to believe it was a mental lapse on her part.

"And who is the Maurice fella that called 911?" he questioned.

"Corey can you please not give me a hard time, I have a really big headache right now," she stated turning her back to him.

Momma Val jumped in instantly.

"Okay Corey, let's not boggle her down with a bunch of questions, she needs to get her rest and so do you," she said beginning to wheel him out.

"Fine, but just let me say goodbye before we go," he said.

"Fine," she replied.

"Mari," he called out.

She half turned her body back around.

"I love you," he said smiling.

"Ditto," she said turning her back towards him while trying hard to suppress the tears that had already begun to fall.

♫♫♫

Daryl left the hospital immediately. It broke his heart to get up and declare his friendship with Amari. He loved her and wanted to be with her. But how could he when Corey conveniently had amnesia and remembered only his life with Amari? Where did that leave him? How could they continue on with their life, if she now had to pretend she was apart of Corey's world?

♫♫♫

The next morning Amari was finally left alone. Corey's doctor said he'd spent more than enough time out of his room, now it was time for him to get himself strong.

There was a knock at the door that Amari didn't feel like answering.

"Amari, are you up?" whispered Xena.

She turned over and there stood Xena holding a pretty bouquet of flowers but looking nervous as ever. Amari smiled and instantly she felt at ease.

"Xena, what's going on?" she asked motioning for her to come in.

She ran towards her and gave her a big hug.

"Amari, I'm so happy to see you. I was so worried about you."

"Yeah, I'm sorry about that. I'm not sure what really came over me, other than the fact that for once in my life I could admit I have too much shit to deal with."

She looked around the room admiring the gazillion bouquets.

"Daryl," they both smiled in unison.

"Where is he anyway, I thought for sure he'd be here," she said.

Amari explained quickly what happened the day before.

"Damn Mari, he must be so upset!"

"Yeah he must be. I tried to call him but he hasn't returned any of my calls."

"And Corey?" she asked.

"Corey is being extremely overbearing. Thankfully his doctor forced him back to his room or he'd be in the hospital longer. It's Momma Val that is really surprising me though."

"Why, what is she doing?" she asked perplexed.

"She is so adamant about me pretending we are still together. I don't get it. She is usually so honest and now she wants to keep this charade going," Amari said frustrated with the whole situation.

The tears began to fall and she couldn't stop them. Xena hugged her and Amari began to feel safe again.

♪♪♪

They kept Amari in the hospital for three days. She spent the first night under suicide watch without even knowing it. Daryl still hadn't answered any of her calls or returned them. It was like he was just ignoring her and she really couldn't blame him. He was hurt, but she was hurting as well. Amari spent so much time worrying about everyone else's feelings, when the hell was someone gonna worry about hers?

Xena promised to pick Amari up and of course she was late as usual. It was her lateness that had Amari thinking so heavily about Daryl and the things they were going through right now. Her mind told her she was losing him, but her heart refused to believe it.

She threw on her charcoal brown velour jogging suit with a white tank top. She slipped her feet into a pair of white flip flops, grabbed her brown Coach bag out the drawer and walked towards the elevator. When she got to Corey's floor, she hesitated a minute before making the long walk down the corridor to his private room.

When she reached his door she heard screaming and immediately rushed in.

"Corey, how can you not remember me? I love you!" shouted Lily.

When Lily saw Amari standing at the door she lunged towards her. They started rolling around on the floor each trying to get decent punches in. Corey hopped out of bed and pulled Amari off Lily.

"Lily, what the hell is wrong with you?" he demanded.

"What's wrong with me? What the hell is wrong with you? We were a couple, not you and her! I love you and now you are just throwing me to the side like yesterday's news," cried Lily.

"Look Lily, you need to get out of here. I told you I don't know you."

"You may not remember me but I'm sure Amari does, don't you?" she said looking at Amari.

At that moment Lissa and Momma Val walked in laughing with each other. They were not expecting to see us all standing in the middle of the room. Momma Val gasped at the sight of Lily. Lissa spoke first.

"What are you doing here? I told you not to come back!" she threatened.

"I know what you said, but I love him and she doesn't deserve him," she screamed pointing at Amari.

All of this was too much for Amari to handle. She grabbed her Coach bag and ran out the door. She ran down the stairs all the way to the entrance. Thankfully, Xena was finally waiting for her.

When she sat down in the car, the tears came rolling down fast. Amari explained what happened and Xena couldn't believe it, just like Amari couldn't.

"Mari, what are you gonna do? Do you want to get back with Corey? I thought you were happy with Daryl," she reasoned.

"I am happy. Daryl was my first love and though he truly broke my heart once upon a time, he really is doing his all to make sure I am happy now. I don't know what it is but there is an unbreakable bond between the two of us. He has such an unexplainable hold on me. But in that same breath how can I count Corey out. I was so happy with him. I honestly feel he completes me. They both complete me as weird as that is. They each contribute a special part to my being. How do I choose between the two? Can I honestly choose?" she asked beginning to cry.

Xena reached her arm over trying to console her. Deep inside she was happy she wasn't faced with this same predicament.

When Amari went home Daryl was there awaiting her return. He could sense something was wrong with her.

"Amari are you okay?" he asked.

Amari looked at him not wanting to break his heart or hurt his feelings in anyway.

"Amari, I can't help you if you don't talk to me," he said hugging her.

The tears came down full force at that moment.

"Daryl I love you, I really do love you," she sobbed.

She felt his body tense beneath her.

"You love me but you need to be with Corey right?" he questioned.

Amari was speechless.

She wasn't sure how to answer him.

He let go of her immediately and began backing out of the bedroom.

"Daryl wait please don't go," she begged.

"Nah Mari, it's okay. I'm gonna make this easy for both of us," he said walking out the front door and out of her life once again.

And just like that he was gone. He didn't stick around to see what she had to say regarding the situation; he just up and left. He left her alone to ponder what the hell she was going to do to get herself out of the predicament she suddenly found herself in.

CHAPTER NINETEEN

After losing Daryl Amari practically threw herself full force into her school work. She continued to visit Corey regularly but did not venture into a relationship with him just yet. As the holidays drew near she found herself spending more time with Corey.

She didn't necessarily like the way things were going between them, but she didn't like to be alone either.

🎵🎵🎵

Corey was finally being released from the hospital. Momma Val planned a surprise welcome home party and Amari was the lucky one that got to pick him up from the hospital and bring him home.

When she got to the hospital, Corey's entire face lit up when he saw her.

"Hey Corey, you ready to go?" she asked sitting down on the bed next to him.

"Yeah, just give me a minute," he said.

The look on his face looked pained.

"Corey are you okay?" she asked again.

"Yeah, I just have a really bad headache all of a sudden," he said lying down and closing his eyes.

"Did you tell the nurse you needed some meds?" she asked getting worried.

"No, it just came on suddenly, can you ask them for me?" he whispered.

"Of course," Amari said heading out the room and towards the nurse's station.

She walked to the nurse's station and politely asked them to please give Corey some meds. She explained his sudden pain to the nurse.

♫♫♫

"Hey D, what's up?" asked Cease walking into the house.

Daryl simply gave him a head nod and continued lifting weights.

"Damn D, what's up with you? You mad about something dawg?"

"Nah just trying to get a little work-out done," he answered.

"Yeah whatever dawg, have you called Mari yet?" he asked.

"Amari? What the hell am I calling her for?"

"To apologize! To tell her how sorry you are for walking out on her and not staying around to hear what the fuck she wanted to tell you."

"I'm not sorry for walking out on her. What I am sorry about is allowing myself to get caught up with her again. She wants to be with Corey, which is very clear."

"Corey? Nigga please, you fooling yourself if you really believe that."

"Fooling myself? What else do you think she was going to tell me?"

"Dawg, do you fucking hear yourself? You are truly un-fucking-believable! She was probably going to tell your simple minded ass that she was silly for going along with his moms plan but it's you that she loves. I've seen her ass around campus and she don't look like someone that is happily in love, she looks like someone who is depressed thanks to love. I can see it in her eyes, dawg she is definitely missing you."

"Come on now Cease, why you tripping? Stop trying to sell me these hoop dreams, I know what's really going on," Daryl yelled.

"Daryl, you my man! Have been my dawg from day one, I'm not tripping! I'm not selling you any hoop dreams I am telling you what I see. If anyone is tripping it's you man, acting like you don't miss shortie!"

"Cease man drop it already. It's a dead issue!" Daryl said slamming the weights down and practically running out the room.

🎵🎵🎵

Amari had been sitting in the hospital for three hours now waiting for someone, anyone to let her know what the hell was going on with Corey.

When she got back to his room from the nurses station he was passed out in the bed. Frantically, she began screaming for the nurses and doctors to come and help him. Within moments his room was filled with the medical staff and they were hurriedly pushing her out of the room.

Amari was terrified as she sat in the waiting room. She got up and walked outside to use her cell phone. Her first call was to Momma Val, she had to let her know what was going on. Momma Val could barely make out a word Amari was saying through all of her tears and sounds of denial.

Her second call was to Xena but her voice mail picked up directly, so she called Ke-Ke to let her know what was going on.

"Hello," she answered barely audible.

"Hey Ke-Ke, you sleep?" she asked not understanding why she sounded so bad.

"Amari," she cried.

"Ke-Ke what's going on? What happened?" she asked.

"Nothing. I am just tired of being alone," she cried.

What the fuck was really going on?

Amari wasn't sure she heard her correctly? Did she just hear Ke-Ke say she was tired of being alone? Ke-Ke was always preaching about the joys of not being tied down to any one person.

"Damn Ke-Ke, are you okay?" she asked feeling at a loss of words.

Usually when her girls would come to her with their issues she would be able to tell them something positive, something they'd get some hope from. She couldn't think of anything to say to her situation.

"I'm fine, just having a real down moment that's all," she cried.

"Damn Ke-Ke, I wish I had something helpful to say to you."

"I know Mari, I'm really not feeling in a partying mood, I think I am gonna have to pass on Corey's party tonight," she said.

Amari had gotten so caught up in her drama she forgot to tell her what she called her for.

"Oh shit, I knew I called you for something. Something is going on with Corey; he passed out right before we were planning to leave the hospital. I'm still here waiting to hear what the hell is going on with him."

"Mari, I'm sorry and here I am going on and on about my bullshit and you've got that to deal with.

"Ke-Ke you had no idea. I'm just worried he may not be able to come home tonight," Amari confessed.

"Is his mom there?"

"No, not yet, I'm sure she is on her way though."

"Mari do you need anything? Do you want me to come down there and sit with you?"

"Nah Ke-Ke, I'm good. But you need to get some rest. I'll stop by later to check on you," she said before hanging up the phone.

Amari turned her phone off and headed back inside. Just as she was exiting the elevator she noticed Corey's doctor standing at the nurse's station writing something down.

"Excuse me Dr. Gordon, how is Corey doing?" she asked.

He looked up from his chart.

"Ah yes, Amari, I was just leaving you a note."

"Is everything okay?" she asked getting nervous.

"Yes and no, we've got him stabilized and out of pain. He will have to stay the night for observation," he said.

"That's it," Amari asked thinking he needed or wanted to say more.

"That's it for now. We will run some more tests on him and observe him for 24 hours and then we will make the decision on when he can leave the hospital."

🎵🎵🎵

Corey ended up staying in the hospital for another seven days before he was finally released. When he finally came home Amari couldn't have been happier. It was hard to see him in the hospital.

She spent a lot of time taking care of him, making sure he had everything and was well taken care of. Most nights she would end up spending the night at the Fowler residence. It felt as though nothing changed with Amari and Corey, she was back to being apart of the family.

Amari tried really hard to push Daryl to the back of her brain. She still hadn't been able to let go of the hurt and pain. She felt completely betrayed when it came to him. They were supposed to be in love, inseparable, and he left her without even giving it a second thought.

Xena blamed Amari for her recent love problems. She felt she was the one that pushed Daryl away. Needless to say, they didn't speak too much these days.

Some days Amari felt like she was losing her best friend. On top of everything she was going through, she couldn't bear to lose her as well. Maybe Amari should call Xena later that night, just to talk.

♪♪♪

Momma Val's doorbell rung as Amari was closing the door to Corey's room. He was lying in his bed playing PS2. She wanted him to take a nap but he refused, he claimed he wasn't tired and was feeling fine. Amari knew he was lying but she allowed him to play his game anyway. She sat down on the bed next to him and just watched him play the latest version of Madden. Before her thoughts could get away from her, there was a soft knock at the door.

"Come in," she yelled.

Ke-Ke walked in and looked like she had spent most of the night crying.

"Hey Ke-Ke, what's up? What are you doing here?" Amari asked motioning for her to sit down.

"Nothing, just really needed to talk to you," she said.

"What's up?" Amari asked sensing her hesitancy.

"My life is so fucked up!" she began to cry.

Amari could tell she was a bit hesitant about speaking her business in front of Corey.

"Corey, I'll be back okay?" she said while getting up and placing a quick peck on his cheek.

She walked Ke-Ke to her old bedroom and motioned for her to sit down on the bed.

"Ke-Ke what's going on?"

"I think I'm pregnant and I'm not sure who the father is," she cried.

Amari sat on the bed next to her and began to rub her back. She felt so bad for Ke-Ke. Amari wanted to comfort her but really didn't know how to go about doing that. Her life was so fucked up at that moment she really wished there was something she could do to make her feel better. They sat in the room for about two hours, she cried most of the time.

🎵🎵🎵

After Ke-Ke left Amari went back to Corey's room to check on him. She was happy to see him fast asleep. She decided to take this opportunity to have some 'me' time. She drove over to Lithonia and decided to have a nice meal at Olive Garden…ALONE! Sure, she could have taken Ke-Ke along with her or waited for Corey to wake up, but she really needed some time by herself. As she asked the hostess for a table for one, she kept looking at Amari strangely. She didn't even care, she was just ready to sit down and enjoy a plate of 'Tour of Italy'.

Amari was sitting at her table enjoying her food and an apple martini when a familiar voice flipped her world upside down.

"Funny seeing you here," he said.

She looked up from her plate and was shocked to see Daryl standing in front of her smiling. Amari's heart began to beat rapidly and she had a family of butterflies swarming in the pit of her stomach. At that moment she knew her heart still belonged to Daryl.

"Daryl, hi, what are you doing here?" she stuttered.

"Hey Boo, anyone sitting here?" he asked referring to the empty chair.

"No," she answered quickly praying he would join her.

Daryl sat down and for the first fifteen minutes they sat there staring at each other not saying a word. She wanted to say something, but wasn't sure what to say to him at that moment. Don't get me wrong, she was glad to see him, but she was still upset with him for hurting her the way he did.

"Amari you look good!" he said finally breaking the silence.

"So good you couldn't be with me!" she retorted, feeling the anger beginning to erupt.

He shook his head.

"Come on ma; don't come at me like that! I was doing what I thought was right. I thought you wanted to be with that cat. I didn't want to make the decision hard for you, so I gracefully bowed out," he tried to explain.

"But I love you," Amari began to cry.

He grabbed her hand, "I love you too."

She couldn't contain her smile.

It felt so good to hear him say that. She had doubted his love for her after all of the pain and heartache he put her through lately.

"Why are you here alone?" he asked.

"Just wanted some time to myself," she answered still holding his hand lightly.

"Do you want me to leave?"

"No."

The waitress came back over and asked if she could get Daryl anything, he declined and started picking at Amari's half eaten plate.

She watched him as he ate and enjoyed the food. For the first time in a long while she felt at ease.

"What are you doing when you leave here?" he asked.

"Nothing," she replied hoping he would invite her back to his house.

"Feel like doing a little shopping?" he asked stuffing his mouth with garlic bread.

"Shopping? Oh you trying to make up for lost time I see!"

"Nah, I just enjoy putting a smile on your face."

"Whateva! Where are we going shopping?"

"We can stay right here and head over to Stonecrest."

"That's cool!"

After he finished her plate of food and she finished her apple martini they headed over to Stonecrest Mall. Their first stop was to purchase her a new Coach bag and matching sunglasses. They spent three hours in the mall buying her outfits and shoes. Just as they were heading out the mall, Daryl stopped her.

"Damn we didn't hit up the jewelry store."

"That's cool, I don't need any," she said flossing her wrists and ears.

"I know you don't need any but I want to buy you something."

Amari didn't even bother arguing with him. They headed back inside the jewelry store. In the display window was a 5 carat diamond princess cut engagement ring that caught Amari's eye instantly. She fell in love with it at first sight. She had to show Daryl.

"When I get engaged this is what I want!" she exclaimed.

Daryl smiled and checked the price tag.

"That shit is more than your damn truck!" he damn near screamed.

She looked at him shocked because the fact he was looking at the price tag let her know he was considering marrying her. Amari's heart smiled at the gesture.

She pulled Daryl into the store to look at the other jewelry. As she was inspecting a two tone pink and blue sapphire bracelet, her Nextel walkie talkie chirped.

"Mari," the voice asked.

She pulled it out of the clip and looked at Daryl as she answered Corey.

"Yeah, what's up?"

"Nothing, I just woke up and was concerned when I saw you were not here."

"I went out to eat and now I'm at the mall," she answered truthfully.

"I should have known you would find your way to the mall. What are you buying?" he asked.

"Whatever catches my eye," she answered winking at Daryl.

"Okay then, will I see you later or are you going home tonight?" he asked.

Amari looked at Daryl. He was mouthing the word 'home' to her. She smiled.

"I'm probably going home tonight but I'll come by after class," she said.

"Okay. I think Greg is coming over tonight, so I doubt if I will be any fun for you anyway."

"Alright then, have fun and make sure you get some rest," she said.

"Will do, I'll talk to you later."

"Bye," she said quickly before hanging up.

She shut her phone and looked at Daryl who was purchasing her bracelet. He walked back over to where she was standing and handed the gift bag to her. She smiled.

"Thank you so much."

In an instant she found herself engrossed in a deep French kiss.

She could hardly pull herself away from him but knew she needed to. She pulled away from him.

"Amari, I'm sorry I shouldn't have done that."

"Daryl, it's not your fault. I wanted it too."

He smiled.

"Daryl can we go back to your place? I'd really like to spend the night with you," Amari said licking her lips.

"Hell yeah!" he yelled.

"Shh," she said grabbing his hand and walking out the mall towards the parking lot.

🎵🎵🎵

Daryl and Amari ended up spending the night together that night. Maybe she should have felt bad about it, but she didn't. Corey was stronger and he'd just have to learn the truth. She loved Corey to death, but she definitely was not in love with him anymore. Her heart sincerely belonged to Daryl.

She was always looking out for everyone else and their feelings. Now it was time to look out for her. She deserved happiness just as much as the next person and right now her happiness was with Daryl.

She was lying in bed at the moment with Daryl by her side and it felt right. She curled up next to him and decided to just allow life to take its course.

🎵🎵🎵

"Ma, has Mari called?" asked Corey sitting down at the table to have some breakfast.

"No, was she supposed to?" Momma Val asked placing a stack of buttery pancakes in front of Corey.

"I thought she was gonna stop by," he said sounding a bit deflated.

"Damn Corey, stop smothering the girl," commented Lissa coming into the kitchen.

"I'm not smothering her. I miss her, that's all!" he said sounding defensive.

"Corey, I know you miss her. But remember she has a life. She's a full time college student. She's got other shit to do besides take care of you," she said with a slight attitude.

"Lissa there's no need to be rude!" interrupted Momma Val sensing something was going on with Lissa.

"Whatever," she said walking back out of the kitchen.

"Lissa," Momma Val called after her.

Lissa stopped at the front door with her hand on the door knob.

"What has gotten into you young lady?" she asked her daughter.

"Nothing, just regretting some decisions I was forced to make."

"Like what?"

"Like allowing you to convince me lying to Corey was the best thing for him. We've ruined Amari's life!" she whispered so only her mother could hear her.

"How do you figure that? She seems happy every time I see her."

"She's miserable without Daryl!"

"Too bad, my concern is not for Daryl. My concern is for my son and his well being. Amari makes him happy."

"Yeah, but does he make her happy?"

"Lissa I can't believe this is coming from you!"

"Ma, Mari is like a sister to me and I don't like to see her moping around the house or the campus. No one should intervene with true love and I think that is what we have done. You may be able to live with that but I can't!" Lissa said before walking out the house.

🎵🎵🎵

"Hello," Amari answered not fully awake.

"Mari, what are you doing?" asked Xena.

At the sound of her voice, she sat up in the bed.

"Nothing, what's up?"

"You tell me, you didn't come home last night and your truck wasn't at Corey's this morning, where are you?" she asked pointedly.

She looked at Daryl lying quietly next to her.

"I'm at Daryl's."

The phone was silent.

"You two got back together?" she beamed.

"Not exactly, I ran into him yesterday and we ended up back here," she said smiling.

"It's about time!"

"Xena wait a minute. This is not public knowledge. Let's keep this between us for now okay?"

"Yeah whatever!"

"So are you staying there all day or will you come home at some point?"

"Nah I'm leaving in a little bit, I have to go and check on Corey."

"Come on Mari, he's a big boy."

"Xena stop! I'll be home later tonight, I'll see you then," Amari said before hanging up.

Amari hung up the phone and glanced at her watch. It was already noon and they were still in bed. She had long since missed her class. Carefully she got out of the bed and headed for the shower. After showering and getting dressed, she decided to leave Daryl a note instead of waking him up.

Daryl, thank you so much for last night. Not just the sex but especially for the love. My heart is yours, know that and don't forget it! Please don't give up on me. I love you!

Amari

🎵🎵🎵

"Amari, where have you been?" asked Momma Val as soon as she walked in.

"Just had some errands to run after class," she lied.

"Oh you had class today, I wasn't aware of that!" she said snidely.

"Yeah," Amari said walking upstairs to see Corey.

She knocked softly on the door before entering. When she walked in he was peacefully sleeping. She grabbed 'Gangsta' by Kwan out of her bag and made herself comfortable on the empty side of the bed.

Before she could get to comfortable, 'We Belong Together' by Mariah Carey began to play on her cell phone. Quickly she snatched it open and whispered, "Hello," as she walked out of Corey's bedroom.

"Hey sunshine, did I disturb you?" asked Daryl.

"No, just with Corey, what's up?" she answered back.

"Okay, I'll make it quick. I want to have you over for dinner tonight. We need to talk," he said.

Amari wasn't sure if she liked the way this sounded but she agreed to go over for dinner. She hung up the phone and started to rack her brain about what he wanted to talk about after thinking about it for half an hour, she realized he probably wanted to tell her how crazy she was for asking him to wait for her.

She got up off the bed and headed downstairs to get something to eat, she was starving. Lissa was in the kitchen eating a sandwich when she walked in.

"Hey girl, I haven't seen much of you lately, what's good?" she asked.

She looked up from her sandwich.

"Hey, how are you?" she asked.

"I'm good," Amari said thinking about the precious night she had with Daryl.

"Did your mom cook any lunch before she left?" Amari asked rummaging through the refrigerator.

"Nah, that's why I'm eating the sandwich," she replied.

"Damn! Do you want to ride with me to Popeye's?" Amari asked.

"Yeah, why not?" she said throwing the other half of her sandwich away.

"Let me grab my purse," Amari said running back up the stairs.

♪♪♪

Lissa and Amari went to Popeye's and ended up having a much needed talk. Lissa apologized for asking her to give up Daryl and their love for what her mother felt was the sake of her brother. She could tell this was weighing heavily on her mind. She told her not to worry about it, that everything would eventually work its way out.

♪♪♪

Amari was walking up the stairs to Daryl's front door. She was so nervous. He wanted to talk and she was petrified that he was gonna tell her he was 'off this', that he no longer could be bothered with her. Before she could ring the bell, he opened the door.

"Damn he looked good in that suit!" Amari thought excitedly to herself.

Instantly her mind was filled with erotic thoughts of her undressing him and pleasing every inch of his body.

"Hey Daryl, what's up?" she said instead.

"Nothing much, why don't you come into the dining room," he said closing the door behind her.

She walked into the dining room and he had the table set impeccably. There were candles and real dishes on the table, she was extremely impressed.

"Amari?" he called.

She turned around. He was standing there holding a dozen red roses.

She smiled.

He walked up to her and took hold of her hands.

"I love you," he said gazing into her eyes.

Amari smiled.

"It makes me so happy to know you want to be with me."

"Daryl, I really do want to be with you, but we have to be careful about this. I don't want to be the one to cause Corey to regress."

"Shh," he said while placing a finger over her lips.

"We will take it slow. We can have a secret romance," he laughed.

She laughed too.

"We can go public whenever you're ready ma."

"Daryl, thank you."

"I don't know about you, but I am horny as hell right now!" he said looking me up and down.

"I'm a bit hungry though," she said teasing him.

"Okay. I got some chocolate covered strawberries and whip cream in the fridge, I'm sure we can find a good use for them," he smiled.

Amari laughed.

She grabbed Daryl's hands, "Can we just have one dance before we head upstairs?"

She just wanted him to hold her, in a non-sexual way for a moment.

"Sure thing, I got the perfect song too," Daryl said as he went and turned on the stereo.

Daryl took Amari in his arms.

At first he was humming along to the song, he wasn't sure what made him want to sing to her, but he felt the need. He wanted her to know how much he loved her and was willing to wait any amount of time for her.

In Daryl's deep and thuggish voice, he began singing along with Mario. Daryl loved the song, Crying Out for Me, by Mario it expressed his feelings for Amari and the situation they were in like no other.

"It's like you caught up in a maze, you keep on going in circles girl, and you're trying to find your way out. But it's time I put on my cape and put that S on my chest. Girl I wanna come and

save you, but I'm stuck in the middle of seeing you hurt. I know when you love him and you wanna make it work. And I can't help but think that I knew you first. It's getting louder, can't ignore it no more. I can hear your heart crying out for me. And it keeps on saying, come on in, come on in, come on in and save me."

At that point Amari and Daryl both were crying. Their love was so tied up and they desperately wanted to be with each other, but neither wanted to be the cause of Corey going into remission. The situation was becoming very tense, so Amari decided to try and liven it up a bit.

"Last one to the bedroom has to go first!" she screamed as she began to run to his bedroom.

He came into the bedroom twenty minutes later.

"I came in here last on purpose. I want to please you!" he said dimming the lights and shaking the bottle of whip cream.

Then out of nowhere he busted out in Snoop's latest song, 'Sexual Eruption', *I'm gonna take my time, she gon get hers before I…I'm gonna take it slow (woah woah), I'm not gonna rush the stroke, So she can get a sexual eruption, so I can get her sexual eruption, so we can get her sexual eruption. Sexual Eruption (woah woah), she might be with him but she's thinkin 'bout me, we don't go to the mall, we don't go out to eat, all that we ever do is play in the sheets.*

Amari couldn't contain her laughter. This was a side of Daryl she wasn't used to. Back in the day, he would never put his feelings out there the way he had tonight. She found herself falling in love with him all over again.

Sex with Daryl was always so riveting, so exciting. Even if she didn't feel in the mood, all he had to do was suck on her breast for a moment, or gently rub the 'to-ta' and he instantly could put her in the mood. Daryl and Amari enjoyed each other for most of the night, she thought to herself, finally she had found happiness! She could finally be at ease, be in love and not have to worry about anyone or anything else. For once, she was not confused in the head on who she wanted to be with. She knew without a doubt, she wanted to be with Daryl for the rest of her life. Little did she know, this night was simply the calm before the storm!

CHAPTER TWENTY

Things started to get hectic after the night she pledged her love to Daryl. Corey started to get better and gain more strength which made him a lot more mobile. He would pop up at one of her classes or her apartment unannounced. Even though she was secretly dating Daryl, they would never stay at her house. They would always stay at his house, because she never wanted him and Corey to run into each other. In the pit of her stomach, she knew what would happen if their paths crossed, she wish she had been wrong, but she wasn't.

Daryl never stayed at her house, but this particular Thursday he did. When they awoke, she told him instantly he needed to leave; something told her the day was going to be an ugly one. He respected her request and got dressed. He sat on her bed saying his good-byes when they heard a tapping at the window. Not sure of what to think, she lifted the blinds and was shocked to see Corey's hands attempting to lift the window.

"Corey, what the hell are you doing here?" she yelled.

"Let me in!" he demanded.

A fear swept over her body. She was so afraid of what might possibly go down.

"Corey, please get off the window," she asked again.

"Open the door and I will," he said.

"Fine," she agreed stupidly.

He let go of the window and walked towards the front of the apartment. Amari tightened her robe and walked to let him in the hallway. Daryl stayed seated on her bed.

"So you fucking him?" Corey screamed.

"What are you talking about?" she yelled.

"Just tell me if you are fucking him or not?"

"I am not gonna justify your dumb ass with an answer!" she said disgusted trying to walking away.

Without warning, his fist connected with her face and she was out cold.

Moments later, she got up off the hallway floor and stumbled into the house. Daryl heard her and came rushing towards her.

"Amari, what the fuck happened?" he asked.

"He hit me," Amari said in disbelief.

Daryl immediately called 911. He sat her down on the couch and gave her a towel to hold on her nose to stop the bleeding. When the EMT workers and policemen arrived, she had a pounding headache and really didn't feel like talking. She managed to give them a description of him along with his address. Daryl sat by her side the entire time, something felt different.

"Daryl can you take me to get a restraining order? she asked.

"Amari, do you really want to do that?" he questioned her.

"What do you mean? You think its right for him to hit me?"

"No, I don't think its right, but you just gave the police all of his information, what do you think he is going to do when he finds out. He's gonna be back and pissed as shit!" he said sounding scared.

"I know he will be back, but I will have a restraining order and I will have his ass arrested with no hesitation!"

"Amari, let's think about this for a moment. This is Corey we are talking about."

"I know who the hell we are talking about! I can't believe you are telling me to just let this shit ride! Who the fuck do you think I am? I am not his fucking punching bag, if he's got an issue with me he better use some words and not his damn fist. He is too goddamn big to be punching me!" she screamed getting angry.

"Peaches, calm down!"

"You fucking calm down!" she spat.

"I can't believe you are so fucking calm about this shit. I'm supposed to be your girl, the love of your fucking life and another man puts his hands on me and you are chill with that? What the fuck? This is not the Daryl I know. The Daryl I know, wouldn't be talking right now, he would be out with Cease handling his business. When the fuck did you get all soft?"

Daryl immediately jumped up, obviously he'd gotten angry. She must have hit a sore spot.

"What the fuck are you trying to say?" he questioned getting in her face.

"I'm not 'trying' to say shit. What I am saying is that you are a punk ass bitch nigga! You sat in here while Corey fucking used my face as his personal punching bag! Who the fuck does that bullshit?" Amari screamed on him beginning to cry.

"You know what, I'm just gonna leave, you sitting up here talking foolishness," he said grabbing his hat off the bed and walking towards the door.

Amari watched him leave and started crying harder. She couldn't believe he actually left. How could he leave her at a time like this? Why wasn't he man enough to deal with the situation. Damn! She needed to go to the courthouse to get a restraining order and she knew there was no way she could drive herself.

Amari picked up the phone and called Xena.

"Hey Xena, where are you?" she asked.

"On my way home, why what's up, you need me to bring something home?" she asked.

"Nah, just hurry up, some shit went down and I need you."

"Alright, I'm turning down our street now," she said wondering what had gone down now.

Within moments, Xena was walking into the house, unaware of what she was walking into.

"Mari, whose blood is all over our hallway floor?" she asked opening the door.

As soon as she saw Amari and her face, she screamed.

She ran over to the couch, "Who the hell did this to you?" she asked.

"Corey," she began to cry.

"Oh my God! Amari, are you okay, did you go to the doctor?"

"No, the EMT's came here. Daryl was here when it happened and he didn't do a damn thing, then he had the nerve to cop an attitude with me because I called him on his bitch ass!" she cried.

"Daryl was here and he didn't handle that nigga?" she asked surprised.

"Nope, 'Mr. Big Time Street Thug' just sat in my room like a little baby bitch!"

"Fuck that nigga too then!" she screamed.

"Mari, don't worry about it, everything is gonna be okay," she said trying to comfort me.

"I know. I need to go down to the courthouse to get a restraining order," she said wiping the tears that wouldn't stop falling.

"Alright, let's go get that then. I dare that nigga to pop up over here while I'm here, I'll fucking stab his ass!" she joked.

♬♬♬

Corey couldn't believe he actually put his hands on Amari. He rushed over to Greg's because he needed to talk to him ASAP.

"Damn C, what's up dawg? What the hell you been doing, why you sweating like a madman?" Greg asked looking at Corey weird.

"Man, I fucked up so bad!" he began to cry.

"Yo, yo dawg what's good?" Greg asked getting worried.

"I just hit Mari," he said not believing what he did.

Gregory Charles was speechless.

"I went over there; she wouldn't return any of my calls. I was climbing through her window and Daryl was there. I lost it when I saw him there with her. How could she be there with Daryl? I love her and I know she loves me too. I asked her point blank if they were fucking and she wouldn't answer me. Next thing I knew, she was on the ground and there was blood everywhere," he admitted.

"Damn Corey man, what the fuck? You couldn't just walk away?" Gregory Charles asked not truly believing what he was hearing.

"I couldn't dawg. Honestly, when she wouldn't answer me the only thing I saw was red. I know she fucking that dude and it pisses me off to think of them together."

"Man I get all that honestly I do, but did you ever stop and think that maybe she really loves that cat? I mean I know he cheated on her and what not but that was a minute ago. Maybe she forgave ole boy and they decided to get back together," Gregory Charles tried to reason.

"How she gonna be with that nigga when we are supposed to be together?" Corey asked.

Gregory Charles laughed.

"Come on dawg; let's be real about the shit. You knew good and well that she and Daryl were back together. That's why your ass is pulling this amnesia card, because it kills you to know they are together. You think I don't know what you trying to pull? You trying to get ole girl back and it hurts you to know that just pulling the amnesia card alone hasn't helped you get her back," Gregory Charles said putting the truth out there.

Corey sat speechless for a moment.

"Okay, so I faked the amnesia. So the fuck what! Point still remains that she led me to believe we were together and on good terms."

"Dawg come on, Amari did what your moms asked her to do which was act like ya'll were still a couple because she thought it would help you to get better. That girl put her life on hold just so you would get better and this is how you thank her? If you really loved her, then you would have just told her that from the get go. You wouldn't have lied to her all this time and had her going crazy and out there trying to kill herself behind all the stress and pressure she has been put under. I'm sorry dawg, but the only thing you care about is your goddamn self! You never once thought about her feelings and what she wanted. Now you done went off and hit her, man you have lost your damn mind!" Gregory Charles said disgusted with his good friend.

Corey sat on Gregory Charles's bed disgusted with himself and his actions.

"I should have just walked away," he mumbled to himself while walking out the door.

♫♫♫

"Cease open up the fucking door!" yelled Daryl.

Cease came to the door in just his boxers, he knew whatever Daryl was about to tell him had better been good.

"Damn D, what's up?" he asked.

"Fucking Corey just punched the shit out of Peaches," he screamed.

Cease looked shocked. He went back upstairs, got dressed and came back downstairs ready to do dirt.

"Alright dawg, let's go I'm ready!" he said patting his waist.

"Whoa, wait a minute son, where the fuck you think you going?" Daryl asked.

"What do you mean where am I going? We going to handle that nigga right?" Cease asked confused.

"Nah, ain't none of that gonna be going on tonight," Daryl answered.

"What? Why the fuck not? That nigga got to get gone! That nigga violated you. How the fuck you gonna let him put his hands on your woman and you not do anything about it? He's lucky you wasn't there?"

Daryl was quiet and redirected his eyes.

"D, what aren't you telling me?" Cease asked.

"I was there," he said quietly.

"What? And you didn't do shit to the nigga, what the hell is wrong with you? That's blatant disrespect and you cool with that? I thought you loved Amari, what's really good?" Cease yelled sitting down.

"I do love her," he said quietly.

"Then why aren't we handling this nigga?" Cease asked utterly confused.

Daryl had no reply.

♫♫♫

The next few weeks were utter hell for Amari. She had been avoiding calls from both Corey and Daryl. Her physical pain had long since subsided but now her heart was aching harder than ever before. Her heart was aching for Daryl and what could have been between them but after the way he acted she knew she could never be with him like that again. It bothered her that he acted that way, she was so used to the 'thug' Daryl, and she couldn't help but wonder where it went when she needed him most. She loved Daryl wholeheartedly and didn't know how she was gonna survive through life without his love and guidance following her every step. Daryl was always there for her even when they weren't a couple.

And then there was Corey. He had been trying his hardest to get things back to the way they were between them, but her heart just wasn't into it at the time. She still held a lot of love for him but something just seemed really off about him. He needed desperately to work on his anger issues before they could even think about having any type of future together.

"Dammit, what the hell is wrong with me?" she thought angrily to herself. Here she was rationalizing her life with both Daryl and Corey and she had to admit she was in love with both of them. How could that be? How could she still hold such a strong love for both men? What the hell was wrong with her?

🎜🎜🎜

"Xena, I have been wanting to ask you something for a long time but you have been going through so much with Mari I was scared to ask you," Jordan began as he inched closer to her.

Xena smiled wondering what Jordan wanted to ask her, she was so nervous.

He smiled at her.

"I know you and Mari are like sisters to each other, but with graduation upon us I thought maybe it would be a good time to move on with our lives."

"Jordan please quit beating around the bush and just let me know what you are trying to ask me, the suspense is killing me," she giggled.

"I think its time we took our relationship to the next level and moved in together. Xena I love you and I want to spend the rest of my life with you. I want to wake up to you each morning and go to bed with you each night."

Xena's smile faded a tad bit. She expected him to ask for her hand in marriage, she was obviously wrong about that. She was happy he was committed enough to her that he wanted to live with her. She smiled again.

"Of course I'll move in with you," she said kissing him on the cheek.

"Yeah, are you sure? Do you think Amari will be okay with it?"

Xena hadn't even thought about Mari and how she might take it. This would have been a lot easier if Mari were seeing someone at the time. Technically Mari was still with Daryl neither of them had actually called it quits they just haven't spoken in like three weeks.

"Yeah, I think Mari will be happy for us," she said hoping that was how the conversation would go.

"Alright good," Jordan said looking happier than usual.

"Look Boo, I really hate to bounce so soon but I gotta go," she said abruptly.

Her whole attitude had changed as she thought about Mari and how she would react to this bit of news. She'd hoped her best friend would be happy for her but didn't know for sure. Amari had been so depressed lately, she wasn't really sure about anything these days. Her moods changed so often. Xena kept praying she wouldn't try to kill herself again.

Xena arrived at the apartment and was happy to find Amari sitting on the couch flipping channels.

"Hey Mari," she said as she hung her keys up on the apple key rack next to the front door.

Amari didn't bother to look at her. She mumbled a hello and kept channel surfing.

"Ya need anything?" Xena asked refusing to give up.

"Nope," Amari said avoiding eye contact.

Xena continued on and went straight to her room and slammed the door. She understood why she took her frustrations out on Xena.

Xena wanted her friend back. They used to share so much of their lives with each other; Xena longed for those days daily. Xena hadn't even realized it but she had begun crying, it had become a daily ritual for her.

♪♪♪

"Damn D, what's good with you and ole girl?" asked Cease.

Daryl looked at him shocked.

"What the hell you bringing her up for?"

"D, I'm your man! I know you dawg better than you know your damn self," Cease said looking him in the eye.

"Amari is off limits!" he yelled.

"Don't get loud with me son! I know you better than you'd like for me to. What's good with ya'll though, have you swallowed your damn pride and called her?"

"Call her? What the fuck am I supposed to say to her? I didn't protect her like I should have," he said thinking back to the day when things changed forever for them.

"Yeah, we never did discuss that son. What happened? Why didn't you see that nigga?" Cease asked still curious to find out what the hell was going on with his man.

"I don't really know. I now she expected me to handle him and I should have but for some fucking reason I didn't. That's part of the reason why I haven't called her. I don't have a reason for why I acted the way I did and she's gonna want an explanation," Daryl thought out loud.

Cease sat and watched Daryl. He could tell that he was conflicted about something, he just didn't know what.

"D man, I think you should call her. If you continue to avoid her she's gonna think you don't care about her and then you're gonna find yourself in a bigger pile of shit then the one you're already in."

♫♫♫

Ke-Ke sat down on her bed looking at her growing belly. She couldn't believe she was actually going through with this pregnancy. She wanted to have an abortion but found out she was too far along to have one. She really wished she knew who her baby daddy was, but she really didn't have a clue.

She didn't see much of her girls these days. Xena was too busy with Jordan to pay any one any attention. Toni was gone, she hadn't heard from her since Tommy's death. Amari had enough drama in her life to keep her busy for three centuries. She wanted to call Amari and talk the way they used to but she knew those days were over.

CHAPTER TWENTY-ONE

"Good afternoon Amari," Momma Val said sounding cheerful.

"Good afternoon," Amari replied not thinking it was a good day at all.

"Graduation day is coming is there anything I can do for you?" she asked wanting to be helpful.

"No, not really. I don't even think I am going to the ceremonies."

"Amari, no don't say that. Graduation is a very important day, you just can't miss it."

"Yeah I know, but I'm just not feeling up to it. I know you don't really want to hear it but I've been through a lot and I just can't bear to be around a crowd of people right now," she said.

"Amari baby you sound so sad and it really breaks my heart. Look Marie and I was just heading out to lunch. We're going over to Olive Garden, why don't you join us?" she offered.

"No, not today."

"Amari, we haven't spent any time together in a long time. This is not an offer to be turned down it's a demand," she said lightly.

Amari lay in bed and thought about it for a moment.

"Fine," she finally answered.

"Good, see you in about an hour."

🎵🎵🎵

Amari pulled up to Olive Garden and was dreading the luncheon. She quickly parked her car and walked inside. She found Aunt Marie and Momma Val at the table enjoying the breadsticks.

"Hello," she said.

"Oh Amari, so happy you were able to make it," Aunt Marie said.

Amari smiled.

"It's so good to see the both of you," she said.

"You too. Please have a seat," Momma Val said.

Amari sat down at the table and picked up a breadstick and started nibbling on it.

Momma Val and Aunt Marie made small talk and she just sat and listened. Amari was waiting for them to get to the questions that were burning their mouths to ask.

Aunt Marie started them off.

"How's Daryl?" she asked.

"I'm not sure we haven't really talked much lately," she answered honestly.

"Why not?" Momma Val asked.

"Not really sure, we had a falling out and neither one of us have bothered to call the other, I guess."

"That's too bad," Aunt Marie observed.

"What about Corey?" Momma Val finally asked.

"You know Corey and I don't talk anymore," Amari said while lightly allowing her fingertips to touch the side of her face.

"He's been trying to call you. Why won't you accept any of his calls?" she asked.

"He hurt me! He punched me and nearly broke my nose," she said trying to remain calm.

Momma Val and Aunt Marie just looked at Amari. The tears were stinging her face as they began to fall down her face.

"Mari girl is that you?" a strange yet familiar voice asked.

She looked up and was shocked to see her Cousin Simeon standing there. She jumped out of her seat and gave him a big hug.

"Birdie, damn nigga I ain't seen you in a minute," she said filled with excitement.

Birdie and Amari grew up together. He was her favorite cousin. They were like brother and sister.

"I know I have been detached from the family lately. I heard about your mom, sorry I didn't make it to the service," he said apologetically.

"Yeah, it's alright," she said thinking about her mother for a moment.

"So let's keep in touch this time around," he said pulling out a piece of paper.

He wrote his number down and they promised to stay in touch. As soon as he left their table Momma Val and Aunt Marie didn't waste a moment getting back to the conversation they had started earlier.

"I'm sure if you'd give him a chance, he'd apologize," Momma Val said mistakenly thinking an apology would make everything better.

"Momma Val I have heard all the apologies I need to hear from him. I'm through with it and the whole situation. An apology is not going to make things better. The fact still remains, he hurt me and there's no changing that no matter how many times he says he's sorry."

Momma Val just looked at Amari stunned.

And what about Daryl, why do you refuse to deal with him?" Aunt Marie asked.

Amari laughed.

"Daryl's not for me. I need…" she paused.

"What I need neither of them seem to be able to give to me," she summarized without going into too much detail.

"Amari, I don't want you to think we just want to get on your case. We just want to see you happy and right now you're not happy," Aunt Marie said sympathetically.

Amari understood completely where she was coming from but she also knew happiness wasn't something that was her friend. Amari felt uncomfortable. She cleared her throat.

"You know what? This was a bad idea. I shouldn't have come here," she said getting up excusing herself.

She didn't give either of them a chance to stop her. The tears had begun falling again before she had even a chance to get completely out of the restaurant. When she got back to her truck she slammed her hands on the steering wheel and began to cry harder.

She was mad at Corey for hitting her and hurting her the way he did. She was mad at Daryl for not protecting her and for showing no concern for her. But most of all she was mad at herself. She was mad that she had such a strong spellbinding love for both Corey and Daryl.

♫♫♫

Cease and Daryl sat in Daryl's living room playing video games. The days of conversations about Amari long dead. Cease stopped trying to figure out why Daryl gave up on her. Time and time again she had proven how much love she had for him. She never let him down; she was always there for him no matter what the situation was. Cease thought it was such a shame to let a good thing like that go. He knew it was literally killing Daryl to not be with her but yet he refused to go to her.

"Damn nigga, I am whipping that ass! You can't see me son!" Cease boasted.

Daryl chuckled.

"Whateva nigga, lucky shot!"

"Oh please, that's not luck that's skill my friend," Cease laughed.

The two friends broke out in a hearty laughter. Daryl's ringing cell phone broke up their fun.

"Yeah, hello," he answered.

"Hey D, what's good man?" Ty said.

"Nuttin just here playing NBA Live with Cease. What's good my nigga?" he asked.

"Nothing much. I just saw Mari and she didn't look too good."

Dilemma

"What do you mean? Where did you see her?"

"Over at Olive Garden she was having dinner with Corey's mom and another woman," he reported.

"Yeah and?" he asked.

"And she ran outta the restaurant crying. I followed her out and when she got to her car she started crying harder and she was banging on the steering wheel," he said recounting the events.

"Alright thanks," Daryl said quickly.

"One more thing, I tracked down that nigga Darvis for you. I find out where he lays his head each night, so we can go take a ride whenever you ready my nigga!" Tyrone beamed.

"Good looks my nigga, let's go handle that tomorrow night," he said quickly before hanging up.

"What's dat about son?" Cease asked puzzled.

"Ty said he saw Mari down at Olive Garden and she didn't look good. She ran outta the restaurant crying," Daryl said.

"Damn D what you think is wrong with her?"

"Man I don't know."

"What you gonna do? Are you gonna call her or not?" Cease said handing him the phone.

"I'll call her later, Ty also said he found out where Darvis lays his head, so we gotta handle that first," Daryl said while giving Cease pound.

🎵🎵🎵

Momma Val and Aunt Marie got back to the house more worried than ever about Amari.

Aunt Marie sat at the table in the kitchen while Momma Val began making a cake.

"I'm really worried about her Val," said Aunt Marie.

"Marie me too, did you see the sadness that was in her eyes?"

"Yeah."

They both were engulfed by a moment of silence, neither of them knowing what to do.

Aunt Marie finally broke the silence.

"I just hope she doesn't try to hurt herself again," she said out loud.

Momma Val stood at the kitchen sink remembering how hurt she was to find out Amari tried to kill herself.

Corey's actions angered her. She couldn't believe what he'd done to Amari. She refused to believe it. She'd scolded him about his behavior but there was only so much she could say and do to him, he was an adult.

🎵🎵🎵

Corey sat at Lily's house on her couch waiting for her to bring him his dinner. The relationship they had was more than tense at this point. She was constantly bringing up Amari which only made him think about her more. He couldn't help it. He was here with Lily but his heart and soul was with Amari. He couldn't figure out for the life of him why he chose to leave her in the first place.

"Corey here," Lily said bringing him back to reality.

He focused in on her and saw she was holding a plate of baked fish and steak fries, with no ketchup. He took the plate from her.

"Where's the ketchup?" he asked annoyed. Everyone knew he couldn't eat anything without ketchup.

"We don't have anymore," she said defensively.

"What? Why the fuck didn't you go the corner store and grab some? You know I can't eat this shit without it," he said getting angry.

Lily stood there shocked. She couldn't believe he was talking to her like this.

"Corey don't fucking talk to me like that. I watched you lay in that bed unconscious. I stepped aside while you recovered and thought your life was with Amari. That was me that did that! So don't think you gonna sit up in my spot disrespecting me!" she yelled breaking into tears.

Corey was over the whole situation. He showed no remorse for hurting her feelings. He got up and grabbed his car keys.

"I'm over it!" was his only reply as he walked out of her apartment and life forever.

🎵🎵🎵

Daryl, Cease and Tyrone cruised the streets of Decatur until they came upon the all white house on Waldrop Road. Cease slowed the car down and watched the house carefully. All three were looking around suspiciously to see if they saw any suspect movements.

Cease parked the car four houses down. They all jumped out of the car, dressed in black and ready for war. Tyrone went to the front door carrying 2 boxes of Dominos pizza. Cease and Daryl stood on the side waiting for the entrance to get secured.

Tyrone rang the doorbell and Darvis quickly answered the door.

"What up? Can I help you partna?" Darvis said.

"Dominos pizza delivery," Tyrone said displaying the pizza.

"Nah, you must have the wrong house, I didn't order shit," Darvis said leaning on the frame of the door.

"Yeah, I think your wife did," Tyrone said smiling.

"What the fuck you talking bout nigga?" Darvis screamed.

Daryl revealed himself from his hiding spot.

"Actually bitch nigga I ordered the pizza for you," stated Daryl with a devious grin on his face.

Darvis took a step back and tried to slam the door but Tyrone was too quick, he already had his foot wedged in the door.

The three gentlemen helped themselves and walked straight into the house.

Cease grabbed Darvis and threw him on the couch.

"You a real stupid muthafucka, you tryna come at my nigga!" Cease spat.

Darvis sat scared. He never really thought out the situation. He didn't think there would be any chance of him getting caught. After he hired them young boys to do his dirty work, he had them all disappear; he never thought word would get around that he was behind the attacks on Daryl and his crew.

"Dawg, please give me a break, I got a baby on the way, please don't kill me," Darvis pleaded.

"A baby? Nigga I don't care about that shit. You didn't give a fuck when you were murking my peoples; you didn't give two shits about their kids so why should I care about yours?" Daryl asked.

Darvis didn't know what to say. He sat there quiet.

"I don't want this to be a long drawn out process, I want this nigga murked and I wanna be outta here," he said getting his nine millimeter out of his waistband.

At the sight of the gun, Darvis pissed in his pants.

Daryl aimed his nine directly at Darvis' head, without warning he let one shot off, caught Darvis' directly in the middle of his forehead. When Daryl saw his body slump down, he walked back to his car.

Darvis was dead.

Cease and Tyrone made sure they left no traces of themselves as they exited the house.

The three drove off and headed back to Lithonia, neither of them felt a bit of remorse for what they just did.

🎵🎵🎵

Xena and Amari were sitting at home on the couch watching the evening news. The news anchor immediately began reporting a murder that happened in Decatur on Waldrop Road. Xena got nervous at once. She sat up on the couch and looked nervously at Amari.

"Reporting live from Decatur, there appears to be a murder, the victim, black male early twenties, was found slumped down on the couch with one single bullet wound to the forehead. He was dead upon arrival. At this time he has not been identified. There are no suspects at the moment..."

Xena saw them standing in front of Darvis' house and she couldn't stop the tears.

"Amari, that's Darvis' house," she cried.

"I know," Amari said picking up the phone.

She called Ke-Ke immediately and asked her if she saw the news. Ke-Ke told her yes and said she was on her way over.

Amari and Xena sat idly waiting for any news on the victim.

There was a knock on the door; Amari assumed it was Ke-Ke.

She got up to answer and received a true shock.

"Amanda, what are you doing here?" Amari asked.

At the mention of Amanda's name, Xena came running down the hallway. Xena already knew what she was there to say.

"NO!" Xena screamed before any words could be said.

Amari stood frozen by shock.

"Xena, I am so sorry, but yes, Darvis is dead," Amanda confirmed.

Xena slumped down and began crying hysterically.

Amanda turned towards Amari.

"I'm sorry, I really am; please let her know I said that. I got the call from Danyale, she was the one that had to go and identify the body. I will be in touch regarding funeral arrangements," she said coldly before walking out the door.

CHAPTER TWENTY-TWO

Xena sat on her bed and thought about her options and what she should do. She knew she should go ahead and have the abortion. She was about 95% sure that this baby she was carrying was Darvis'. Ever since his funeral she hadn't been able to stop thinking about him. She secretly wished he was still around to hold her and comfort her.

Jordan was a great guy but lately she didn't feel the same type of happiness she felt when she was with Darvis. Darvis and Xena would fight religiously over his many side relationships. But through it all they still held a deep love for each other.

The last time they saw each other, he nearly cried trying so hard to apologize to her for all of the pain he caused her. Thinking back on that day Xena strongly feels that Darvis knew he was living his last days.

When he kissed her, he did so with such passion. When he looked into her eyes and asked her to let him make love to her one last time she quickly obliged. As they snuck off to the Marriott hotel they looked like newlyweds unable to keep their hands off one another. Once in the room they wasted no time getting undressed. Darvis for the first time treated her with care. He was gentle and full of an undeniable passion. When she asked him to wear a condom and he responded by saying, "I wanna give you something to always remember me by," she thought he meant some good sex, but now she wondered if he felt or hoped she'd get pregnant that night.

Xena wasn't sure if she was ready to be a single parent. She watched Ke-Ke and knew the struggles she faced and Xena wasn't sure she was ready for that.

She knew it was time for her to go and meet Jordan. They were meeting at the Cheesecake Factory for lunch; she'd decided she'd tell him then. She got up off the bed and headed to the bathroom to get ready.

♫♫♫

"Cease you think I'm making a mistake don't you?" he asked.

"Nope, I can't believe you didn't think of it sooner."

"Yeah you're right," he said.

Daryl picked up his cell phone and called Amari. She picked up sounding happy as can be.

"Hey Daryl what's up?"

"Nothing."

"Are you okay?" she asked.

"Yeah, I'm fine. Would you like to go out to dinner tonight?" he finally asked.

"Sure," she said after a brief silence.

"Cool," he smiled. "We're going to Justin's I'll pick you up around 7pm."

"Okay, Daryl," she said hanging up the phone.

"Alright Cease she agreed."

"Man I don't know why you thought she wouldn't."

Daryl nodded his head.

They went back to playing the latest version of NBA Live and waited patiently for the time to pass until Daryl's big date with Amari.

♫♫♫

"Corey?" yelled Lissa from downstairs.

He stuck his head out his bedroom door with an annoyed look on his face.

"What do you want?" he asked.

"Do you wanna go to the mall?" she asked excitedly.

"No," he said going back into his room and slamming the door behind him.

Corey flopped down on his bed wanting to shake this nasty state of depression he'd found himself in but not able to. He missed Amari so much he didn't know what to do with himself. He thought once Amari knew he wasn't with Lily anymore she'd take him back with open arms, boy was he wrong. Amari refused to talk to him and it was killing him inside.

Lissa tapped lightly on his door and entered without waiting for the okay from Corey.

"Corey, can you please come to the mall with me, it may help to get your mind off Amari."

He sat there not really wanting to be bothered but knew how relentless his sister could be.

"Fine," he said half smiling.

"Oh thank you so much," she said excitedly.

"She left him alone so he could get dressed."

🎜🎜🎜

Amari hung up her phone. She just got off the phone with Daryl; he wanted to take her out for dinner tonight. She'd agreed but she wasn't sure why she'd agreed. She was still hurt by his actions but she knew it was time to forgive him.

"Who was that on the phone?" asked Tee.

Amari looked up and saw her standing in the doorway smiling.

"Damn you ain't changed, still nosey as a muthafucka!" Amari laughed.

"Whateva bitch," she replied.

"It was Daryl; he wants to take me out to dinner tonight at his favorite joint, Justin's."

"Dinner huh?" she asked puzzled.

"Yes dinner," she replied realizing what her friend was implying.

"Well what are you going to wear?" Tee asked.

Amari sat there with a blank look on her face.

"I don't have anything to wear, we gotta hit up the mall," Amari said suddenly.

Amari got up outta her bed and rummaged through her closet quickly and looked for a quick sweastsuit to throw on.

After finding her baby blue Rocawear sweat suit, she threw it on along with a pair of baby blue and white air forces. She tied her hair back in a tight ponytail grabbed her white coach bag off her dresser and headed out the door.

She decided to go over to the Lenox Mall. Daryl said he was taking her to Justin's for dinner so she knew she needed a somewhat elegant dress for dinner.

She was able to find a midnight blue Dolce & Gabbana dress with a swoop neckline and the back completely exposed. She went to Saks and picked up a pair of midnight blue Jimmy Choo stilettos. She stopped by La Perla and picked up a black lace thong. As she was driving back home she realized just how excited she'd become in anticipation of her date with Daryl. Truth be told she missed him immensely. It'd been so long since she'd felt his touch and she was more than ready to allow the past to be the past.

🎵🎵🎵

"Damn dude! You are doing the damn thing!" Cease complimented Daryl on his midnight blue Armani suit.

"You think I look alright?" he asked glaring at himself in the full length mirror.

"Yeah Amari will no doubt drool over you," he agreed.

Daryl couldn't stop the smile from forming on his face.

"Alright my nigga, go get your wifey back," Cease said nearly pushing Daryl out the door.

Daryl went to his garage and decided on his latest purchase the latest model of the Mercedes CL edition. He got in and quickly searched through is CD collection until he found one of his favorite homemade mix tapes. It had only songs that reminded him of Amari on it. From P.S. I'm Still in Love with You by Rihanna to I Gotta Be by Jagged Edge. He skipped all the way to number 12 on the

CD, his favorite song when it came down to his feelings about Amari, Song Cry by Jay Z. That song spilled out his every thought of her. It always choked him up when he heard Jay Z voice that he was 'just fucking them girls he was gonna get right back..' and then to hear him say, 'I have to deal with the fact I did you wrong forever' always blew his mind.

Daryl thought about that line heavily. He hated he was so immature in dealing with Amari. He wished repeatedly that he'd never gotten mixed up with Nikki. He thought constantly about the pain he put Amari through. He would often think about how different his life would have been if Nikki hadn't made Amari lose their child.

Before Daryl knew it he was parked in front of Amari's apartment. He sat in his car a moment continuing to travel down memory lane.

♫♫♫

Amari couldn't believe how nervous she was about going out with Daryl. She hadn't been out with anyone in months. She viewed her reflection in the mirror and had to admit she was looking damn good.

"Damn ma, you bout to have that nigga going bananas! Your booty is banging in that dress," exclaimed Xena.

Amari turned towards the door and saw the approving looks of both Ke-Ke and Xena.

"Whateva! Does it really look that big?" she asked getting self conscious and trying to examine her butt at the same time.

"Oh girl please, you know you can't hide that thing no matter what you put on," laughed Ke-Ke.

"Anyways, Daryl's outside sitting in his car, he's been out there for like ten minutes playing the same song over and over," Xena said peering out the window.

Amari walked over to the window and sure enough Daryl was sitting in his car seemingly lost in thought. She cracked her window and could hear Song Cry by Jay Z blasting from his car.

Amari couldn't help but smile. She loved that song. She grabbed her purse and headed out the door.

As she walked towards his car she could see Daryl sitting there with his head resting on his head rest. She lightly tapped on his window. He jumped apparently startled by her presence. He rolled his window down and smiled.

"Hey," he said trying to open his door.

"Don't bother, I can get in on my own," she said walking around to the passenger side.

As she got comfortably in her seat she could see how nervous Daryl was.

Amari lightly touched his hand.

"Are you okay?" she asked.

He smiled a smile full of tension.

"Yeah, I'm good, you ready?" he asked shifting the car to drive. She nodded her head yes and relaxed in her seat while listening to the sweet music playing from Daryl's CD player.

♫♫♫

The time for Xena had finally come. She realized she could no longer continue to lie to Jordan. She had to tell him the truth. She had to confess that before Darvis passed they had a continuous affair and as a result of that she was now pregnant. She assumed there was a chance Jordan could be the father but her heart continued to tell her he wasn't.

She picked up the phone and called Jordan. She could hear the eagerness in his voice. He was more than happy to hear from her. He was ready to put all of this behind them and get back to their happy lives.

"Hey Jordan, I'm in the mood for Waffle House, would you like to join me?" she asked praying he would agree.

"Sure, do you want me to pick you up?" he asked.

"No, that's okay, I'll meet you there. Let's meet at the one on Wesley Chapel in about 20 minutes?"

He quickly agreed.

♫♫♫

Daryl and Amari were seated at a beautiful table at Justin's. She couldn't believe the lengths Daryl had gone. There were two dozen red roses on the table awaiting their arrival. He quickly ordered a bottle of Cristal and they were left with their thoughts. She broke the silence.

"Daryl you look good tonight," she smiled.

She caught him blushing.

"Thanks, but I could never compare to you," he said.

Now it was her turn to blush.

"I want to propose a toast," he said filling her glass.

"To what?" she questioned.

"To us," he answered.

They both drank.

Amari ordered chicken and waffles and Daryl ordered smothered chicken, baked macaroni and cheese and collard greens. They both ate like it was their last meal, hardly coming up for air.

When the waitress came to remove their plates, Daryl informed Amari that he took it upon himself to order her favorite apple pie a la mode. She couldn't help but smile.

Daryl hadn't lost his thoughtfulness.

"So...Daryl, have you been?" she asked.

"I've been doing well. I've been doing a lot of thinking lately," he said staring at her.

"Really, about what?" she inquired.

She was secretly trying to figure out if he still thought about her.

"Life," he said being vague.

"Do you want to be more specific?" she asked getting a little annoyed.

"Nah, not right now, I hear Ginuwine is gonna be here tonight," Daryl informed her.

She looked up shocked.

"What? Are you sure?"

"Yeah, that's what they told me when I made the reservation."

Now she was excited. Ginuwine was one of her favorite R and B singers. They started making idle conversation and then the announcement was made that Ginuwine would be on in five minutes. When he came to the stage she put her full attention on him while sipping on her glass of Cristal. He started off with "So Anxious" and she quickly found herself in heaven. He went ahead and performed "My Pony" and "Betta Half". And then Amari's life changed forever. The music was off and

Ginuwine started walking into the crowd. He began speaking.

"The next song, 'Differences' is dedicated to Amari from my man Daryl," he said standing right at their table.

Her heart began to flutter as she looked at Daryl and saw the big kool aid grin that was plastered on his face. She allowed herself to get lost in the words as she thought about Daryl feeling this way about her. For so long she longed for Daryl to call her and tell her how much he loved her. She was so lost she hadn't realized Ginuwine had stopped singing and now Daryl knelt before her.

"Amari, we have been through the fire and back. You held me down even when I turned my back on you. I've tried to live without you and I can't. I love you. I need you in my life. This life is not worth living if I can't live it with you. I want you to be my wifey, legally. Amari, please will you marry me?" he asked kneeling in front of her holding a small ring box that housed a four carat diamond engagement ring.

Her eyes bugged out at the huge rock he had in front of her. She smiled. So long she waited for this day to come and finally it was here. The entire restaurant was silent awaiting her response.

She hugged Daryl tightly and whispered in his ear.

"You know I love you, but I really do need to think about this."

"No doubt," he said slipping the ring on her finger.

At the sight of this the restaurant burst out in applause. Daryl and Amari both allowed them to believe she had accepted his marriage proposal. Moments later the waitress appeared with another bottle of Cristal.

"This is from the owner," she said pointing to the corner of the restaurant where the infamous owner sat amongst his guests.

Amari sat baffled.

"Daryl I can't believe you did this," she began, unable to take her eyes off the rock that now weighed down her ring finger.

♫♫♫

Xena and Jordan sat at Waffle House enjoying their food, Xena more so than Jordan. He quickly noted how much Xena was eating. She was never much of an eater but she was cleaning up her plate well he noticed.

"Jordan, I don't know how to tell you this," she began.

He started squirming in his seat not liking where this was headed.

"Jordan, I'm really sorry. I cheated on you with Darvis and now I'm pregnant," she said not holding anything back.

Jordan sat back in the booth. He couldn't believe the news Xena just hit him with. He was heartbroken. Xena was his world and now she was telling him she was pregnant with Darvis' child.

Xena sat and watched Jordan's behavior. She hated to hurt him but knew she couldn't go on living this lie.

"Jordan, I'm really sorry," she said again.

Jordan was near tears.

He got up from the table and swiped all the dishes to the floor. He stormed out of the Waffle House leaving her to look stupid amongst the other patrons. She quickly got up and headed towards the counter to pay the bill. Once she settled that she hurried out the restaurant and practically ran to her car. Once inside she thanked God she'd decided to meet Jordan there, if she hadn't she'd be searching for a way home.

She drove home in silence, left to thinking about everything she'd done. She'd made some poor decisions in her life. She silently began crying.

🎵🎵🎵

Amari danced around her apartment astounded by Daryl's actions. She couldn't believe he'd actually proposed to her. She figured the night would be about how foolish they both had been trying to stay away from each other. She would never forget the look in his eyes as he got down on one knee. At that moment she knew without a doubt he loved her. She had no idea in her mind or her heart that he truly and sincerely was ready to spend his life with her exclusively.

Amari couldn't wait to go home and share the news with her two best friends. To her dismay when she got home she found the house was quiet. She went to her room and quickly undressed, she was headed to the shower.

As she stepped into the shower and started lathering her body with the Pure Seduction body wash from the Secret Garden Collection by Victoria's Secret her mind raced to Daryl. She leaned her wet body against the tile and imagined Daryl was standing behind her, rubbing her back. Her hands began to travel up and down her body. She wasn't sure how or when but somehow her middle finger found its way inside her sweetness. At this point it was overflowing with juices, she hated to let these juices go to waste but there was nothing else she could do. She continued to insert her finger in and out while simultaneously eagerly rubbing her breast. She was in heaven, all the while fully believing it was Daryl that was taking her there.

She giggled at herself when she heard the moans escaping her lips. She suddenly couldn't control herself. She started to please herself harder and harder, before she knew it she had inserted two fingers inside herself. She was moments away from climbing the walls. She had got so wrapped in her thoughts of Daryl that before she knew it she had released all over her hand. As the liquid began to drip down her leg she laughed at herself again for not being able to wait for Daryl.

Amari quickly washed herself and got out of the shower. She went straight to her room and started lotioning her body. She was startled when she heard, Justin Timberlake's song, "Until the End of Time" playing from her cell phone. She quickly leaned across her queen sized bed and picked up the phone.

"Hey Boo," she beamed.

"Hey cutie, whatchu doing?" Daryl asked.

She smiled thinking about what she was just doing.

"Well, I just got out of the shower," she began.

"Really, so what you got on?" he asked getting comfortable on the couch.

"Well nothing because I just go out," she smiled.

"So what was you doing oiling your body down?" he asked while quietly grabbing his keys.

"Yeah, I was until you called. Now I'm just lying on my bed talking to you."

"So you're naked?" he confirmed while quietly getting into his car.

"Yep," she answered.

"Wow! What I wouldn't give to see you right now like that," he said sounding disappointed.

"Well, why don't you come over?" she finally suggested.

Daryl beamed ecstatic they were finally on the same page.

"I wish I could but I'm waiting for Cease to come through. He's gotta pick up a package," he lied as he parked his Mercedes next to her Acura.

He quickly jumped out of the car careful to not slam the door. He nearly ran to her front door; he was so excited to see her face when she saw him.

"Alright, I guess I understand," she said sounding obviously disappointed.

"Don't sound so sad," he said getting more excited.

Amari started pouting thinking about how much she wanted to see him at that moment.

Ding...Dong...Amari's front door bell rang.

"Shit!" she screamed in panic at the chime of the bell. She quickly realized she wasn't dressed.

Daryl started laughing as he listened to her fumble with her drawer trying to find something quick to put on.

Again he rang the bell wanting her to think that whoever was at the door was in an urgent need to get inside.

"Just a minute," she yelled while throwing on one of Daryl's oversized Rocawear t-shirts along with her chili pepper red bathrobe.

She rushed to the door and swung it open without asking who it was. She was stunned beyond relief when she saw Daryl standing there with a big kool-aid grin plastered on his face.

"Daryl," she shrieked.

He put his finger to her lips and hushed her quickly. He forcefully pushed her backwards and shut the door with his foot. In one swift movement he had her red robe off and his hands were freely roaming her body. They kissed passionately and Amari couldn't have felt better.

They tumbled onto the couch and neither of them stopped or cared. Daryl forcefully laid her back and began kissing her body from head to toe. Amari's body was tingling all over. She never wanted this feeling to go away.

"Peaches, I missed you so much," he said in between kisses to her inner thighs.

Amari sat up and began to pull him closer to her.

"I can't wait to become your wife," she said while taking hold of his manhood.

Daryl smiled instantly. Amari always knew how to handle her business.

She took his manhood and placed her lips around it. She smiled as she realized how much she was pleasing him. He began to moan softly at first and within a few seconds his soft moans turned to loud screams. Feeling himself about to erupt he quickly pulled himself out of her mouth and attempted to lay her back. She stopped him.

"Daryl would you please hit it from the back, I've been craving that," she said aggressively.

Daryl happily obliged he wasn't used to her being so aggressive. She was usually so laid back. Daryl was in absolute heaven. He knew he was handling business, with each thrust he could feel her pressing her body on him wanting and needed more. Daryl let himself go completely within five minutes. It had been way too long since he had any of her loving.

Daryl couldn't contain himself. Daryl and Amari fucked all over the house that night. They didn't make it sleep until the wee hours of the morning. It was then Amari realized her and Daryl didn't use a condom all night. Since they were getting married she didn't sweat it too much.

CHAPTER TWENTY-THREE

Ke-Ke sat back on the couch and was preparing for a night alone at Amari's and Xena's apartment. She had just bought the latest Tyrese movie, 'Waist Deep' and the latest movie from the crazy Wayans Brothers, 'Little Man' and she was dieing to see them both. She poured herself a glass of Hennessey mixed with Coke. She was satisfied. She hated being alone.

🎵🎵🎵

Gregory Charles and Corey sat on Gregory Charles' couch watching ESPN.

"Corey man you want to hit up 112 tonight?" asked Gregory Charles tired of staying in the house.

"Nah not really, if you wanna go you can go ahead; I'll just head back to the crib."

"Come on man, stop that pity party bullshit! You stay with Amari on brain, if it's that serious for you, why don't you just pick up the phone and call her already?"

"Man, what the fuck am I suppose to say to her?"

"Tell her whatever is weighing on your mind. Tell her the truth, tell her you love her and can't live without her."

"I wouldn't know where to start. I really fucked up!" Corey finally agreed.

Corey sat on the couch pondering Gregory Charles's words. He knew he couldn't avoid talking to Amari forever. He just didn't know how he could make her understand what he was going through being without her.

He picked up his cell phone and dialed her house number. He was shocked a bit when Ke-Ke told him Amari went out. He called her cell phone next and was angered when he repeatedly got her voice mail. He decided to give her an hour and then he was going to call her back.

♫♫♫

Ke-Ke sat back on the trying to enjoy her movie. She had just got up for the tenth time to answer the phone. Corey had called repeatedly looking for Amari. She had just got comfortable on the couch when she heard a light tap on the porch door. Annoyed she got up and prayed Corey hadn't resulted to stalking Amari. She slid the blinds back and was shocked speechless at who was standing before her.

♫♫♫

Corey waited patiently in front of Amari's apartment complex. He called the house repeatedly and each time Ke-Ke answered the phone highly annoyed with him. He'd tried calling Amari's cell phone and each time he was sent straight to voice mail.

He sat in the car and listened to an old Dru Hill CD. The lyrics to each song seemed to speak directly to him and Amari's situation. As each minute passed he became angrier and angrier. He wondered where the hell Amari was and what was was taking her so long to get home.

He leaned back in his seat and noticed Amari's Acura MDX parked on the opposite side of the street. This enraged him even more.

♫♫♫

"Oh my God," Ke-Ke nearly yelled.

Ke-Ke was so excited and still in shock. She didn't know what to do with herself. Her visitor walked into the apartment and planted herself on the couch.

"What are you doing here? How have you been?" she asked hurriedly.

"Fine, just trying to get some things together," the visitor said nonchalant.

"Getting some things together, damn you make it sound like you went away on vacation."

"I know. I gotta go down to the police station and turn myself in." the visitor said looking at her hands nervously.

Ke-Ke walked over to the couch and gave her best friend Toni another hug.

"I'm so happy to see you, I was so worried about you," Ke-Ke admitted.

Without warning Toni started crying. Ke-Ke hugged her tighter only imagining the type of emotional distress she was under.

"Ke-Ke, I still can't believe he's gone," she barely whispered.

"I know, but it was going to be either you or him. It may be mean but I much rather it was him instead of you," she answered honestly.

Ke-Ke and Toni hugged each other tightly both reflecting on the issues they both were facing in their lives.

🎵🎵🎵

Xena went to the clinic on an emergency visit. She couldn't stop throwing up and she suddenly found herself having hard time breathing. She walked from her front door to her car which was all of seven steps and she was hunched over gasping for air. She didn't really know what was wrong with her but she knew it needed to get checked out.

Since the day Jordan walked out of her life she didn't know what to do with herself. She hated what she did to him but Darvis was her first true love.

Xena rubbed her stomach as she thought about him. She missed him so much. She would sometimes go out to the gravesite just so she could be closer to him.

As a single tear fell for her one true love the medical assistant called her name to go to the back.

♪♪♪

Daryl and Amari finished their evening and they both were riding on a pretty big high. Daryl was pretty secure that Amari would eventually say yes, he just hoped she didn't make him wait to long. He was ready to start planning the wedding of the century. Amari was steadily trying to figure out if this was truly what she wanted. She loved Daryl with everything that was in her but she loved Corey as well. Apart of her wished there was a way she could clone the good qualities they both had into one man, but she knew that would be taking things to the extreme.

They pulled up to Amari's apartment oblivious to the drama that was about to go down. Daryl parked his car and turned the alarm on and together they walked to her front door. No one had mentioned anything but it was understood that he was spending the night.

"Oh if this ain't some bullshit!" Corey yelled from his car as he got out approaching the two.

Amari instantly became nervous. She had no idea what Corey was up to but the look in his eyes and the swagger in which he walked let her know this situation was not going to turn out good. She grabbed onto Daryl's arm.

Corey walked right up on them.

"What are you two love birds now?" he laughed.

Daryl and Amari remained silent. Corey looked Amari in the eye and stood directly in front of her.

"What's up? You still fucking this nigga?" he said nearly spitting on her.

Daryl instantly went on the defensive.

"Come on dude, get outta her face like that," he warned.

"Whatchu gonna do nigga? You ain't gonna do shit just like the last time," Corey yelled getting in Daryl's face.

The two men stood face to face each waiting for the other to make the first move. Daryl wasn't flinching and neither was Corey.

Amari stood by not sure of what she was going to do. She hugged Daryl's arm.

"Come on Daryl, let's just go inside."

Daryl could hear her but there was no way he could back down from Corey, AGAIN. He couldn't allow himself to be looked upon as a punk but in the same breath he didn't want to stand outside all night standing in this nigga face.

"Would you two cut it out already? This is bullshit!" she yelled getting angry.

"Nah boo, he wanna act like a man, then he gonna need to stand up here and be a man," Daryl responded still staring Corey down.

"Nigga please, I'm more man than you'll ever be!" he spewed back.

Without any warning Corey cocked back and punched Daryl square in the mouth. The punch didn't faze Daryl at all. He chuckled and served Corey with the worse ass whipping of his life.

"Daryl stop it!" she screamed beginning to get concerned for Corey's safety.

Daryl eased up off him without putting up a fight with Amari. Daryl looked down at Corey who was curled up on the sidewalk, with hatred in his eyes.

"Listen up nigga, don't come around here no more you ain't welcomed," Daryl said giving him one last kick.

Amari hurriedly pulled Daryl into the house just to get another shock.

♫♫♫

Xena pulled up to the house minutes after Daryl and Amari walked in. She was caught off guard when she saw Corey lying on the sidewalk in an obvious amount of pain. Forgetting all of her pain and the devastating news she just heard from the doctor, she quickly walked up to him.

"Corey you okay?" she asked concerned.

In one quick movement he pulled a gun on her and had her at his mercy. She was horrified and didn't know what to do as he forcefully made her walk to the door.

🎵🎵🎵

"Toni?" Amari said in disbelief.

Toni smiled.

Quickly Amari rushed over and gave Toni a big hug.

"Damn girl, are you okay?" Amari asked.

"Yeah, I am, I see you doing okay as well," she said pointing to the diamond that sat on Amari's ring finger.

They both smiled.

"Hold the fuck up! What is that?" Ke-Ke said getting up to get a better look.

The three could barely hold their excitement. When the knock at the door came and Daryl answered it, their excitement quickly turned to fear.

Daryl spoke first, "Corey what the hell you up to now?" he asked trying to diffuse the situation.

Corey ignored him. He forcefully pushed his way into the house.

"Sit the fuck down!" Corey yelled.

Ke-Ke, Toni, Xena and Amari quickly turned to the couch. Tears began to trickle down Amari's face as she thought about what was happening and what could eventually happen. Daryl remained firm at the door; he wasn't budging for this bitch ass nigga. Daryl wasn't sweating the nigga he had his nine tucked tightly in his waistband.

Corey shut the door and locked it. He had no idea what he was going to do but he knew he couldn't turn back now.

"Corey?" Amari said above a whisper.

He turned his head quickly towards her.

"What?"

"Why are you doing this? Whateva your beef is, it's between us, let my friends go," she pleaded.

He laughed.

"Sorry, no one's going any damn where!"

Amari sat next to her friends trembling.

"Dawg, you taking this bull shit a bit too far. How you gonna hold niggas hostage and they don't know why they being held," Daryl asked easily getting annoyed with the situation.

"So what I'm yo bitch and gotta answer to you?" Corey asked getting in Daryl's face.

"Nigga please, you are what you are!"

"Corey, why are you holding us hostage?" Amari asked hoping to distract him so that maybe Daryl could get that 38 away from him.

Corey laughed.

"Where have you been?" he asked pointing the 38 directly at her.

The terror was written on her face. All she could see was the gun pointed at her. She thought her life was nearing its end. Different thoughts were swarming through her head.

He walked closer to her, he kept the gun pointed at her and watched Daryl out the corner of his eye.

"I asked you where you have been."

Amari opened her mouth but couldn't manage to get any words to come out.

"She was out with me," Daryl said clearing his throat and trying to get the attention taken off Amari.

Corey walked over to Daryl.

"I would advise you to stop fucking with me. I'm tired of you and your bull shit," he yelled.

"Look dude, this is some bull shit! All this coming in here waving your gun tryna act like you bout to kill somebody is some real pussy shit. You wanna get at me then holla, I'm right here dawg!" Daryl said getting annoyed.

Corey stared him down. They both stood face to face neither blinking. With one quick thrust, Corey snatched Amari up by her hair and held the gun to her head.

She could no longer contain the tears. They fell all at once.

"Corey please don't do this," she begged sniffling.

She looked at Daryl and could tell how angry the situation had made him. She locked her eyes on his and pleaded with him to get her out of this mess. He winked at her and she knew he wouldn't let me down.

Corey pressed the 38 harder against the side of her head. She instantly felt a headache coming on.

"Corey you're hurting me," Amari said through clinched teeth.

He ignored her. He directed his comment towards Daryl.

"How would you feel if I killed her right now!" he asked laughing.

"Come on dawg you don't really want to do that," Daryl said through clenched teeth hoping Corey wouldn't really go through with it

His grip on her hair got tighter.

"Corey you're really hurting me," she cried.

"Shut the fuck up!" he screamed.

Amari could hear Xena, Ke-Ke and Toni crying.

"Now look this is what we're going to do," he began waving the gun around.

"You three can go but Amari and Daryl stay."

Xena, Tee and Toni quickly got up to leave. As they reached the door he grabbed Xena by the collar and pointed the gun at her. If you so much as call anyone over here you can kiss your friends ass goodbye because I will kill her, ya hear me?" he asked.

She nodded her head yes and turned down the stairs behind Toni and Tee. She couldn't get Amari's pleading eyes out of her head.

Corey slammed the door shut and locked it.

"Now what should I do with you two?" he asked no on in particular.

He could feel Amari's body trembling in his grasp but he didn't care at the moment.

He laughed a sinister laugh.

"I've been calling you for hours and not once did you bother to call me back, why is that? You were too busy being laid up with this dude?" he asked.

Why I felt the need to explain myself to him was beyond me. Maybe him waving that 38 all around was cause enough.

"Corey, I wasn't laid up with him. We went out to eat, that's all," I began.

"What the fuck ever! If it was just dinner why didn't you take any of my calls?" he asked.

She honestly didn't have a legitimate answer for him. She was out with Daryl and didn't feel like being bothered with Corey at the moment.

Once Corey got Amari and Daryl alone he wasn't sure exactly what he wanted to do. He knew he couldn't really go through with hurting her but he was crushed at the moment. To see Amari and Daryl together killed him.

Corey momentarily zoned out giving Daryl enough time to get Amari out of the room. Amari dashed to her bedroom and locked the door. She grabbed the cordless phone off the charger and went to hide in the bottom of her walk in closet.

She contemplated calling the police but remembered her vow to Corey to never again do that to him. She just hoped she wouldn't regret her decision in the end.

Instead of the police she decided to call Gregory Charles. She quickly dialed his number.

"Yeah," he answered in his laid back tone.

"Gregory Charles, I need your help," she whispered.

"Who this?" he asked.

"It's Amari and Corey's lost his mind," she said beginning to cry again.

"Amari, what's wrong?" he asked.

"Corey's over here and he has a gun," Amari said.

"Shit, I'm on my way," he said not asking anymore questions.

Amari hung up the phone hoping Gregory Charles would get there in time.

♪♪♪

"Punk ass nigga!" Daryl screamed before landing a hard punch directly to Corey's skull.

Corey snapped out of his daydream and instantly went on the defensive.

The two started rolling around fighting. Somehow Corey managed to have Daryl pinned down. Corey went into his waistband and grabbed his thirty-eight.

"Die bitch nigga!" he screamed before letting off a shot.

In an instant Daryl managed to move slightly, instead of the bullet entering his head he managed to get away with only a shoulder wound. He winced in pain.

Corey was shocked at his actions and immediately ran out the back porch.

♪♪♪

BOOM! Amari heard the gun shot and panicked. She rushed out of her bedroom afraid of what she might find. She saw Daryl laying on the floor in obvious pain, her stomach dropped. She rushed to his side.

"Daryl," she called out.

He didn't respond.

"Daryl," she cried again.

He began to move.

Slowly he opened his eyes. He hated to see her crying.

"It's okay, I'm fine," he said trying to reassure her.

She jumped up and ran back to her room to grab the phone.

After she got it she knelt beside him. She clicked the phone on. At the sound of the dial tone, Daryl grasped her hand.

"Who are you calling?" he asked.

"You need an ambulance," she replied.

He shook his head no.

"Just call Cease, he'll handle the situation. Calling an ambulance will only bring five oh over here and you don't need that kind of heat," he reasoned.

Amari shrugged her shoulders as if to say she didn't care.

"Are you tryna see that nigga in jail?" he asked.

Realizing that she wasn't, she broke down and called Cease.

♫♫♫

All at once her apartment was filled with people. Gregory Charles came over and was frustrated that Corey had fled; he spent most of the time pacing in the living room. Cease was tending to Daryl's wound. Xena, Toni and Ke-Ke had returned. Amari could feel herself beginning to go insane. She walked out onto the porch unnoticed for a breath of fresh air. She stood on the porch gazing at the moon. Deciding she wanted to sit, she walked down one flight of stairs and sat on the second step. She put her face in her hands and began to cry. She couldn't believe the kind of situation she had once again found herself in.

She glanced on down by her foot and was shocked to see a small ring box. She picked it up and looked around to see if anyone was watching her. Slowly she opened it up. She was taken aback by the beauty of the simple ring that sat inside the red velvet box. At most it was a two carat three stone diamond engagement ring. She smiled, thinking of how the recipient of the ring would feel when she saw it.

Amari lifted the ring out of the box and tried it on for size. She had a funny feeling when she put it on. She quickly slipped it off and put her own extravagant engagement ring back on her finger. She started inspecting the ring, she noticed the ring was engraved and strained her eyes in the dark so she could read it.

When she read it, a tear instantly fell from her eyes. It read, "An unbreakable bond". She knew it was from Corey. She remembered some time ago when they had the conversation of their love and they both said they had an unbreakable bond. Amari was speechless she couldn't believe Corey was gonna propose to her.

Amari began to cry harder trying to figure out what she would do now.

🎵🎵🎵

"Wait til I see that nigga his ass is dead!" yelled Daryl while punching the wall.

Cease had cleared his wound, removed the bullet and stitched him back up.

Xena, Toni and Ke-Ke sat stunned as they watched the whole process. Daryl looked around quickly and became nervous.

"Where's Peaches?" he asked no one in particular.

Everyone just sort of shrugged their shoulders because no one had seen her.

Daryl searched her room and was disappointed when he realized she wasn't in there either.

Xena opened the front door and was spotted Amari's Acura and informed Daryl.

Now Daryl was really worried about her.

Gregory Charles stepped on the porch and called her name. He too got no response.

"D man, maybe she went for a walk, let's go look for her man," Cease offered.

"Good idea," he said gingerly grabbing his jacket and heading towards the door.

"Mind if I help?" Gregory Charles asked.

"Yeah, that's cool, come on. But while we out, you need to call your boy and find out where the hell he's at," barked Daryl.

♫♫♫

Amari snapped out of her daydream and headed back up the stairs. She carefully opened the screen door and walked into her apartment.

"Damn where the hell you been?" Ke-Ke asked getting up off the couch to give Amari a hug.

"I had to get some air," Amari said.

Ke-Ke hugged Amari real tight and once again Amari started crying.

"Are you okay?" Ke-Ke asked.

Amari really wanted to tell her what was going through her head but she couldn't.

"Yeah, I'm fine. Where's Xena?'

"In the shower and Toni is laying down," she said sitting back down.

"Alright, I'm gonna go lay down too," Amari said headed towards her room.

"Mari, you should call Daryl first, he's worried sick about you," Ke-Ke said getting comfortable on the couch again.

Amari nodded her head yes and continued to her room.

♪♪♪

After taking a long hot shower Amari plopped down on her bed and prepared to call Daryl.

The phone rang one full ring before he answered.

"Peaches is that you?" he asked.

"Yeah, I'm here," she said.

"Where have you been?" he asked getting ready to blast her with numerous questions.

"I went for a walk," she said telling half the truth.

"You couldn't let me know, I would have went with you," he said letting her know how disappointed he was.

There was a pause on the phone.

"Look Daryl, I am really tired. I just need to get some rest," she said trying to usher him off the phone.

"Alright that's fine. I'll be there after awhile, I'll just use my key," he said.

"Actually Daryl, I really just want to be alone tonight, I'll call you in the morning okay," she said hoping he wouldn't give her too much of a hassle.

Daryl could sense that he was losing her and he was getting scared.

"Amari, please don't do this," he nearly begged.

Amari tried so hard to hold the tears back. She hated to hear Daryl sound so defeated. But she just couldn't see him right now. She needed to be alone for a moment. She needed a moment to breathe to figure out where her life was headed.

"Daryl please, I just need to be alone tonight. I promise I will call you first thing in the morning okay," she said hoping he would just let it go.

Feeling defeated he agreed.

"Okay, call me then. Peaches, I love you. Please don't forget that," he said barely above a whisper.

"I love you too," she said hoping to reassure him.

Amari hung up the phone and laid down in her bed. She pulled the ring from under her pillow and just stared at it. She wondered where at that moment Corey was and what he was doing. She was still in shock about everything that happened but she still felt a need to speak to Corey. She needed to talk to him to figure out where his head was at.

She picked up the phone and decided to give Corey a call. Slowly she dialed his cell phone number and prayed he would answer. She felt let down when she heard his voicemail pick up.

"Corey, its Amari, please give me a call on my cell phone when you get this message. We really need to talk," Amari said before hanging up quickly.

Amari lay down and replayed the events of the day. She couldn't believe what was going on around her. Once again she quickly found herself torn between both Corey and Daryl and she wasn't quite sure how she'd gotten to that point.

She placed Corey's ring on her nightstand right next to Daryl's and wrapped herself in her comforter and headed off to sleep.

♫♫♫

"Oh God, I feel so damn sick!" Xena thought to herself as she sat once again in the bathroom throwing up all of her insides.

She really hoped no one would hear her that was why she turned on the shower. She didn't want to tell anyone what happened when she went to the clinic the day before. She knew her news would crush Amari and after the day she had she couldn't do that to her best friend. She wouldn't do that to her best friend.

♫♫♫

Daryl arrived at Amari's house bright and early. He couldn't wait to see her and he truly felt she just needed a hug. She needed him to be there with her. He used his key to open the front door. He saw Ke-Ke laying on the couch and Toni on the love seat. He heard the shower running and hoped it wasn't Amari in there. He knocked softly on her room door.

♫♫♫

Amari heard a soft knock on her door and was instantly annoyed.

"Yeah," she said looking towards the door.

"It's Daryl," he said poking his head in.

Amari jumped up out of the bed and quickly snatched Corey's ring off the nightstand and met Daryl at the door.

"Hey," she said giving him a quick peck on lips.

"Are you okay?" he asked noticing how quickly she jumped up out of the bed and snatched something off the nightstand.

"I'm fine," she said holding the ring tight in her hand.

"I brought you some breakfast," he said holding up the bags.

Amari smiled. Daryl was so thoughtful and he was making an honest effort to make sure she was okay.

"Thanks," she said. "Let me just go wash my face and hands," she said before heading out of the room.

Amari walked quickly to Xena's room. She knocked once and let herself in. Xena was sitting on her bed crying.

"Xena you okay? What's wrong?" Amari quickly asked.

"I'm fine," Xena said trying to brush her off.

Amari sat down on the bed next to Xena.

"Girl we have been friends way too long for you to try and lie to me."

Xena laughed.

"I know, I just didn't want to burden you with my troubles you got enough shit going on," Xena said honestly.

"Xena, come on now, you know I always got time for you, no matter what I am going through," Amari said hugging her.

Xena sat there and decided to just go ahead and let it all out.

"I went to the doctor yesterday because of how sick I have been. They told me I was HIV positive," Xena said bursting into tears.

Amari sat shocked. She couldn't believe what she was hearing. She didn't know what to say. She couldn't imagine herself going through life without her best friend to go along on the journey with her.

"Xena no," Amari cried.

The two friends just sat there and hugged each other, not saying a word.

♫♫♫

Daryl sat in Amari's room not sure what was taking her so long. He could feel that she was hiding something but he had no clue what it was. He noticed her engagement ring sitting on her nightstand and he picked it up. He admired it. He bought it for her the day they were in the mall and she saw it.

Dilemma

That was the kind of guy he was. Whatever she wanted he felt the need to give it to her. He had treated her so wrongly in the past he just wanted to make up for it. Apart of him felt she was going to turn his proposal down. He wasn't prepared for that.

He lay back on her bed and made himself comfortable. He ended up falling asleep thinking about her and the life they could have together.

🎵🎵🎵

"Xena what happened?" asked Amari.

"I'm not really sure; I just know when I went to the clinic that is what they told me. I have a good chance of passing it off to the baby and they want me to consider abortion. But I can't this is Darvis' baby. I can't kill this child!" she cried.

"Xena don't cry," Amari said trying to comfort her.

"Are you okay?" Xena asked looking at Amari.

Amari looked down at her balled up hand, and opened it.

"No," she said handing the ring to Xena.

"Daryl gave you two rings?" she questioned.

"No, I found this one on the steps outside in the back. I think Corey dropped it when he ran out of here. Look at the engraving," Amari said pointing to the inside of the ring.

Xena whispered the words, "unbreakable bond".

"Oh my God, Amari, what are you going to do?" she asked putting everything together.

"I have no idea. I love Daryl to death; I really do, but the thought of Corey proposing to me. I have dreamed of that moment," Amari said finally being honest with herself.

"Go with your heart," Xena said hugging her friend.

"My heart is so torn," Amari cried.

"I don't want to hurt either one of them. I love them both."

Amari and Xena sat there just holding each other and trying to comfort each other.

🎵🎵🎵

Corey sat in his car still not believing what he had done. He couldn't believe he actually let the gun go off and shot Daryl. His intentions were not to go over there and hurt anybody. He just wanted Amari to hear him out. He had to tell her how much he loved her.

Corey reached into his pants pocket to pull out the ring. He was confused when he couldn't find it. He searched frantically for it.

When he couldn't find it he slammed his fist on the steering wheel realizing he must have dropped it when he ran out of Amari's apartment.

"Shit!" he yelled.

Corey sat there trying to figure out how he was gonna get that ring back. He didn't want Amari to see it until he was ready to give it to her.

CHAPTER TWENTY-FOUR

Amari was suddenly awakened by a tap at her bedroom window. She had no idea who it was but she was annoyed that someone was waking her up. These days it took her so long to get to sleep. It had been three weeks since the incident in the living room that changed her life forever.

Amari and Daryl had grown apart a little. He was ready for her to commit and she suddenly wasn't sure if she should. She knew she loved him and nothing would ever change that but just the mere thought of knowing Corey wanted to propose to her had shaken everything up for her.

She had gotten to the point where she would only talk to Daryl a few times a week. She knew Daryl wanted revenge on Corey for shooting him and she wasn't sure if she would be able to live with the fact if he had caught up with Corey.

She got out of her bed and threw on a pair of shorts and walked to her bedroom window. She lifted her blinds and nearly screamed at who stood outside her window.

She hurriedly lifted the window and screen so he could come in.

"Corey, what are you doing here?" she asked.

"I need to talk to you," he said looking around.

"Corey, you really shouldn't be here, if Daryl catches you over here he's gonna kill you," she said suddenly fearful for his life.

"I'm cool," he said nonchalant.

Amari sat on her bed not believing he was standing in front of her.

"We really need to talk," he said looking at her.

Corey still felt she was just as beautiful as the first day he laid eyes on her. She had grown and matured over the years but her beauty had simply intensified. He sat down on the bed next to her.

"I don't know where to begin," he said chuckling to himself.

"This really isn't a funny situation," she said.

"I know, I just don't really know where to start with you," he said lowering his head.

"I've always been a big fan of the truth," she said looking at him.

Corey sat beside her and nodded his head. He knew he had to just come straight out with the truth, but he was so afraid of rejection from her that he didn't know what to do. He sat there and looked around her room trying to get the courage to come out with it. As he glanced next to her bed, he looked at her nightstand and saw the ring he had bought for her and next to that was another ring, a much bigger engagement ring.

"Amari, I love you," he said hoping that would be enough.

"Corey, you came over here after all this time to just say that? You have said that so many times, but then your actions tell me something different," she said.

He got up and walked to her nightstand. He picked up his ring and knelt down before her.

"Since the day that I met you I knew I had something special. We were so young and very much wet behind the ears. I didn't know much of anything but I knew I loved you. I've watched you grow from a teenage girl into a sexy lady. Amari you are the light that helps me see, the wind beneath my winds and the spark that lights my fire. You are my air, you are my everything. I will be your strength when you are weak; you're happiness when you are sad. Amari, I love you so much. There is no me without you. Would you please marry me?" he asked while handing her the ring.

Amari sat numb. She knew his intention was to propose, but she just didn't think he would do it so soon after everything that had happened.

"Corey, I don't know what to say," she said admiring the ring again.

He glanced at her nightstand at the other ring that was there.

"What did you tell Daryl?" he asked.

"What do you mean?" she questioned not sure how he knew of Daryl's proposal.

Corey nodded his heads towards the engagement ring on Amari's nightstand.

"I told him I had to think about it, which is the same thing I am telling you," she said.

"Amari, please don't make me wait too long," he said getting up off his knees.

"Corey, I have to ask you. What were you thinking when you came here and held me at gunpoint?"

"I wasn't thinking. I just knew I needed to talk to you, I needed you to understand how much I love you, there's nothing I wouldn't do for you," he said tilting her head so he could look her directly in the eyes.

"Corey I know you love me but you shot Daryl, he's not gonna let that go you know?" she asked, hoping he was fully aware of what was going on.

"Yeah I know the big tough guy is out for my head. I know his boy is out of jail and they got a bounty on my head. I don't care about any of that though, I just want to be with you," he said again.

Corey stood up and headed back for the window.

"I'm gonna go, but I'll call you and please think long and hard about what I said," he said before slipping out of the window.

Amari was left to her thoughts and what she should do. Her mind was even more confused than previously. She didn't know what to do, she loved them both and had no idea how she would ever choose between the two.

CHAPTER TWENTY-FIVE

It had been four long months since Amari's life had changed drastically for the worse. Everything in her life had been turned upside down.

Amari and Xena persuaded Toni that the right thing for her to do was to turn herself into the police. They had been looking for her ever since they pronounced Tommy dead. After a thirty day trial, Toni was found guilty and sentenced to ten years in prison for the murder of her abusive boyfriend Tommy. She was sentenced to Metro State Prison in Atlanta, Georgia, a female maximum security prison. Two weeks later she committed suicide in her cell.

When Toni was pronounced dead, Ke-Ke stopped talking to Amari and Xena; she blamed them for her best friend's death.

Xena decided not to have the abortion she couldn't see herself killing Darvis' child. She loved Darvis so much and just couldn't do it. She thought about him daily and vowed to help the police find his killer by any means necessary.

Xena was preparing for the birth of her baby boy whom she would name Darvis Junior.

Daryl and Amari grew farther apart. Corey and Amari grew apart as well. Amari stopped all communication with them. She needed that time to get her thoughts together to figure out who she would indeed marry.

She finally made a decision a month ago. She went to his house and told him the good news. He was ecstatic. He couldn't believe that after all this time, she chose him.

They planned a small wedding that was how she wanted it. She picked out her Vera Wang gown and had Xena at her side, she was ready to walk the aisle and become his wife.

♪♪♪

It was Amari's wedding day and she couldn't believe the day was finally here. She was a recent college graduate and she was getting ready to marry the love of her life.

Dilemma

Xena came in and told her which guests had arrived. She could care less about any of them. The only one she cared about was the one she turned down. She wondered if he would come to her wedding. She wondered if he could stomach the pain to watch her marry someone else. When Xena told her he wasn't there she felt a bit sad. She knew she would end up hurting someone, but she had to follow her heart.

Amari was left alone with her thoughts. She had doubts, she wasn't sure if she had made the right decision. She admired herself in the mirror. She had the perfect gown, the perfect tiara, the perfect set of pearls on her neck and dangling from her ears. She was ready to walk the aisle. She stood up and fluffed out her dress. She was getting ready to walk out and to wait for the song, You by Jesse Powell to play. That was the song she had chosen to walk to on her way to meet her groom.

She left her private bridal suite right after she said a special prayer to her mother. She stood at the doors alone waiting for them to open them so she could reveal herself to her groom. In one swift movement the doors swung open and the guests rose to their feet. She could see the smiles of her friends and family admiring her beauty.

She took two steps to her groom and looked to her right and there he stood holding a dozen red roses.

The one she said no to. She smiled. She was happy he was there. At that moment in her heart of hearts she knew they would love each other forever.

She faced forward and continued on to her groom. The walk seemed endless when she finally reached him, she saw he was full of tears; looking into his face, she knew she had made the right choice.

The wedding went along as planned. The time had finally come, they were officially married and the priest had just given her groom permission to kiss his bride. After embracing in a very passionate kiss he let her go.

It was time for them to be announced to their guests.

The minister cleared his throat, "By the powers invested in me, I know pronounce you husband and wife. Ladies and Gentleman, I present to you

Mr. and Mrs……."

To find out the conclusion please stay tuned for Book Three in the Drama Series; No More! Available December 2008

Latifa Sanchez

Made in the USA